FREUD'S
Sister

FREUD'S
Sister

A NOVEL

Goce Smilevski

Translated from the Macedonian by
CHRISTINA E. KRAMER

PENGUIN BOOKS

PENGUIN BOOKS

Published by the Penguin Group

Penguin Group (USA) Inc., 375 Hudson Street, New York, New York 10014, U.S.A.
Penguin Group (Canada), 90 Eglinton Avenue East, Suite 700, Toronto, Ontario,
Canada M4P 2Y3 (a division of Pearson Penguin Canada Inc.)
Penguin Books Ltd, 80 Strand, London WC2R 0RL, England
Penguin Ireland, 25 St Stephen's Green, Dublin 2, Ireland
(a division of Penguin Books Ltd)
Penguin Group (Australia), 250 Camberwell Road, Camberwell, Victoria 3124, Australia
(a division of Pearson Australia Group Pty Ltd)
Penguin Books India Pvt Ltd, 11 Community Centre, Panchsheel Park,
New Delhi–110 017, India
Penguin Group (NZ), 67 Apollo Drive, Rosedale, Auckland 0632, New Zealand
(a division of Pearson New Zealand Ltd)
Penguin Books (South Africa) (Pty) Ltd, 24 Sturdee Avenue, Rosebank,
Johannesburg 2196, South Africa

Penguin Books Ltd, Registered Offices:
80 Strand, London WC2R 0RL, England

First published in Penguin Books 2012

1 3 5 7 9 10 8 6 4 2

The Macedonian edition published as *Sestrata na Zigmund Frojd* by Dijalong in 2011 has been
edited and translated for this publication.

A portion of this book appeared as "Fourteen Little Gustavs" translated by Ana Lucic, in *Best
European Fiction 2010*, edited by Aleksandar Hemon, published by Dalkey Archive Press.

This is a work of fiction based on real events.

LIBRARY OF CONGRESS CATALOGING IN PUBLICATION DATA
Smilevski, Goce.
[Sestrata na Zigmund Frojd. English]
Freud's sister : a novel / Goce Smilevski ; translated from the Macedonian by
Christina E. Kramer.
p. cm.
"The Macedonian edition published as Sestrata na Zigmund Frojd by Dijalong in 2011 has
been edited and translated for this publication."
ISBN 978-0-14-312145-9
1. Freud, Adolphine, 1862–ca. 1942—Fiction. I. Title.
PG1196.29.M58S4713 2011
891.8'193—dc23 2012020979

Printed in the United States of America
Set in Electra • Designed by Sabrina Bowers

ALWAYS LEARNING   PEARSON

Author's Note

*T*HIS IS A NOVEL BASED IN FACT. ALTHOUGH Sigmund Freud wrote that "reality will always remain unknowable," we do know about Freud's exit visa and the opportunity it represented for his sisters, and about Freud's final months spent in exile in London—they are documented in detail. We also know about the fate of Freud's sisters. Their final months, however, are lost to history.

In one of his letters, Freud refers to Adolfina as "the sweetest and best of my sisters." His son Martin is not as kind toward his aunt. Reading the few lines that refer to her in Martin's book about his father, we can conclude that Adolfina was underestimated by her family, and sense the pity that family members felt for her. From letters we also know that she was mistreated by her mother, that she lived with her parents as an adult and cared for them until their deaths, that she spent her life in loneliness. And that is all we know about her. The silence around Adolfina is so loud that I could write this novel in no other way than in her voice. The well-known facts of Sigmund Freud's life were like scenery, or like the walls of a labyrinth in which I wandered for years, trying to find the corridors where I could hear Adolfina's voice so I could write it down, and in this way rescue in fiction one of the many lives forgotten by history.

AN OLD WOMAN LIES IN THE DARKNESS. Her eyes closed, she sifts through her earliest memories. Three drift into her mind: at a time when many things in the world still have no name, a boy gives her something sharp and says, "Knife"; at a time when she still believes in fairy tales, a voice whispers to her the tale of the bird that pierced its breast with its beak and tore out its heart; at a time when touch tells her more than words, a hand approaches her face and strokes her cheek with an apple. The boy in her memories who strokes her with the apple, who whispers to her the fairy tale, who gives her the knife, is her brother Sigmund. The old woman dredging up memories is me, Adolfina Freud.

"Adolfina," said a voice in the darkness, "are you sleeping?"

"I'm awake," I said. My sister Paulina was lying beside me in bed.

"What time is it?"

"It is probably around midnight."

My sister woke up every night, beginning the same story with the same words:

"This is the end of Europe."

"The end has come to Europe many times."

"They are going to kill us like dogs."

"I know," I said.

"Aren't you afraid?"

I said nothing.

"It was like this in Berlin in 1933," continued Paulina. I no longer tried to stop her from telling me what she had told me many times before: "As soon as the National Socialists and Hitler came to power, young people took to marching down streets to the beat of martial music. Just as they are marching here now. Banners with swastikas flew from buildings. Just as they are flapping in the wind here. You could hear the Führer's voice from radios and public-address systems that had been set up in the squares and parks. Just as we hear it here now. He was promising a new Germany, a better Germany, a pure Germany."

It was 1938. Three years earlier, my sisters Paulina and Marie had fled Berlin and returned to the apartment they had left when they married. Paulina was nearly blind, and someone always had to be at her side; she slept in the bed where our parents had slept, and Marie and I took turns sleeping beside her. We took turns because Paulina woke up every night, and either Marie or I, depending on which of us was in the room with her, would be kept up all night.

"It will be the same here," continued my sister. "Do you know how it was there?"

"I know," I answered sleepily. "You've told me."

"I've told you. Men in uniform burst into Jewish homes at night. They broke everything; they beat us and ordered us to leave. All those who did not support the Führer, and who dared to express their views publicly, disappeared without a trace. People said that anyone opposing the ideals on which the new Germany would be built would be taken to camps and put to hard labor. There they were tortured and killed. That is what will happen here, believe me."

I believed her, but I said not a word, because every word I said would compel her to say more. Several weeks earlier, German troops had marched into Austria and set up a new government. Sensing danger, our brother Alexander had fled with his family to Switzerland. On the following day the borders were closed, and anyone wishing to leave Austria had to report to the newly opened emigration office. Thousands applied for exit visas, but only a few were granted permission to leave.

"If they are forbidding us to leave, it means they have a plan for us," said Paulina. I said not a word. "First they will take everything from us, and then they will fill ditches with our bodies."

A few days earlier, uniformed men had entered our sister Rosa's apartment and shown her a document stating that her apartment and everything in it was to be taken from her. "Now there are officers sleeping in the beds where my children slept," said Rosa on the afternoon she moved into the building where I lived with Paulina and Marie. She brought nothing with her but a few photographs and some clothing. So now we four sisters were living together in the same home, just as we had so long ago.

"Are you listening to me? They are going to fill ditches with our bodies," Paulina said more emphatically.

"You tell me the same thing every night," I said to her.

"And still you do nothing."

"What should I do?"

"You could go see Sigmund and persuade him to request exit visas for the four of us."

"And then where would we go?"

"To New York," Paulina replied. Her daughter lived in New York. "You know that Beatrice will take care of us."

When we awoke the following day, it was already noon. I took Paulina by the arm, and we went for a walk. While we were walking down the sidewalk, I saw several trucks roll by. They pulled to a stop, and some soldiers jumped out and shoved us into one of them. The truck was filled with people, all of them terrified.

"They are driving us to our death," said my sister.

"No, we're taking you to the park, to play with you," one of the soldiers guarding us said, laughing. The vehicles circled around the Jewish quarter where we lived, and stopped from time to time to load in more people. Then they did indeed take us to a park, the Prater. They pushed us out of the trucks and forced us to run, squat, stand, jump; almost all of us were old and weak. When we fell down from exhaustion, the soldiers kicked us in the groin. I held Paulina by the hand the whole time.

"Spare my sister at least," I said to the soldiers. "She's blind."

"Blind!" They laughed. "Wonderful! That'll be even more fun."

They forced her to walk alone, her hands tied behind her back so she could not touch things in front of her. Paulina walked until she bumped into a tree; she collapsed on the ground. I caught up with her and bent down, wiping her face clean of the dirt and blood that ran down her forehead. The soldiers laughed, a sound sweet with carelessness and sour with the enjoyment of someone else's pain. Then they led us to the edge of the park, lined us up, and aimed their rifles at us.

"Turn around," they told us.

We turned our backs to the rifles.

"Now run home if you want to save your lives!" one of them shouted, and hundreds of old legs set off running. We ran, we fell down, we stood up, we began running again, while behind us we heard the soldiers' laughter, sweet with carelessness and sour with the enjoyment of someone else's pain.

Rosa, Paulina, Marie, and I passed the evening in silence. Paulina trembled, perhaps not so much out of fear for her life as at the thought that she would never again see the one closest to her, the one who had come from her womb. Rosa's and Marie's children were dead, and the sole remnant of the family I never had was a fading bloody trace on the wall by my bed. They say it is more difficult for those with offspring to depart from this world: death separates the one who received life from the one who gave it. Paulina sat in the corner of the room and trembled, sensing that separation.

The next day, I went to see Sigmund. It was Friday afternoon, the time he devoted to his ritual cleaning of the antiques in his study. I wanted to tell him what had happened to Paulina and me the day before, but he showed me a newspaper clipping.

"Look what Thomas Mann has written," he said.

"Marie and Paulina are more and more afraid," I said.

"Afraid . . . of what?" he asked, setting the clipping down on the table.

"They say the same thing is going to happen here that they saw in Berlin."

"That they saw in Berlin . . ." Then he picked up one of the antique objects from the table, a stone monkey, and began cleaning it with a small brush. "None of that is going to happen here."

"It is already happening. Violent gangs are breaking into apartments in our quarter, beating up everyone they meet. Hundreds of people committed suicide last week; they could not take the pressure. Crazy people entered the Jewish orphanage. They broke the windows and forced the children to run across the shattered glass."

"Forced the children to run across the shattered glass . . ." Sigmund passed the small brush across the monkey's body. "All this will not last long here."

"If it is not going to last long, then why is everyone who can getting an exit visa and fleeing the country? Out on the street, have you met any of the people fleeing? They are leaving their homes, leaving them forever; they have gathered up their most important things in a bundle or two and are fleeing to save their lives. There are rumors that death camps are going to open here, too. You have influential friends here and around the world; they can arrange for you to get as many exit visas as you want. Ask for enough for the whole family. Half of Vienna is trying to get these visas, without success. Use your friends to get us out." Sigmund set the monkey down and picked up another figurine, a fertility goddess. He began to brush the nude body. "Are you listening to me?" I asked, my voice dry and tired.

My brother looked at me and asked, "And then where would you go?"

"To Paulina's daughter in New York."

"What is Paulina's daughter going to do with four old women in New York?"

"Then at least try to get an exit visa for Paulina." He was looking at the nude mother goddess, and I was not sure he had heard me. "Are you listening? Nobody needs to see Rosa, Marie, or me. But Paulina needs to be with her daughter. And her daughter needs to be with her mother. She wants her mother to be safe. She calls every day, begging us to beg you to request an exit visa for her mother. Are you listening to me, Sigmund?"

He set the mother goddess down.

"Would you like me to read just a few words from Mann's article? It is called 'Brother Hitler.'" He picked up the clipping and began to read: "'How a man like that must hate analysis! I have the deep suspicion that the fury with which he carried out the recent invasion of a certain capital city was fundamentally directed at the old analyst who lived there—his true and authentic enemy—the philosopher and unmasker of neurosis, the great deflator, the very one who knows and pronounces on what "genius" is.'" Then he set the essay on the table and said, "Mann wrote that with such subtle irony!"

"The only true statement in what you have read is 'the old analyst.' I am telling you this with no subtle irony. And regardless of whether the assertion that you are Hitler's worst enemy was written with irony or not, it sounds like common nonsense. You know the reason for the occupation of Austria is the start of Hitler's grand campaign to conquer the world. Then he will wipe anyone who is not of the Aryan race from the face of the earth. Everyone knows that: you, Mann, even I, a poor old woman—even I know that!"

"You needn't be so alarmed. Hitler's ambitions cannot be fulfilled. In just a few days, France and Britain will force him to withdraw from Austria, and then he will be defeated in Germany as well. The Germans themselves will beat him; the support they are giving Hitler now is only a temporary eclipse of their reason."

"That eclipse is lasting years."

"Correct, it is lasting years. But it will end. Dark forces guide the Germans now, but somewhere inside them is smoldering that spirit on which I, too, was nurtured. The nation's madness cannot last forever."

"It will last long enough," I said.

My brother had been infatuated with the German spirit since childhood, and even then had inculcated that love in us, his sisters. He convinced us that German was the only language in which one could fully convey the greatest achievements of human thought; he passed on to us his love of German art; and he taught us to be proud that, even though we were of Jewish blood, we belonged to German culture because we lived on Austrian soil. Even now, when he saw how the German spirit had been in decline for years and how the Germans themselves were trampling the most significant fruits of that spirit, he continually repeated, as if to convince himself, that this was a temporary madness, that the German spirit would regain its luster.

SINCE THAT DAY IN his study, whenever we called Sigmund we were told that he was not at home, or that he was busy with patients, or that he was not well and could not take our call. We asked repeatedly whether he was going to file an application for exit visas, but his daughter Anna, his wife, Martha, and his sister-in-law, Minna, said they knew nothing about it. A whole month passed without our seeing our brother. On the sixth of May, his eighty-second birthday, I had resolved to drop by his place with Paulina. We took a small gift, a book we thought he would like, and set off toward Berggasse 19.

At my brother's home, it was Anna who opened the door for us.

"You have caught us working. . . ." she said, making enough space between herself and the door to let us in.

"Working?"

"We're packing. We sent off ten large boxes yesterday and ten the day before. We still need to select which of the many gifts my father has received we will take with us."

"You're leaving?" I asked.

"Not immediately, but we want to get everything packed as soon as possible."

In my brother's study there were souvenirs, books, boxes large and small, antiques strewn everywhere, everything anyone had ever given him and he had saved. Sigmund sat in his large red armchair in the middle of the room, surveying the objects spread about on the floor. He turned toward us, barely nodded, and turned his attention back to the disarray. I told him we had come to wish him a happy birthday. He thanked us and set our gift on the table beside him.

"As you can see, we are leaving," he said. "For London."

"I could help you," I said. "With the packing."

Anna said she would hand me the things to be discarded; I would put them in a box while she organized the objects in the boxes they would later mail to London. Paulina remained standing by the wall.

"This cigarette case?" asked Anna, turning toward her father, displaying a silver box set with several green stones.

"A gift from your mother. We will take it."

Anna put the cigarette case in the box beside her.

"This ivory domino?" asked Anna.

Sigmund thought a moment or two, then said, "I do not recall who gave it to me. Throw it out."

Anna handed me the domino, and I dropped it into the box beside me.

"This?" asked Anna, picking up a book and bringing it closer to Sigmund's eyes.

"That Bible was a gift from your grandfather Jakob for my thirty-fifth birthday. We will take it."

Anna said she was tired because she had been working since morning and wanted to take a small break. She went into the dining room to stretch her legs and get a drink of water.

"So you requested exit visas from Austria after all," I said to my brother.

"I did," he said.

"You assured me there was no need to flee."

"This is not fleeing. It is just a temporary departure."

"When are you leaving?"

"Martha, Anna, and I are leaving at the beginning of June."

"And those of us left behind?" I asked. My brother said nothing. "When are Paulina, Marie, Rosa, and I leaving?"

"You aren't."

"We aren't?"

"There is no need," he said. "I am going not because I want to but simply because some of my friends, diplomats from Britain and France, have insisted that the local offices give me exit visas."

"And?"

My brother could have staged a farce, could have told us that some foreign diplomat had pleaded that he and his wife and children be allowed to leave, and that he himself was powerless to do anything to save others. He could have staged a farce, but that was not his genre.

"They allowed me to make a list of people close to me who would leave Austria with me," he said.

"And there was not an instant in which you thought to put our names down?"

"Not an instant. This is only temporary. We will return."

"Even if you do return, we will no longer be here." He did not say a word. Then I said, "I have no right to ask, but I will anyway. Who is on the list of those close to you that you need to save?"

"Indeed. Who is on the list?" asked Paulina.

My brother could have staged a farce, could have told us that he had written down only the names of his children, his own name, and his wife's—those whom the officials would have expected to be on a list of people to be saved—only his closest relatives; he could have staged a farce, but that was not his genre. He pulled out a sheet of paper and said, "Here is the list."

I looked at the names written on the paper.

"Read it to me, too," said Paulina.

I read it out loud. My brother, his wife, their children, and their families were on the list, as were his wife's sister, two house-keepers, and my brother's personal doctor and his family. And at the very bottom of the list: Jo-Fi.

"Jo-Fi," said Paulina, laughing. She turned toward the sound of Sigmund's voice. "Ah, yes, you are never parted from your little dog."

Anna came back into the room and said, "I didn't ask whether you wanted something to drink or whether, perhaps, you were hungry."

"We are neither hungry nor thirsty," I said.

Paulina continued as if she had not heard Anna's words or my own: "It really is lovely that you thought of all these people. You even thought of your little dog, and your housekeepers, and your doctor and his family, and your wife's sister. But you could have thought of your sisters, Sigmund."

"If it were necessary for you to leave, I would have thought of it. But this is only temporary, because my friends insisted that I leave."

"So why did your friends insist that you leave, if it really isn't dangerous to stay here?" I asked.

"Because, like you, they do not grasp that this situation will last only a short time," said Sigmund.

"Well then, if this terror is going to last only a short time, why aren't you going alone, for only a short time, to placate your friends? Why aren't you going alone, rather than taking not only your family but also your doctor, his family, two housekeepers, and even your little dog and your wife's sister?" I asked.

Sigmund said not a word.

"Sigmund," said Paulina, "unlike Adolfina I believe you. I believe that this whole terror will last only a short time. But my life will last a shorter time than this terror. And I have a daughter. You, Sigmund, you could have thought of your sister. You could have remembered me, and that I have a daughter. You surely remembered, because ever since I came from Berlin, and my Beatrice left for New York, I have spoken often of her. I have not seen her in three years. By just writing my name, you could have helped me see my daughter one last time," she said, and at the word *see* she turned toward him her eyes that see only contours. "You could have put my name down, between the name of your wife's sister and the name of the dog. You could even have written it below your dog, and that would have been enough for me to be allowed to leave Vienna and be with Beatrice. I know now that she will never see me again."

Anna tried to get us back to separating the things to be packed from those to be left behind.

"And this?" she asked. She held a wooden object in the palm of her hand—a gondola the size of a finger.

"I do not know whom it is from," said Sigmund. "Get rid of it."

Anna handed me the gondola, the present I had given my brother for his twenty-sixth birthday. I had not seen it since, and now here it was, floating down through time. I placed it gently in the box among the other objects to be thrown away.

My brother stood and walked toward the opposite wall, toward the canvas on which seven decades earlier we had been painted, the Freud brothers and sisters. Alexander, who was a year and a half at the time the portrait was made, later recalled that when he had grown up a little, Sigmund told him, pointing to the painting, "With our sisters we are like a book. You are the youngest and I the oldest. We need to be the sturdy covers that hold and protect our sisters born after me and before you." And now, many years later, my brother stretched his hands toward the painting.

"We will pack this separately," said Sigmund, reaching to take the canvas down from the wall.

"You have no right to that painting," I said.

My brother turned toward me, holding the painting in his hands.

"It is time for us to go," said Paulina.

At the entrance to the building we met Sigmund's sister-in-law coming in. She said that she had been buying some basic things she needed because she was to leave Austria the following day.

"Have a nice trip," Paulina said.

I led my sister homeward, holding her by the hand. From her clenched fingers, I knew how she felt. I looked at her from time to time; on her face flickered that smile which some blind people have fixed on their faces, even when they are feeling fear, anger, or terror.

ON A HUMID DAY at the beginning of June, Paulina, Marie, Rosa, and I set off for the train station to see my brother off, along with Martha and Anna, the last on Sigmund's list to depart from Vienna. The three of them were standing at the open window of their compartment; the four of us were standing on the platform. My brother held his little dog in his arms. When the whistle announcing the train's departure shrieked, the dog shook with fright and, panic-stricken, bit Sigmund's index finger. Anna took out a handkerchief and tied it around the bleeding finger. The whistle sounded once again, and the train set off. With one finger bandaged, the other four curled tight, my brother waved goodbye, the outstretched finger and bloody handkerchief moving through the air.

$\mathscr{T}$HE EVENING OF THE DAY OUR BROTHER left Vienna for good, my sisters quietly discussed how important it now was for him in London, with his friends' help, to make it possible for us, too, to leave as quickly as possible. I listened to my sisters' reports of horrors, but in place of the apocalyptic events they spoke of, there appeared before my closed eyes only my brother's bandaged index finger waving through the air.

In the months after my brother's departure, Martha and Anna called us occasionally from London. They told us that Sigmund had had new operations on his mouth, that he was getting better, but that he could no longer speak. The cancer had also damaged his hearing so much that he communicated with them in writing. I recalled the time when we were children, and my brother was teaching me how to write. Martha and Anna told us that they were living in a beautiful house in a quiet London suburb, and they reassured us over and over that Sigmund's friends were doing everything they could to help us get visas out of Austria, and then we would all be together in their house.

The four of us learned to live with our fear; it was a fear not of death but of torture. We had to wear the Star of David on our sleeves so that the restrictions imposed on all Jews could be enforced: we were no longer able to go to the theater, the opera, a concert; we could not go to restaurants or parks; we were not allowed to ride in taxis; we were allowed to board trolleys, but only the last car; we were allowed to leave our homes, but only at strictly defined hours; our phone lines were cut, and we were allowed to use only two post offices in the city.

It was a September day when one of the sons of my friend Klara's brother came to our home to tell me that Klara had died at the Nest, the psychiatric clinic where she had lived for years. He asked me whether I would go with him to the burial. My sisters were at a neighbor's; on a piece of paper I wrote them a note telling them where I had gone.

Several months prior to this, the new municipal leaders had decreed, as one of the many changes in Vienna, that those who died in a specialized clinic could not be buried in public graveyards, but only on the grounds of the clinic. And so these dead were buried there in shallow holes, placed not in a coffin but in a sheet.

I entered the room where Klara's body lay. I was told that she had died in her sleep; her face was so peaceful that no trace could be seen of her sleep, of her life, or of her death. She lay curled up as she always was when she slept, with her legs folded up, her head down on her chest, and her hands clenched to her stomach. Her body was already rigid. We wrapped her, still curled like this, in a sheet.

"Just like a fetus," I said, when they carried her from the room she had called a womb.

"Too big for a fetus, too small for a person," replied one of the doctors.

In fact, no one would have thought there was a human body wrapped in that sheet.

It was raining hard, and there were barely twenty of us who went outside. The others remained standing by the hospital windows, where they watched through the bars. We laid the sheet with the body in the waiting hole. People shoveled mud onto the sheet.

Later that afternoon, I returned home. My sisters were sitting at the table in the dining room. Rosa looked at me with red-rimmed eyes and said, "Anna called. Sigmund died last week."

"Klara died. Last night," I said.

"They cremated him."

"We buried her today on the hospital grounds. We dug a shallow grave. We didn't have a coffin. We wrapped her in a sheet. It was raining."

It was raining outside. The raindrops struck hard at the windows. The sound they made struck at our words.

I went to my room and lay down on the bed. I thought of my brother. I did not try to imagine the last moments of his life. I did not try to imagine him barely moving. I did not want to hear how the last drops of strength forced him to inhale and exhale, nor did I want to know what was going through his head in those moments—whether he was tormented by the thought of his sisters who had repeatedly called his home, begging for some way to be found to get them out of Vienna, whether he had any weight on his conscience from suspecting that they, too, would be taken to the death camps. I did not try to think of the last moments of his life. It was enough for me to know that he was dead, that he was at peace, without bodily pain, without spiritual torment, because surely in the next world the soul is liberated from all suffering and self-reproach. It is only while it is here that the soul cannot be completely assured that everything is as it should be, and that it has done what it had to do in order to fulfill some higher, yet unfathomable, plan.

I woke up in a sweat. Outside, the rain had stopped, and the darkness was descending through the dark purple of the clouds. I remembered my dream. In it, Sigmund was dead.

"I am very much alone," he said, "although *alone* is not the right word. One can be alone only as long as others exist. Look, there is no one around. There is no one here."

"Everyone is right here," I said to him.

He shook his head.

"No, there is no one," he said.

"Everyone is here," I said. "You just need to look for them."

"I am looking," he said. "But no one is here. Everything here is empty. Take a look. Here there is only light, and nothing else. And when the light is alone, without anything around it, it is empty, bare. It is the most awful prison, from which there is no escape, because there is nowhere to escape to. The deadly light is everywhere. And there is no one else in it."

"Everyone is here," I told him. "It's just that you are looking too much at yourself, so you cannot see the others."

"No," he said. "There is no one here. But perhaps that is what death is: to exist forever, to be conscious, and to be completely alone. Completely alone. It would have been better if I had simply vanished after death, better if I were not present. I once believed that that is what it would be like after death. Even a vision of the most terrifying hell is less dreadful than this hellish detachment, this eternal wakefulness in a deathly emptiness."

"No," I told him. "We are all here. Just turn your gaze away from yourself. We are all here, the living and the dead."

"You stay here at least," he said.

"I am staying here. We all are. You just need to see us."

"This is punishment," he said, and he clenched his fists and slowly raised them toward his head. "I am being punished with this frightening emptiness." He lowered his head and banged his forehead on his fists. "And I know why I am being punished."

"You are not being punished," I said.

"I know my own guilt," he said, and he looked at his fists. "Forgive me."

"There is nothing to forgive," I said. "You have not done any evil. You neglected to do a good thing; in our lifetime, all of us neglect to do many good things. And we cannot measure which lapse will allow evil to swallow someone."

"Forgive me," he said.

His appearance slowly began to change. He began to return to a time many years before. He was getting smaller, and he reached an age at which I had not known him, an age before I was born. He kept getting smaller and smaller, until he was a tiny nursling. A naked, crying baby. I scooped him up in my arms, uncovered my drooping shriveled breast, and brought it to his lips. As my brother pulled milk from my withered breast, I felt a wondrous pleasure from the contact of his lips on my nipple. And, as I woke, I knew that I was waking, and I regretted that the bliss of nursing him would not last.

AFTER THE DEATH of our brother, Paulina, Marie, Rosa, and I sometimes went to the building in which he had lived prior to his departure from Vienna and looked through the windows of his apartment. A man in uniform now lived there. From time to time, a neighbor or a friend would drop by our apartment for a visit, and the conversation would turn to the impending war. "Yet another great war"—that is what everyone was saying, and then, in fact, the war did begin. Young people were mobilized and taken to the front; lists were compiled of the residents of our quarter, who were then loaded onto trains and carried away from Vienna forever. Although it was said they were being taken off to perform hard labor, we knew they were being taken to death camps. We knew, and we waited for our turn to come. One morning, soldiers distributed lists to the buildings along our street, informing us of what we would be allowed to take with us, and ordering us to be at the train station at the end of the quarter at six in the morning, on the twenty-ninth of June of that year, 1942.

The morning of the day prior to our departure, we packed in small suitcases everything we would need until the end of our lives. I spent that afternoon walking about our apartment; I went from one room to another, my way of saying goodbye to our home. My sisters spent that time looking through old photograph albums; they laughed at the clothing we had worn a half century before, at our serious faces, at bodies frozen at the moment the photograph was taken, and from time to time I heard a sigh, probably for someone in the photographs who had died, most likely one of Rosa's or Marie's children. It was not yet dark when I grew tired and stopped walking about the apartment; my sisters, however, continued looking through the albums. Marie and Rosa told Paulina what was in the photographs, and Paulina asked questions while running her hands over their smooth black-and-white surfaces.

I slept peacefully that night, and when I woke at dawn I turned to the bloody trace on the wall by my bed. That faded trace, more faded than old age, will remain even when I no longer exist, and then that trace, too, will disappear, together with the wall, together with my home. With my lips set for the release of my soul, rather than for a kiss, I kissed that dried stain of blood. Then I woke my sisters; we ate breakfast, picked up our suitcases, and set off. But, just as we were stepping out of the apartment, Paulina said, "Let's not forget the photographs."

Rosa and Marie protested, but I cracked open my small suitcase and stuffed in two photo albums.

"Your suitcase is so full it's going to fall apart," said Marie, and she was right. We were walking down our street when the suitcase split open, spilling all my things to the ground, including the photo albums. From the albums I took a single old photo—one of all of us, sisters, brothers, parents—and tucked it by my right breast. From the torn suitcase I took the one thing that was not mine and tucked it by my left breast.

"What's that baby bonnet to you?" Marie said with reproach.

"Baby bonnet?" asked Paulina.

"Yes," Marie explained to her. "She pulled a baby bonnet out of her things—it is half fallen apart—and placed it by her heart."

"Her heart?" Paulina wondered.

"Between her left breast and brassiere," Marie clarified for her.

"Give us your things—we'll divide them among our suit-cases," Rosa suggested. Their suitcases were already overstuffed.

"We need to be at the station soon," I said. "And the photograph and the bonnet are sufficient."

"I don't know why you have that bonnet," said Marie. "But you're leaving behind so many things that you will need."

"I have already said that I have taken what I need."

We continued toward the train station, and along the streets everything seemed ghostly. Every image spoke of life—an um-brella leaning against a bench, flowers on balconies, a multicol-ored ball on the sidewalk—but everything was emptied of human presence, as if no one had ever lived here. From one part of the quarter, though, life was audible, and we headed toward those sounds. We reached a long column of people, walking as quickly as possible, as fast as their heavy suitcases allowed. Behind some of them ran their children.

I watched the people with their suitcases held tightly in their hands. Some held them in their arms, pressing them tightly to their chests; they hugged them firmly, as if they had packed their entire lives inside and now they only hoped that by clutching the suitcases to their chests they would preserve life, they would sur-vive. We knew they were going to the railway station. We stepped in among these people and continued with them.

At the train station there were soldiers who looked over our documents and then ordered us to board the freight train that was waiting for us.

I do not know how far we traveled. When we got off the train, soldiers were waiting for us; they brought us to a small fortified town. They gave us bread and water, and lined us up in a row to examine our documents, to write down our names, the years of our birth, where we had lived, and to determine where to put us. They put Rosa, Marie, Paulina, and me with a group of twenty other women our age, and they led us—hunchbacked, walking unsteadily with canes, our glances attempting to discern something more, something beyond several feet away—to the nearby barracks. They brought us inside one of them, where, in the long dark room, hundreds of beds were arranged along the walls in two rows. Old women were lying on most of them. Some of the women turned to look as we entered; others continued looking where they had been looking—at the ceiling, toward the floor—or kept their eyes closed.

The soldiers told us to pick out a bed that was still empty, and they left the room. My sisters and I looked for four free beds side by side. We found only three unoccupied beds together; I took the closest free bed. All of us new arrivals put our belongings under the beds we had selected; I had nothing to put under my bed. Then we lay down on the beds: boards with old blankets spread on them. I felt fleas biting me. Occasionally, a rat ran across the floor.

It slowly grew dark in the room. The light outside the barracks, near the window above my bed, illuminated the space around me. The rest was swallowed by the darkness. I tried unsuccessfully to fall asleep. I rubbed my roughened skin where the fleas had bitten, listened to the groans of some women. The bed to the left of mine was empty. At some point during the night, in the darkness, the door to the room creaked open, and I heard footsteps. A woman lay down on the empty bed. She did not belong with us—she was too young, about fifty years old. I slowly moved to the edge of my bed, and in a whisper I crossed the distance between her bed and mine.

"Where are we?"

She opened her eyes and said, "In Terezín."

I asked nothing further.

When I awoke the next morning, the bed to my left was empty. Soldiers arrived and led us to the dining room, in another part of the barracks. We sat down on the long, narrow benches, at the tables stretching from one side of the room to the other. We ate a breakfast of bread and tea, then stepped out in front of the barracks. The summer sun could not warm our bones—we shivered and rubbed our palms together and along our legs, from our thighs down to our knees. When we went again to the dining room, the woman who had slept in the bed next to mine appeared. She sat down beside me.

"The menu is always the same." She smiled. "For breakfast: bread and tea. For lunch: bread and lentil soup. And for dinner: bread and lentil soup once again."

I nodded. I listened to the women around us talking about themselves. They all spoke about their lives—about their husbands, their children, their grandchildren. The old woman sitting across the table from us, whose name I later learned was Johanna Broch, spoke about her son, Hermann. The old woman beside her, Mia Krauss, who had traveled with us from Vienna, spoke about her grandchildren. The woman sitting next to me noticed that I was listening to the others' conversations, and that I was trying not to.

"This is how they protect themselves from the here and now. They talk about what was there and then," she said. Then she asked, "Is your whole family here?"

"I am here with my sisters," I said, and with a glance to the right I indicated where my sisters Paulina, Marie, and Rosa were sitting. "And you?" I asked.

She said she was from Prague. She had daughters; she was divorced. She said she was lucky that her daughters at least, thanks to their father's blood, were secure in Prague. I mentioned my

sister Anna, who had moved to America right after she married; I
also spoke of my brothers, Sigmund and Alexander.

"We are three sisters," she said, "Elli, Valli, and I. We are all
here. We also had a brother, Franz." We fell silent again. I sipped
my lentil soup. She set her spoon down in her empty bowl and
said, "I always eat quickly. I have to. I help out in the barracks
where they house children from the orphanages in Prague and
Vienna. I'm going there now." She stood up and placed her hand
on my shoulder. "My name is Ottla," she said, "Ottla Kafka."

"I am Adolfina," I said.

She pressed my shoulder with her fingers, smiled, then drew
her hand away, turned, and left the room.

THAT EVENING, Ottla was in the dining room again. I slowly
chewed the lentils. She asked me, "Have you gotten used to being
here?"

I did not know what to say. I said that for a person to get used
to "here," one needed to know what "here" was, and I did not.

Ottla said, "This is a camp, you know that. Until last winter,
it was a small town; then they expelled all the residents so they
could bring us here. People younger than sixty work twelve hours
a day. They build barracks for new groups who will be brought
here, or else they work in the gardens so we can have food. After
those twelve hours, those who aren't dead-tired can engage in
whatever it is they did before being brought here. There are musi-
cians and painters, actors and ballerinas, writers and sculptors.
During the day they mix mortar, carry sand, nail down boards, or
dig in the fields. But at night they prepare concerts or ballet performances. Or they compose, paint, write. . . . You should go to
one of the concerts, or to a performance."

"I have not been to a concert or performance in a long time,"
I said. I broke off a piece of bread, put it in my mouth, and chewed.

"It is best if you do something here," she said. "They put me in the barracks where you are so the older women can find me at night if they get sick. During the day, several other women and I teach the younger children to read and write, and the older ones the basics of mathematics, geography, and history. The children help us clean the barracks, and we prepare food together. It is best to do something here."

The following day, Ottla brought me to one of the barracks where the children were housed. We entered a room where dozens of children were divided into several groups, and there was a woman with each group, explaining something. Ottla noticed that even though I was trying to hear what the women were telling the children, their words went past me.

"Let's go out," she said to me.

We sat on one of the benches near the neighboring barracks.

"This is where they put the women who are in their last weeks of pregnancy. They stay here for a few days after they give birth, then they are sent back to the barracks where they were placed when they arrived in Terezín, and they begin working immediately. There is one barracks where several women take care of the newborns." She put her hand in her pocket; I thought she would pull out a drawing of a woman perched on the edge of an abyss. In her hand she held two photographs. "These are my daughters, and these—my sisters, my brother, and I." She ran her fingers over the surface of the photographs. "This is all I have from my former life." She put the photographs back in her pocket. "My brother has been dead for so long that it is becoming harder and harder for me to remember his face." She ran her hand across the pocket of her dress. "I remember only one of his stories: 'The Bachelor's Misfortune.' I might not remember it exactly right, but I repeat it to myself sometimes." Looking at her pocket, she began to tell the story:

"It seems simply dreadful to remain a bachelor when you are old and struggling to preserve your dignity, to have to beg for an invitation whenever you wish to spend an evening in company, to be ill and look out from your bed in the corner at an empty room for weeks on end, always to say farewell at the front door, never to dash up the stairs alongside your wife, to have in your room only side doors that lead into the dwellings of others, to carry home your supper in a sack, to ooh and aah at others' children and not be able to say, 'I haven't any,' to cultivate your appearance and bearing on the basis of one or two bachelors you remember from your youth. That is how it will be, except in reality, you will stand there with a body and an honest-to-goodness head, and hence also a forehead for smiting with your hand."

Then she turned to me and said, "It is as if all that is left of him is contained in these words. But where are all those moments, days, and years, and everything that was in them? It is as if he never existed."

Two women came out of the barracks and sat on the bench next to ours. They put their hands on their bellies, as if to protect their unborn children. We introduced ourselves—their names were Lina and Eva. We struck up a conversation, but then Ottla told me that it was bath time, and we headed to our barracks.

Half an hour later, a group of young people carried several large empty basins and vats of water into the room where we slept. They set the basins in the middle of the room, between the two rows of beds, and the vats of water beside them. Then they left.

Ottla said, "Now hurry while there's water."

I saw all the old people undress as quickly as possible. With half-stiff fingers, we removed our clothing; we stood there naked, with only our sagging flesh, our drooping breasts and stomachs, our legs covered with purple veins, our twisted hands, and our rank breath that mixed with the stringent smell of our bodies. An old woman said something, but her words were lost among the sounds we made in our attempts to get to the basin first, to scoop up water from the vat with a bowl, and to pour water over our bodies, to start rubbing and to keep rubbing to clean ourselves of as much of the filth as possible. This lasted no more than a few minutes; there was water enough just to rinse off the filth, not wash it completely away. We dried ourselves with blankets and sheets, and then we got dressed. Ottla said, "Be happy that you came here in summer, so you can get used to this kind of bathing little by little. When I first washed up like this here, everything outside was frozen."

The young people who had brought the basins and vats came in and carried them away. Only then did I notice that Paulina had been sitting on the edge of her bed the whole time. I sat down beside her. She recognized me by my breathing, and she said to me, "I didn't get to wash up."

Ottla left the barracks and returned when most of the women were already asleep. When she had lain down on her bed, I quietly asked her, "How long will we remain here?"

"The longer the better," Ottla replied. "This is not a true camp but a transit camp, a way station. Trains, each holding a thousand people, occasionally depart from here for the other camps. It is different there. The work there is more severe, severe to the point of death. That is what people who have found out something more about those camps say. They say that people are sometimes brought into rooms where, they are told, they are going to shower. And there really are showers there, but only as a guise. Poisonous gas is then released, and they suffocate. Other horrors are spoken of as well, but it is better that I not tell you. So it is best for us to remain here as long as possible. Until this evil subsides. Then we will all go home." And she shut her eyes. With her eyes closed she said, "Do not tell the others what I have told you. There is enough suffering here, even without thoughts of the other camps. I should not have told you." She was silent a moment, and then she murmured "Good night" before turning to the other side of the bed.

Good night . . . I tried to fall asleep; for a long time I tossed in bed, thinking about what Ottla had told me.

IN THE MORNING, after breakfast, I went to the front of the barracks for pregnant women. There, seated on one of the benches, were the two women I had met with Ottla the previous day, Lina and Eva, and two other women. I sat down on one of the benches a short distance from theirs, and when, a few minutes later, Lina and the other two women went into the barracks, Eva came over and asked whether she could sit beside me. We began to talk; we asked each other where we were from. She said she was born in Prague; her father was a merchant, and her mother worked in the Bureau for the Protection of Workers. She had fallen in love with a classmate just after finishing high school; they married several years later. She was pregnant when she and her husband received word that they would be transported.

"Sometimes the most wonderful things happen at the most difficult times," she said, and looked down at her belly. "They brought us here with the first group in the winter. They gave me light work, in the kitchen. I did not have a problem with hard work as others do here, nor did I ever feel hungry. And at least during the day I was warm beside the stove. Other than in the kitchens next to the cooking stoves, there was no heating anywhere. In the evenings I was afraid I would freeze, that my child would freeze. My husband gave me his blanket as well, but even that was not enough to keep me warm. During the night I would lay my hands on my belly to keep my baby warm. Then spring came. I did not measure time according to dates or months but according to which week of pregnancy I was in. Thirty-nine weeks have passed; I have just a few days left." She placed her hands on her belly. "But a few days ago my husband was transported with hundreds of others to another camp," she said. She lifted a hand from her belly and touched first one cheek, then the other, drying them. "Before they left, they were told it would be better for them there."

"Surely it is better for them," I said.

When I returned to our barracks, I went straight to the dining room, to breakfast. Ottla was not there. I raced through my lentil soup and went to the room with our beds. Ottla was the only one there. She was sitting beside her bed, arranging her suitcase. She put some of her clothes on my bed. She said, "I will not be needing these any longer, and I know that you came without your own things."

I thanked her and asked, "You are leaving?"

"I am leaving," she replied. "They are sending a railroad car with a hundred children to another camp. The soldiers wanted an adult to go with them. I volunteered." She took my hand between hers. "I told the children that I am taking them on a trip."

She hugged me, then took the small suitcase in her hands and left the room. I remembered the words she used to describe the executions in the other camps.

I imagined her traveling with the children in the freight train and, with the children pressed together in the dark of the railroad car, telling them about the trip that awaits them, promising them the sea, games on the sand, and swimming. "But I don't know how to swim," says one of the children. "You will learn," Ottla encourages him. I thought of them being unloaded at the camp and led to a room where they're ordered to strip off their clothes. I heard Ottla tell the children they must shower first, and advise each of them to pay attention to exactly where they were leaving their clothes, because after the shower they would need to get dressed as quickly as possible so they could get to the beach. While I was imagining her, I saw her ashamed of her nakedness in front of the children, although a person feels least ashamed when he knows he is only a few steps from death. And they take those few steps; they enter the room with the showers. They look toward the showers, she and the children. They are laughing; they will finally wash up with warm water, with enough water. Some of them extend their arms, expecting jets of water. But then, instead of water from the showers, a poisonous gas spreads out from somewhere. Ottla looks at the children's faces, sees the contortion of their faces, sees those faces turn green, sees their mouths gape open, searching for air, sees them fall to the floor, one on top of another, and feels her own weakness as well, her own gasping, and curses herself that her body is so tough, that she will die last, watching their deaths, and finally she falls, falls on the children's bodies, sees their eyes roll back, blood flow from their mouths, and then she feels something breaking in her chest, her eyes roll back. She exhales her last breath.

I did not leave the barracks all afternoon. I sat on my bed, looked at Ottla's empty bed, tossed the things she had left me from one hand to the other: several pairs of underwear, a dress, a skirt, two shirts, socks . . .

Several days later, Eva gave birth. While she was in labor I sat on the bench in front of the barracks, and after the little one had been bathed I was allowed inside. They handed me the little body; I held Eva's little daughter. I was happy. I looked back and forth from the newborn to the mother, who lay exhausted on the bed.

"I do not know what name to give her," Eva said. "My husband and I never came up with a name for the child; our only concern was for it to be born alive and healthy. If only I could tell him now," she said, and began to cry. When she calmed herself, she begged me to give it a name.

"Amalie," I said.

"Amalie," Eva repeated.

I went every day to the barracks for pregnant women and those who had just given birth. I sat on the bed beside Eva and looked at this new life. This new life breathed, looked, blinked, cried,

slept, nursed. I listened to Eva when she told me how much she
hoped that she and her husband would meet again.

One morning I told Eva that all the old women in our barracks were being taken to another camp.

"Promise me," she said, "promise me that you will look for my
husband there. Pavel Popper. Please, remember his name. Pavel
Popper."

"Pavel Popper," I repeated.

"Promise me you will look for him in that camp. And if you
find him, tell him he has become a father. Tell him his daughter
is named Amalie. Tell him that she and I are well. And that we
will meet again one day. Promise me."

"I promise you," I said.

And then I had to go. I stood up, kissed Eva on the forehead,
kissed Amalie on the crown of her little head, and, before I left,
reached my hand in above my heart, between my brassiere and
left breast.

"I did not give you anything for the birth of your daughter. I
had nothing to give you. But now I remembered . . ." I said, and
from above my heart, from between my brassiere and left breast, I
pulled out the linen baby bonnet. "I bought this bonnet many
years ago. It is older than you are." I laughed. Eva laughed, too.
"Look at it—it is falling apart. I did not know why I took it with
me, but now I do. Maybe in the wintertime Amalie will need it."

Eva took the hand with which I held the bonnet out to her,
and she kissed it.

Looking at the palm of my hand that held the invisible trace
of Eva's lips, I slowly set off toward the door leading out of the barracks. And when I got there, I opened it; then I turned around,
and I saw Eva nursing Amalie. I looked at them, my view wavering
between fear and hope. I looked at Eva and Amalie as if wanting through them to look back in time, down the long chain of

mothers and daughters, not only the mothers and daughters who flowed through their blood, but all mothers and daughters, from the beginning of the human race to that moment, each one blood to blood. Then I turned and left.

I spent that afternoon in bed. From time to time, I propped the blanket up on my fingers a few inches above my head, and I looked into the white linen sky.

The following day they shoved us into a freight train, and our trip began. In the dark railroad car, which had earlier transported livestock—one could smell the animals—we sat on the floor, pressed one against another. Closest to me were Paulina, Rosa, and Marie. We traveled a long time.

It was night when they shoved us from the railroad car. Then they loaded us into trucks, and several minutes later they unloaded us in front of the entrance to a building sunk in darkness. A woman in uniform told us that we needed to shower before being housed. She told us that before we went into the next room we were to get undressed, and each of us should remember where we left our clothes. We undressed slowly. When I took off my brassiere, out fell the yellowed photograph of all of us: the Freud sisters, our brothers, and our parents.

They ordered us to move toward the door. We entered a dark room. They closed the door behind us. Almost immediately there was an audible hissing sound. I sensed the bitter smell. Someone's fingers pressed my fingers. I knew it was Paulina. I knew that on her face, even in that moment, flickered the smile that some blind people always have, even as they shrink before terror and mortal fear. Some of the old women around us screamed. Others prayed. Death was coming near me, death was before me, and I closed my eyes before my death.

$\mathcal{A}$T THE BEGINNING OF MY LIFE THERE was pain. Like the quiet dripping of blood from a hidden wound. Drop by drop. Although I was sickly as a child, my pain was not my illnesses but my mother. Perhaps I was also the pain of her life, or I was the point at which all her pains converged and dispersed. My mother, Amalie Nathansohn, was still at the age of innocent daydreams when her parents, without asking her, agreed to give her in marriage to the wool merchant Jakob Freud, who was already a widower and had just become a grandfather. With her husband, who was older than her father, she had to leave Vienna and move to a small town, where she forgot both to dream and to cry. In 1856, in a rented room above a blacksmith's where she lived with her husband, she brought Sigmund into the world; the following year she gave birth to Julius, who died eight months later; and then she gave birth to Anna. For months the only food in their home was bread and salt, and when they were down to a few handfuls of flour they decided to move to Vienna, where Jakob assisted Amalie's father in his textile business. They moved from one apartment to another in the Jewish quarter Leopoldstadt, and on each street they lived on, yet another child was born to them: Rosa on Weissgerberstrasse, Marie on Pillersdorfgasse. I was born on Pfeffergasse, Paulina on Glockengasse, and Alexander on Pazmanitengasse.

I was sickly as a child, and Mama was constantly at my bedside. I would see her face just as I awoke, then for several hours she would leave to scrub the floors in the homes of wealthier families, and when she returned home she would stay with me, leaving my bedside for only short periods, to straighten up or prepare something to eat. At some of those moments, while coughing, vomiting, or feverish, when I was on the brink of unconsciousness, I would hear her say, "It would have been better if I had not given birth to you."

At the beginning of my life there was pain, a wound wounded by the thought that my existence meant Mama's unhappiness. Perhaps Mama could not help but cut that wound in me. I was the point at which all her pains converged and dispersed: the premature conclusion of her dreams, her marriage to a man who had just become a grandfather, the death of her second son and the raising of her children in poverty, the constant move to smaller and smaller apartments, the scrubbing of floors in the homes of the wealthy. All these things converged in me, in my illnesses, in her fear for my life. That is why she hated me so much, speaking in a voice in which one would pronounce the fatal judgment, "It would have been better if I had not given birth to you," and why she loved me so much. She loved me to the point of forgetting her unhappiness.

Sometimes, when I breathed heavily, she would sing me a lullaby about the mother who kept watch over her child the way the moon keeps watch over the earth. Sometimes she would take me in her arms and we would go outside the building and walk along the avenues lined with trees; with one hand she would support me, pressing me to her breast, and with the other she would reach up and pick flowers from the lowest branches of the lindens, the chestnuts, and the acacias, and then she would hold the flowers between our faces. Sometimes she would take me in her lap, and while we sat by the window with the snow falling beyond it, she would tell me fairy tales in which good always triumphed over evil.

At the beginning of my life there was love, like a breeze that comes to warm you when life turns cold. And since then, whenever life brought cold that froze my soul, I longed for that warm breeze as for a balm. At the beginning of my life there was love: my mother's look, her hand on my forehead, her concern for my health. In those hours in bed with fever, in my half-consciousness I could see Mama, her look of concern for my life, her hands that placed cold cloths on my forehead, that removed my clothes, damp with sweat, and that dressed me in new ones. Yet sometimes, while my look drank in hers, her eyes would suddenly change, and where there had been concern, there would now appear hatred, and her lips would utter the words I feared as much as death: "It would have been better if I had not given birth to you."

Because of those words, I wanted to die and for Mama to grieve over my dead body. That change in her look and the utterance of those words lasted an instant, just an instant, but they stayed with me even when love returned to her face and to her voice; that hatred and those words slipped even into my dreams.

During the night, I often awoke from dreams in which Mama was leading me to a river and we stopped in the shallows, but then she took hold of my small head and shoved it underwater until I lost my breath and I saw fish biting me in the face; or Mama turned into a wild beast and tore me to pieces; or I was a bird that she did not know was her daughter, and she would capture me, cut off my head, and then scald my headless body and pluck my feathers. I would wake up in the room where I slept with my four sisters and carefully get out of the bed I shared with Paulina, then on tiptoe go to the window. I wiped away the condensation that had collected on the windowpane, but I did not wipe away my tears. I looked through the window at the street, or else at the reflection of my face in the glass, and I repeated my mother's words: "It would have been better if I had not given birth to you." And much later, when it was too late for everything, I understood those words. Saying them to me, speaking them about my existence, she really wanted to say to herself, "It would have been better if I had not been born." She lived in such a way that her hatred—toward her own existence, toward those things in her life that were more horrible even than nonexistence—was divided in two.

At the beginning of my life there was love and pain. To the very end they went together, as balm to a wound, but sometimes the balm itself turned to a poison that inflamed the wound still more. My mother's hatred hurt me most, but no one loved me as she loved me. No one, not even my brother Sigmund.

Sigmund was six years older than I was. I remember him coming near my bed and bringing me a spoonful of honey, or an apple he would first stroke my cheek with and then bring close to my mouth. While I slowly ate the apple, he would tell me about two lovebirds. This was a story not written down anywhere, a story my brother dreamed up for me, or that I thought up much later, trying to recall my childhood. As I swallowed, he told me how, one morning, one of the birds flew off and never returned, and the other, from grief, pierced her breast with her beak and tore out her heart. When all that was left were the inedible parts of the apple, my brother would put his lips to my forehead, to check my temperature. Perhaps, because of my sickliness, my brother was more tender toward me than toward his other sisters, and before I slept he always kissed me on the forehead, in secret, because Mama would ridicule any gesture of closeness toward me. He showed his tenderness only when she was not at home, when she went to scrub floors in the homes of the wealthy, or to help my grandfather and father in the textile store.

With the end of my early childhood came the end of my illnesses. I could now go to the back garden with my sisters, who
played there with the neighborhood children, but a vague fear
compelled me to remain by the window. As soon as I awoke—and
I always awoke earlier than my sisters—I would go into the kitchen.
I knew that Mama would be there—lighting the fire, sewing, or
preparing food—and that Father would already be at the store. I
would sit beside Mama, and she would give me a boiled potato or
a piece of bread and butter, and while she worked, while I chewed,
I would wait for my brother to come into the kitchen. I knew he
was already awake and was reviewing the lessons from the previous day. After Sigmund had left for school, my sisters would go out
into the garden behind the building, but I would stay near Mama
and watch her work. I looked at her hands and face as she did
laundry, scrubbed the floor, patched, embroidered, cooked. When
my illnesses ended, Mama even stopped repeating to me that it
would be better if she had not given birth to me. From then on she
began to compare me with other girls, to tell me that I would
never be like them, to tell me that my life would always be a pain-
ful void.

When Mama was not at home, I went to Sigmund's room. In
each of our homes, he had his own room—these were usually tiny
rooms that had been rearranged, rooms that had been pantries
before we moved in. I would enter his room, with its small window that looked more like a crack in the wall, and I would stop by
the bed. I would stand in one place, and only my gaze traveled:
along the walls, the floor, the shelves, where my brother's books
and clothes were neatly arranged. I took care not to spend too
much time in that little room, so that my mother would not return
before I left it. Even before she gave birth to him, she believed he
would be, as she used to say, "a great man." When she was pregnant, my mother met an old woman who prophesied just that, and

my mother often repeated the woman's words: "a great man." But she always called him by diminutives: "my golden Siggie," always little, always hers.

I wanted to be in my brother's room most of all when he was there. I sat in the corner and watched as his eyes moved along the pages of his books, as his lips moved, silently uttering the words he read. When he had time, I begged him to read aloud to me in one of the languages he knew, or to tell me about what he was studying at that moment, which was often as incomprehensible to me as if he were speaking in an unknown language.

My father would return from the store only after it was dark, and even then, in the little time he spent with us, he seemed absent. He would exchange a few words with Mama, ask whether everything was fine with us children, with our home, and then he would take down the Talmud and, sitting apart from the rest of us, read quietly in Hebrew, a language sacred to him but that none of us, his children, ever learned. When they came to Vienna, our parents had decided, as had many other Jews in the city, that they would pass their Jewishness on to their children only through their blood, not through religion. They hoped that their quiet assimilation, the preservation of only those invisible marks of our ancestry—those in our blood—would make us equals with the other citizens, while they themselves kept their faith as silently as Father read the Talmud. Our father drew near to us only when he shared the stories of Noah, Jacob, and Moses recast as fairy tales, but beyond that he kept his distance, always conscious—in the way that some people are conscious of having done something much later than when it should have been done—of the difference between one time and another. He looked at us children, who were younger than the children of his children from his first marriage, and perhaps his consciousness of this was the greatest gulf between us, a gulf that led us to call him *Father*, not *Papa*—

Father, with the resonance of *Sir*. He froze all his warmth before it reached us.

On the day I was to set off to school for the first time, I begged my parents to allow me to stay home. I stayed home the next day as well, and the days that followed. After that, when my brother returned from school I went into his room, where he took out one of his textbooks and leafed through the pages, telling me what he thought I needed to know.

Every Sunday, Father and Mama went for a stroll in the Prater with Anna, Rosa, Marie, Paulina, and Alexander. Sigmund stayed home with me, with the excuse that he needed to study. But as soon as we were left alone he would put his book aside, and we would lie on the bed that I shared at night with Paulina and cover ourselves with the blanket, propping it up with our fingers about a foot above our heads, and then we were transported to a blissfulness where we felt like joined vessels. In that closeness—would it endure forever and a moment more—as we simultaneously inhaled and exhaled under the white blanket sky, Sigmund told me about the wonders of nature, about the longevity of stars and about their death, about the unpredictability of volcanoes, about waves that erode the shore, about winds that can caress but also kill, and I felt the intoxication of his words, of his breath, of the touch of our bodies lying one beside the other. We remained in that intoxicated state until we were exhausted, until I fell asleep, though I would wake at the bustling sounds of Mama and Father and my sisters and little brother when they returned. Sigmund most likely awoke long before I did, or he did not sleep at all; when the commotion woke me, he was never in the bed beside me.

On one of those Sunday afternoons, after listening to Sigmund's words mixed with the beating of my heart, I felt myself breathing more and more slowly, my eyes closing tight. I was lying there neither awake nor asleep, in some half dream, and I heard

my brother quietly, barely audibly, ask whether I had fallen asleep.
I lay still, breathing calm and level, not because I wanted to deceive my brother, but because I did not want to interrupt my pleasure. Gently he slipped out from under the blanket and left the
room. I remained lying there awhile and then slowly pulled off
the blanket and got up. I headed out into the hallway and toward
my brother's little room, and then pushed the door open a crack
and stood in the doorway. Inside, Sigmund was lying on his
bed. His pants were unbuttoned and resting just above his knees,
and he was looking up at the ceiling. He was moving his right
hand down that thing I was seeing for the first time. I felt my heart
beating in my throat and heard his panting. He was breathing
faster and faster. Then I watched as he closed his eyes, and his
whole body stiffened, his mouth opened, and he quietly cried out.
I heard myself shrieking. Startled, my brother turned toward me.
I darted back to the hallway and to the room where my bed was.
Lying down, I covered my face with my hands and cried. I felt
that the whole world of my childhood—the hours in which my
brother had taught me in his little room, where I sat in the corner
and observed how he noiselessly moved his lips while he read,
the hours in which he passed on knowledge to me, the way we
lay on my bed and felt that we would never be parted—all this
was extinguished forever. The sense that my brother and I were
parting hurt me. It was my first awareness that he and I would
set off on separate paths. I tried to catch my breath. I heard his
voice.

  "Please, don't cry." His fingers, sticky and with a strange smell,
stroked my fingers that covered my face. I felt my heart beating in
my throat. "Don't cry, please," he repeated. He was beside me, so
close and so distant. With his hands, he took my hands from my
face. I looked at him, and it was as if I were looking at a different
Sigmund and some other I were looking at him. I closed my eyes
and felt my tears welling up. I hugged my pillow. He remained by

my bed with his hands on my head. My sobbing quieted down, my rapid, broken inhaling and slow, drawn-out exhaling grew softer and softer. I remained with my head in the pillow; my brother remained beside me.

We heard the apartment door open.

"I will tell them you are sleeping," he said, and he left the room, closing the door behind him. At that same moment I felt my tears overpower me again, and I pressed my face firmly into the pillow, clenching it so that no one could hear my voice. I lay there awhile, and then I fell asleep.

The following day I avoided my brother. I left my room only after he had gone to school, and I returned to my bed before he got home. I did not go to his room, as I had always done when he was at home, nor did he come looking for me, as he had done when I failed to knock on his door. That day, everything disgusted me, from the water to the food, my body, words, and the air, which, with repulsion, I inhaled in shallow gulps and quickly exhaled, then waited as long as I could until the next breath. A strange fever gripped me; it simultaneously exhausted me so I could not stay awake, yet shook me so I could not fall asleep. I spent the next day in bed. In my delirium, my body and soul found a way to keep me from thinking about the changes that a single sight had wrought. I do not know whether my brother had told me, or whether I had made it up myself, the fairy tale about the bird that lost its beloved and, in its grief, pierced its breast with its beak and tore out its heart. While I lay there half conscious, I felt that something was pecking at my chest, as if it wanted to reach my heart.

Those evenings, from the moment I lay down until I fell asleep, I remained turned toward the wall with my eyes closed, and I felt pain and fear beat inside me with the same rhythm. I was afraid of life, of what must come with it, and I ached with that fear. It was my awareness of the difference between my body and

my brother's that hinted at the changes that must come, and that
I did not know about. Much as I feared that difference, and much
as the thought pained me, I was equally afraid of, and pained by,
the mystery of relations with other bodies. It is something that is
passed down from generation to generation long before one hears
of it, before it is seen or experienced, a record carried in the blood,
firmly etched but cloudy and inexplicable in childhood. I began
to experience pain, and fear of that trace written in the blood,
with my awareness of the difference between my body and my
brother's.

Many years later I read a study in which Sigmund, then
middle-aged, explained how one becomes a woman. He wrote
that the female child begins to become a woman "when she sees
the genitals of the opposite sex for the first time. She immediately
notices the difference and, it must be admitted, its significance."
With this observation, every girl "feels that she is seriously damaged," and therefore "becomes a victim of penis envy. All this will
leave indelible traces on her development and the formation of
her character." If womanhood is indeed achieved not through
something essential within a woman but through something external to her, her observation in childhood that she does not have
the same sexual organ as a male, her observation, as my brother
stated, that she has been "castrated," then why is the result of that
awareness envy, and not sadness, or fear, or indifference: sadness
that the sexes are different; fear of that difference, fear of the other
sex; indifference toward the difference? My brother did not allow
that observed difference to give rise in any of the girls-who-are-
becoming-women to other feelings except envy; he placed that
envy as the locus around which the *I* in every woman is created.
When my brother communicated this to the world as absolute
truth, he did not recall my pain that afternoon when he was thirteen years old, and I was seven, that pain and fear produced by the

sight of the differences in our bodies, of the thought of growing up and separating from childhood, from the presentiment that my life and his life were not going to continue together and would march on separately toward death. He forgot that afternoon and the sadness and fear that flowed from it and descended on me like a shadow transforming itself into a different sorrow, into a different fear, pouring into other sorrows and fears. He forgot. And to the maturation of every girl, that process he called "becoming a woman," he attributed one trait only—envy.

In my childhood, in my fear and my pain, only Mama noticed that something had been severed between my brother and me. She knew, not only because in the mornings I began to come to her in the kitchen only after I had heard my brother leave for school and to withdraw to the bedroom I shared with my sisters before he came home, but also by the way my face changed when my brother and I happened to be in the same room, how we avoided looking at each other, how our breathing altered. My brother no longer went on walks with me, nor did he play outside with children his age, because his time for games was over; his friends sometimes came to see him in his room, and when he went out to visit one of them Mama would come over to me and say, "Today is a beautiful day," as she drew back the curtains to let the sun enter the room. Slowly, I began to go out with Mama. We went to the market or to the shop where Father was. Sometimes I went down the stairs alone and out the front door of our building, down to the end of the street, and back again. From time to time, without saying hardly a word, Sigmund would give me a book he had borrowed for me from the school library. Likewise, after I had read it, I would silently return it to him and wait for him to bring me another. Even when he was not at home, I never entered his room. I avoided being in the same room with him; however, just as before, I waited for his return from school, or from visiting a friend. And when I heard his steps in the hallway I lay down on my bed, pulled the cover over my head as we had once done together, holding it with our fingers above our heads, and in place of my former joyful intoxication I felt a pain pecking at my chest, as if trying to reach my heart.

*S*HADOWS, WITH THEIR HINT THAT PERHAPS we, too, are shadows of some essence that will remain a mystery to us until we return to it, are one of the wonders of daily life that often go unnoticed. Only occasionally will someone peer into the shadow thrown by clouds or by a tree, or into his own shadow, and that moment will seem to hint at some revelation.

There was something of that union of shadows, that touch of reflections, that weaving of two intangibilities, in those moments when Rainer and I were together. I met him when he was nine years old; I was two years older. He had eyes that were different from the eyes of every child I had seen. His were eyes that cried inward, with tears that fell somewhere deep inside him, and they did not bring him the release that comes with weeping. Until then, I had been afraid to get close to other children (to me, my brother Sigmund was never a child); some sort of strange unpleasantness washed over me even in the presence of my sisters. But as soon as I saw Rainer I wanted to be near him. Little by little I drew close, and once I called to him so our shadows could play. It was autumn, and I said, "Our shadows can touch each other even if we don't touch." And our shadows played together.

That was the year my brother enrolled in medical school. It was a time of changes. Grandfather had died, and his store had passed to my parents. Mama no longer scrubbed floors in the homes of wealthy families but helped my father in the store. We moved to a larger apartment on Kaiser-Josef-Strasse. That year I wanted to learn to paint. Sigmund and I had long been distant, but this desire of mine renewed our closeness. We were eating dinner when I said I wanted to learn to paint. Mama had a good laugh at that. She said I had not wanted to go to school because I was incapable of basic learning. She said I also did not know how to converse, and so I did not play with other girls; she said painting was not for girls.

My brother remembered my wish, and a week later he told me there was a painter who gave free drawing lessons in the home of one of his professors. The painter, whose name was Friedrich Richter, was from the area around Munich. He and his wife had lived in Vienna when their son was born, and had then returned to their estate near Munich, but now they had come back to Vienna because they had heard that Dr. Otto Auerbach, my brother's professor, could help children whose souls were filled with sorrow. Because Dr. Auerbach believed that proximity to other children would help Rainer, he allowed Friedrich Richter to hold drawing classes in his home for the children of the professors in the medical faculty who were the age of his son. My brother had asked that I be allowed to attend the classes, and every Sunday afternoon he brought me to the home of his professor.

Out in the garden, when weather permitted, or in the house when it was cold, Friedrich Richter taught us how a point develops into movement and line, how a line widens into a surface, how a surface becomes space. When the classes were held in the garden, we often noticed Sarah, Dr. Auerbach's daughter, watching us from the window of her room. Sigmund told me that Friedrich Richter gave her drawing classes on other days, because Sarah Auerbach had difficulty walking, and our drawing classes were more of a game, a pastime, child's play, and less about mastering the skill of drawing. The game's purpose was to cure Rainer, but he remained distant from the other children, distant from everything in this world.

I knew only a few things about Rainer, things my brother had heard from his professor, Dr. Auerbach. Dr. Auerbach refuted his colleagues' hypotheses that Rainer's sadness stemmed partly from the fact that his mother and father became parents in their later years and seemed more like his grandmother and grandfather. He had grown up near Munich, but was still steeped in nature; while his father painted, he stayed near his easel in the fields, near the brooks, and in the forest around his home; the remainder of the day he spent with his mother, who sometimes read him poetry and played for him on the piano. Yet that idyllic existence did not lessen Rainer's sorrow. The child remained immersed in his pain, as if sunk in water, as if some torment had pushed his head down and forced him to sink into this pain, and only occasionally allowed him to surface above the water to catch his breath.

No one knew where his melancholy came from, or what provoked his sighs or turned his gaze aside. Even when his mother stood before him and explained something, Rainer stared into an absence, as if he were staring in the direction where something had disappeared and would never return. His gaze fled from everything and fastened on the emptiness. Sometimes a child would pass a ball to him, but Rainer did not stretch out his arms; another child would say something to him, but Rainer would not respond; yet a third child would tug him by the sleeve, but Rainer would not move or shift his gaze. The other children went on with their games, but I stayed beside him.

Many pains occur in the course of a life. Some disappear; others stay with us until death. But only that first pain is our true one. Every other pain aches through that pain; every pain that follows hurts deeply only if it approaches that first one, only if it contains something akin to it. My pain had a name: the pain preserved in my first memories, and to which all later pains attached, had the name of my mother. Rainer's pain was nameless. Although it was always present and always with him, he had forgotten it, and his gaze, which drifted somewhere to the side of people who stood near him, somewhere into the emptiness, seemed to seek out that pain, the pain his parents also sought, hoping, with the help of doctors, to cure him.

We were children, and we were at the time of our first pain; our pains met each other, and perhaps that is why we became so close, close like wound and balm, closer than two happy children, because pain is the strongest bond. And so we stood alone, one beside the other. All around us the other children hopped on one leg, tossed a ball, skipped rope, chased one another around the trees, but Rainer and I stood there. I looked at him, and his gaze sometimes fell on me for a second, and then fled again into the emptiness. I sometimes told him tongue twisters, riddles, fairy tales, and once I began to tell him about my mother, about her words of contempt and ridicule about how I ate, how I laughed, how I walked, about how when her friends visited us at home with their young daughters she would tell them, in front of me, that I did not know how to talk, to laugh, to walk as they did. I told him what words she used to wound each of my delights and each of my joys—my delight in his father's talent, my joy at meeting him, Rainer, each Sunday afternoon, even though he was silent.

Then, for the first time, Rainer spoke to me. "But my parents love me," he said, yet there was such pain in his voice. Pain such as children have when someone close to them has just abandoned them.

For a moment or two I looked at him in silence, and then I said, "My parents love me, too. I know Mama hates me because she loves me. And when she says those words to me I no longer listen to her. That is, I do listen to her, but her words do not hurt me. They go past me, because I am thinking of you."

For the first time Rainer looked me in the eye for longer than a second. A ray of happiness crossed his face and took the sadness away. I wanted to ask him what it was that had made him happy, and he also seemed to want to tell me something, but his parents, who were sitting on a nearby bench, had noticed the change.

"Rainer smiled," cried his mother. His father came running. But the sadness had fallen once again across their son's face, and his gaze was lost in the emptiness.

The following Sunday, when the grown-ups had gone into Dr. Auerbach's house and the children were running about the yard, I proposed to Rainer that we play with our shadows. He said nothing, but I told him that our shadows could touch, even if our bodies were far apart. We began to play with the shadows of our fingers, holding our hands apart, mine from his, but on the ground the shadows of our hands intertwined. Slowly, we moved our fingers closer through the air, moved them around, and watched as their shadows joined together and moved apart. Rainer watched the shadows, and for the first time his eyes refrained a long while from fleeing into the emptiness. I held out my hand toward his and told him that I sometimes dreamed I was falling and held out my hand to grab on to someone else's, and my hand really does reach out while I am sleeping, and it strikes the wall, and the impact wakes me up.

"Sometimes," I told him, "when I am awake and things are hard for me, I want to have a hand near me, and for that hand to grasp mine."

Then the shadows of our hands overlapped, and his hand and mine entwined their fingers.

Mr. and Mrs. Richter were grateful to Dr. Auerbach, because their son pulled his gaze more and more often from the emptiness, and he sometimes answered other people's questions, not only his parents'. Occasionally, he even smiled.

Soon, owing to Rainer's improvement, his parents decided to return to their estate near Munich.

"One day we will be together again," Rainer said to me at our parting.

"But until then," I said, "it will be hard for me until you come back."

"For me, too," Rainer said. "So that it will be easier for us, let's think of that day when we will be together." Then he handed me a piece of paper he held in his hand. "This is for you," he said. "A remembrance."

I took the sheet of paper, and there was Rainer. It was a portrait his father had sketched in pencil. I looked at the drawing, and then I looked at Rainer. I looked at his eyes that cried inside and imagined the tears falling inside him. I wanted to give him something, too, something he would remember me by, something that would remind him how our shadows played together, how he touched my hand, what he promised me at our parting. I wanted to give him something, but I did not have anything, and then I thought of tearing off the pocket of my little red dress, a hand-me-down from my older sisters.

"It is very hard for me that you are leaving," I said, and I began to tear the pocket from my dress.

"It is for me, too," said Rainer, and he placed his hand at the pit of his stomach, as if he were placing it on a wound. "It hurts me here for you."

I tore the red pocket off the dress. I stared at that small piece of cloth the size of a child's heart.

"This is so you can remember me," I said, and I scrunched the little pocket into the palm of his hand.

When he left Vienna, Rainer was ten and I was twelve. Often, some boy on the street would look like him to me, and I would set off toward him, my heart beating joyously, and then my steps would stop abruptly, because the face was not the one I expected.

I would recall his look whenever I awoke during the night at the moment when my hand, seeking in my dreams someone else's to take hold of mine, struck against the wall. And then I would hug my pillow, thinking of his words that one day we would be together, and I wanted to fall asleep and sleep through all the days and nights that had to pass until that promised day, and then awaken.

. . .

IN THE MORNING, WHEN MY SISTERS AND MY YOUNGER brother left for school, and Sigmund went to his lectures at the university, after Mama went to help Father in the store, I pulled from under the carpet where I had hidden it the piece of paper with the drawing of Rainer's face. My gaze caressed the paper. I looked at Rainer's full lips, at his carefully combed hair, at the thoughtful line between his eyebrows, at the eyes that cried inside, and I thought that perhaps at that same moment Rainer was sitting in his room, and just as I was looking at this piece of paper he was looking at the red pocket I had given him to remember me by.

Sometimes, sitting in the corner of the room, leaning against the wall, I would fall asleep staring at Rainer's face resting on my knees. I was wakened from one of those dreams by the sharp voice of my mother, who had returned early from Father's store.

"What is that stupid face?"

I saw her look at the piece of paper with contempt. My hand trembled with the desire to hand her the paper and beg her to bring Rainer back for me. My hand hesitated, but my mother's hands were already tearing the paper with all the abandon of a murderer who has long thirsted to take a life, and who finally carries out his crime. She tore Rainer's face into tiny pieces, as when the murderer, after killing his victim, continues to strike, not because there is any doubt that the person is dead but because death seems too small a torment, or because not even the act of killing has extinguished his rage. My mother crumpled up the torn pieces, then opened the window and tossed out what only a few moments earlier had been Rainer's face. She closed the window and left the room.

I bowed my head on my knees, felt my chest shaking, my knees becoming wet with my tears, and I heard myself crying. That piece of paper with Rainer's face had been for me a presence in his absence, a sign and a promise that our separation was not forever. And while Mama was tearing his face I felt she was destroying not only my one tangible memory of him, the one thing that reminded me of his face, but also, with his hair, his eyes, his face now only a hazy memory, the promise that our separation would not be forever.

• • •

ONCE AGAIN, MY MOTHER BEGAN TO RECITE THE WORDS THAT
had been engraved in my first memories, and that I had long forgotten: "It would have been better if I had not given birth to you."
At one time, she had said them to me when I was ill and on the
edge of unconsciousness, but now she said these hateful words
when I told her some naive thing that was appropriate to my young
age. She also said them when I made a mistake, one that could be
expected of a girl my age; and eventually she began to say "It
would have been better if I had not given birth to you" instead of
"Good morning" or "Good night," instead of "How are you?" or
"Do you need anything?" I heard her words even when she did
not say them to me; I moved in a circle circumscribed by "It would
have been better if I had not given birth to you." I wished to free
myself from that circle, and in the morning I wanted to go into the
kitchen as before, when my mother would give me a hot potato
and I would sit in the corner of the room, watching her work. There
were many such mornings when I hoped I could again go in, and
then I would ask her what I could do to expiate my guilt. Perhaps
something in me hoped that my mother would greet me with her
former look and we would again be close. I went into the kitchen,
but now I was cut off by the coldness of her look, the roughness
of her words, the way she skirted around my body as she moved

about the room, and my question stuck in my throat. It remained there, and later on I wanted to vomit it up, to toss it out as one discards spoiled food, but it remained, like rotten food, stuck to me, refusing to let me go, and I carried it everywhere, a sign of some horrible guilt that does not know its crime.

When I lay in bed at night, huddled next to the wall, my whole body trembled from fear and sadness. Falling asleep, I struggled for air, struggled to inhale and exhale. Sometimes, during the night, the strike of my hand against the wall would wake me; in my dream I was falling, and I reached out for someone's hand, trying to grasp it, to save myself from the fall. Even in my dreams, my life turned into an undeserved gift, and the one who had given it to me reminded me continuously of this. I said nothing during these moments of humiliation, and I felt something pecking at my breast. That feeling of rejection plunged its beak into that which trembled in my breast, and that pecking bird cried with the cry of a newborn left alone, who feels that its entire world has disappeared because its mother is not there before its eyes. That is how something cried within me. I did not cry, but a tormented expression crushed my face, as if a stone had been hung around my neck and I were condemned to move with it through my childhood and beyond. I met that expression whenever I looked in the mirror. I hated my hypersensitivity. I trembled, and I wanted to be able to smother that trembling. I pitied myself, and I hated my self-pity. Once, after another "It would have been better if I had not given birth to you," when my self-hatred wanted to kill my hypersensitivity, I hid under the bed, put my hands around my throat, and sank my fingers firmly into my neck above my collarbone, until I lost consciousness.

Sometimes I borrowed a piece of paper and a pencil from my brother. I would sit in the corner by my bed, and I would try to draw that gaze looking into the horrible emptiness, two eyes that cried inside, but my attempt ended in a single point—the movement of my hand stopped where it had begun. Then I looked a long time at that point on the piece of paper, or I stood and looked out the window, or else I stabbed the tip of the pencil into the palm of my left hand.

   •   •   •

MY FRIENDSHIP WITH SARAH AUERBACH BEGAN SEVERAL months after the cessation of the drawing classes held in the courtyard of her family's house. Until then, I had known her as only a face that watched through the window. Later, her father told my brother that Dr. Ernst von Brücke, an amateur painter and a colleague of his, would be coming to their home to hold classes for his daughter and that he was seeking the participation of another child in order to create a more dynamic work environment.

Sarah was a year older than I was, and she had a sister, Bertha, who was three years older. Sarah wore metal braces on her legs. "I need to wear these because my legs are not strong enough to hold me up," she told me. Someone needed to accompany her when she walked. Often she would ask me to support her, and so we walked, our sides touching, from one end to the other of the spacious room with silk-covered walls, and imagined we were walking about a park. Sarah told me that with the help of the metal braces she could walk alone, but, should she happen to fall, her bones could break, because she was anemic, and therefore someone had to support her when she walked. I did not know what it meant to be anemic, but I was uncomfortable asking. Once, as we walked about the room, our sides touching, I told her how beautiful her hair was.

She said to me, "That's because I am anemic."

I told her I did not know what being anemic meant.

"If you're anemic, you have moments in which all of a sudden you cannot hear anything around you. You feel completely weak. You cannot see anything. And you lose consciousness. It is all wondrous and beautiful. I don't know why. All at once, in complete weakness, you do not know who you are," she said, and, falling silent, she brushed back the lock of hair that had fallen across her face. Then she added, "If that is how one dies, then I am not afraid of death."

Instead of speaking about death, we spoke about life. Sarah tried to explain to me what menstruation was, and how she would feel the day before its onset. She would have a high temperature, and at the same time tremble from cold.

"That is the first step toward becoming a mother," she said.

"When will you become a mother?"

"That will come much later, many years after this first step. That's what my mother told me." Then she put her hands on her belly. "It must be a wonderful feeling, to have another life here."

"It seems frightening to me," I said.

"Perhaps," she said. "Terrible and simple, like menstruation, the first step toward becoming a mother," she said, as she stood halfway with difficulty, then hesitantly stretched out one leg, as if she would take a step, but in fact let it hover just above the floor, and then sat down again in her chair. "My steps are always too slow. . . ." She stood again and began to take some steps across the room. I went over to hold her steady while she walked, but she gently brushed my hand away. "Mama did not want to tell me exactly how one becomes a mother. She said, 'This is the first step.' And she said there are still many steps until one becomes a mother. But when I asked her what those steps were she did not want to tell me."

I thought about Rainer and my brother, and I asked Sarah, "What is the first step toward becoming a father?"

"I don't know," she answered.

Several months later, my first step toward motherhood arrived. From that day on, the memory of the thick red fluid has stayed with me, the feeling that I was somehow cut in half, and that horrible heaviness when I told my mother, and she said to me, "From now on you will need to know your obligation, the fundamental obligation of every woman: to repay the debt for your life with the birth of new lives."

. . .

ONE SUNDAY MORNING DR. BRÜCKE TOLD US HE HAD TAUGHT us everything he knew about drawing, and he advised us to enroll in the School of Applied Arts, where we would be able to deepen our drawing skills and learn to paint. Sarah was then fifteen, and I was fourteen; she did not even try to enroll, and I did not pass the entrance examination. The two of us continued to draw whenever we met. I drew at home as well, in secret, and sometimes, when my mother was at the store helping my father, I would lay the drawings out in the kitchen. Once, my mother returned early and stared at the drawings laid out on the table, on the chairs, on the stove, beside the window. She looked first at me, then at the drawings, as if she had caught me doing something shameful. She thought that since I had stopped attending lessons with Dr. Brücke, and had not succeeded in enrolling in the School of Applied Arts, I had stopped drawing.

"Why do you draw at all?" she asked, as I slowly gathered the drawings, one by one, as if gathering up my shame. "Your drawing is meaningless." I looked at the drawings that I had crumpled between my fingers. "Do you know what meaninglessness is? Meaninglessness is when something is done for no purpose. When what you do does not lead to something else. You learn to walk so you can get somewhere. You learn to talk to communicate with someone. You give birth to a child to continue life. But you, why are you drawing? It is meaningless. Since you are doing something as meaningless as drawing, perhaps even those things that do have meaning will become meaningless in your life. You will not get anywhere, even though you have learned to walk. You will have no one to communicate with, even though you have learned to talk. You will not continue life, even though you could give birth." She covered the drawing closest to her with the palm of her hand. "Stop drawing if you want to save the meaning of your life."

I stopped drawing. I stopped not because I believed that if I stopped drawing I would save myself from the meaninglessness of my existence. I stopped because every time I wanted to take a pencil in my hand I recalled my mother's words and my fingers tightened. And that afternoon, when she had ended her rebukes but continued to look at me with contempt, I crumpled the drawings, put them in the stove, and lit the fire.

• • •

WHENEVER I WANTED TO GO WITH MY BROTHER TO THE
library, where he spent hours, my mother would say that she and
my father needed me at the store, and I would go with her. Later,
I figured out what I had to do. As soon as my mother started a
conversation with a customer, I begged my father to let me go and
read, and he did; I would leave the store quickly and set off for the
reading room. My brother read books for his studies at the medical faculty, while I tried to understand some philosophical works.
During our reading breaks we talked, and, if he had already read
what I was reading at the moment, he helped me understand what
I'd found incomprehensible. When we returned home together,
my mother would again greet me with reproach, blaming me for
all the work she and my father had to do without my help, or she
would explain again that girls belonged in the kitchen. But the
hours spent beside my brother in the reading room while he looked
at his books and I at mine, hours spent in conversation, had somehow made me strong, and more and more often my mother's
words rolled off me; they did not penetrate me, they did not pierce
my breast, the coldness of her look did not bore into the center of
my eyes. My mother sensed this, and at times her look lost its
assuredness. We no longer shared equally the poison that had entered the thread between her and me but flowed only toward her.
It was too powerful for her alone; it smothered her in her power-

lessness. That ray of happiness that more and more often suffused my face, that hint of joy that tinged my voice whenever my brother and I returned home together, smothered her.

When we took a break from our reading and went into the library's courtyard, my brother explained things that were difficult for me to understand, but still I listened attentively. I knew how important it was for him to have someone to hear him out, because his friends were dedicated to medicine alone, while he wanted something more; he wanted to unravel the secrets of being human beyond anatomy. Sigmund was convinced that those secrets could be deciphered at the intersection of reason and emotion. He said that both thinking and feeling were essential parts of us, and only through the "cooperation" of those two parts could a person understand himself. Sometimes my brother would reread one of the books he had recommended to me. He liked Sophocles, Shakespeare, Goethe, and Cervantes. He asked me not to read Balzac and Flaubert, because they were filled with immoral things. He forbade me to read Dostoyevsky, whom he had just discovered, because his work was filled with dark thoughts. He tried to help me understand Hegel and Schopenhauer, and I told him what I was reading of Plato, whose works he knew indirectly through John Stuart Mill's writings.

Sometimes, at home, I opened the Bible, and the part I liked most was when the Queen of Sheba said to Solomon, "O that thou wert as my brother, that sucked the breasts of my mother! when I should find thee without, I would kiss thee; yea, I should not be despised. I would lead thee, and bring thee into my mother's house, who would instruct me: I would cause thee to drink of spiced wine of the juice of my pomegranate." I opened that book only when my brother was not near me; he had read only short sections and said it was full of nonsense. This was where the slender thread was broken between us and our forgotten ancestors. We were the first nonbelievers in the long line of generations from the time of

Moses to our own, the first who worked on Saturdays, who ate pork, who did not go to synagogue, who did not say Kaddish at the burial and on the anniversaries of the deaths of our parents, who did not understand Hebrew; German was our sacred language. We were enraptured with the German spirit and did everything to become a part of it. We lived in Vienna, the capital of Austria-Hungary, which was termed the "Holy Empire of the German Nation." And with a strange enthusiasm with which we hid our shame toward our own tradition, we adopted the customs and mores of the Viennese middle class of that era.

My brother believed that Charles Darwin had discovered man's true place in the animal kingdom, asserting that with Darwin begins our true understanding of the human race—a natural creation that arose through the transformation of one living form into another, not a divine creation from dust and a puff of divine breath. He believed that with intellect it was possible to resolve the puzzle of our existence, that Darwin's theory concerning the origins of man was just a beginning and what must follow the discovery of man's origin was an understanding of what man is, what it is in him that makes him what he is. "I want to understand the complex texture around which what are referred to as fate and chance intertwine," he said. In order to see each layer of that texture, in order to know each component of all these layers that constitute a human being, it is necessary to take the first step, to expel illusions, and he considered religion, with its dogma, the greatest of all illusions. He believed that only the mind can destroy these illusions, and he sought his predecessors in all those who believed more in intellect than in religious dogma.

Whenever he noticed that I was not following what he was telling me, my brother would make a certain gesture that we used as both our greeting and as a sign that we should change the topic of conversation. With the tip of his index finger he would touch my forehead, the tip of my nose, and my lips, and then we would begin to talk about our dreams, how we wanted to go to Venice, just the two of us; Venice, which, in our longing for a shared existence in that city, shimmered as we imagined the moon shimmered in the waters of the Venetian canals. With its lacelike architecture that we had seen in books, Venice appeared in our minds more real and powerful than it did to many who had been there. Venice—whenever we mentioned it, I would playfully press my two wrists together at the spots where my pulse beat, curve my fingers slightly, shaping them into a gondola, and sail my gondola-hands through the air. Through books, we discovered its painters as well: Carpaccio and Bellini, Giorgione and Lotto, Titian and Veronese, Tintoretto and Tiepolo. Through books, we also discovered painters who had never set foot in the city my brother and I dreamed of living in. We searched among the figures in the paintings of Brueghel and Dürer for fools, that subspecies of *Homo sapiens* that had vanished centuries before, whom we recognized by their marvelous caps, often with donkey ears or two or three points shaped like horns, and sometimes with little pompons attached; the fools, who were already amusing the rulers during the time of the pharaohs, telling them nonsense, yet concealing within it great wisdom; the fools, who were always found in the European courts alongside the kings, princes, counts; the fools, who, all the way up to the sixteenth or seventeenth century, could be found everywhere in Europe, as they wandered from city to city, village to village, receiving a groschen or two at holiday celebrations; the fools, the part of the human race that, perhaps wisely, rejected their intellect, deciding, perhaps consciously, to serve as jest for others, thus mocking the whole world, as well as the one who had so misassembled it; perhaps that awareness that the world had been put together incorrectly was the main reason to abandon one's intellect.

• • •

EVERY WEDNESDAY EVENING A GROUP OF TEN YOUNG PEOPLE gathered in Bertha Auerbach's drawing room, located on the floor above Sarah's room, to show off in front of one another, attempting to say something clever about life, love, music, literature. It was like a competition to see who would leave the strongest impression. Sarah did not socialize with her sister's friends. When I visited her on Wednesdays, we stayed in her room, talked as we normally did, and only occasionally would we hear the loud laughter, the lively discussions, or the sounds of the piano and the voices singing in concert that wafted down from the floor above.

During one of those evenings, Bertha came down to Sarah's room and asked us to come up to her salon to meet the artist who was to paint their family portraits. As soon as I saw him, his face seemed familiar to me, and when he began to talk about himself I remembered. Four years earlier, I had been seated next to him at the entrance exam for the School of Applied Arts. His name was Gustav Klimt. He was now eighteen years old, the same as I was. Even though a thick beard covered his face and his hair was already thinning, I recognized him by his pug nose, his gaze, and his self-assured smile.

That evening he was talking about shameful things that were kept hush in every home and among all but the very dregs of society. Even when Bertha's friends attempted ever so gently to steer

the conversation in another direction, or asked him where he had
completed his first commissioned works, he described how at fifteen he had painted certain acts on the walls of a brothel, and
then he went on about everything he did there besides painting.
They asked him whose portraits he had painted in the past few
years, and he reeled off the portraits of the wives of butchers,
bankers, doctors, and professors, but he spoke less about the portraits and more about what he did with those whose portraits he
painted. He spoke, we blushed, and Bertha Auerbach decided,
likely that very evening, to tell this young man she was canceling
the commission for the family portraits.

There, next to Klimt, sat his sister Klara, two years his senior,
who from time to time, completely inappropriately for the gathering, struck him roughly with her elbow and rebuked him, but he
justified himself by saying his behavior was part of the freedom
every human being required. She told him that the manner
in which he expressed himself did not demonstrate he was free,
rather that he had contempt for women, that he ridiculed and
degraded them. He was silent for a moment, waiting for someone
else to say something, and then he started in again with his inde-
cencies. When Klimt's vulgarity became so intolerable that Bertha's friends excused themselves, said they had to leave, and
quickly left the drawing room, Klara cut her brother off and said,
"My brother is right when he says that sexual expression is a path
to freedom, but his understanding of both sexuality and freedom
is incorrect. Sexuality is, in fact, freedom, a freedom that society
fears because of its potential to break down the hierarchies and
systems that support it, causing the very society that exists today to
fall apart. So it attempts to have sexuality wrapped in mendacity
and hypocrisy."

One of the young men sitting by the piano said, "We all know
that, but we do not know how these things can be changed without turning in a worse direction."

"For a start," said Klara, "mothers must stop advising their daughters to submit to their husbands. The advice mothers give their daughters can be summed up in one sentence: Obey your husband, because in that way you are submissive to God, because God gave him to you as your lord, and, even if he behaves badly toward you, suffer everything; try to please him, and do not complain to anyone."

A discussion concerning women's rights ensued between Klara and Bertha's friends, who belonged to the young Viennese intelligentsia. The discussion was more like an argument. The young intellectuals said that even so, the male gender must rule in the world, and Klara, before leaving the salon, stated, "Evidently, we young women must take for ourselves what the world and this era do not want us to have."

Klara did not come again to Bertha's salon, but that is when our friendship began. Sarah and I socialized with her almost daily, and so, little by little, we learned about her life. She spoke of beautiful things and ugly ones. She spoke about her father, who painted miniatures on tiles that later decorated the kitchens of the wealthy. Not only could he paint magically; he could also tell his children stories about the paintings that appeared on the tiles under his hand: the rooster and the hen, the windmill and the cow, the milkmaid and the river. Sometimes he got drunk and beat the children and his wife, Anna, who at that time earned money scrubbing floors in the homes of the wealthy. When she went to work, Klara's mother tied her sons and daughters to their chairs. She punished them harshly when they bickered, when they were naughty, when they went out of the house without asking her. Klara's brothers somehow, even as children, managed to save themselves from this terror by going to their father's workshop and helping him paint tiles, and later, when he would get drunk, they would run down the street so as not to be near his hand when he began to strike. It was more difficult for the sisters, but even for them salvation appeared: Hermine and Johanna went to live with their mother's parents, where they remained until their grandparents died, and Klara went to live with her father's sister.

When Klara moved to her aunt's house, her aunt had just become a widow and had returned from London, where she had lived with her husband. She had no children and devoted herself fully to her niece. She taught Klara to speak English and French; she gave her not only popular novels but also the works of Olympe de Gouges and Mary Wollstonecraft—a bit premature for Klara to understand them in their entirety, but just the right age for her to make up her mind to fight for women's rights. The two of them lived together for five years, but later, after her aunt died, Klara had to return to her parents. She was then sixteen years old, and her mother burned all the clothes and books she brought with her.

Klara was now dedicated to the idea of making women aware that they must win for themselves what belonged to them. She made posters on which she wrote that girls' education should be preparation not for their role as homemakers but to enable them to be independent. She pasted them on the walls of the schools; she demanded that wives have the right to seek divorce; she organized groups that petitioned for women's right to vote. For this, the political parties turned her in to the police. She was put in prison and charged with acting against not society but humanity.

When she was released, Klara would meet with Sarah and me. Her prison terms were short, several days, and she always came out with bruises. But she never wanted to tell us anything about prison brutality, nor did she talk about her mother's brutality. We learned about their relationship later, from Gustav, but Klara said nothing about it; laughing, she described how people threw stones at her when they saw her riding a bicycle or wearing trousers.

With distress she described how children were abandoned on the streets after their parents' death and died frozen and hungry. With anger she described the injustices women suffered in their marriages, and she repeated, "We young women must take for ourselves what the world and this era do not want us to have."

．　．　．

I OFTEN THOUGHT OF THAT WORLD AND THE TIME WHEN we were girls. I thought about this long after we were no longer girls. I thought of the young women of our era, who Klara said must ultimately liberate themselves, the young women whose place, my mother said, was in the kitchen. We were the first generation of girls born after the introduction of the word *sexuality*, in 1859; we were girls at the time when some called intimate relations between male and female bodies "bodily acts," others "venereal acts," yet others "instincts for procreation." From this union of two bodies one expected the elevation of souls to some heavenly sphere, but it was also regarded as an animal act that sullied the soul.

When I was no longer young, and I tried to recall the young women from that period when I, too, was a girl, I recalled the fearfulness of their gestures, the quavering of their voices, the restraint that further accentuated their bridled excitement. At that time, love was something that trembled between two souls and two bodies, a time in which passion was described as the rumbling of a volcano and longing as the rampaging of a hurricane, a time in which the words *soul* and *passion* and *longing* were spoken and written down so often—most often, by those whose bodies and souls had barely ever trembled with passion and longing—

that they became as worn as old shoes. It was a time when young people, or at least the young people of my acquaintance, lived in anticipation of the realization of that love, and believed that the beginning of their shared life would be as if the heavenly kingdom had descended to earth. But later they were sobered by the banality of the daily life that awaited them, because every anticipation that is greater than the reality, like each love that is greater than those who are loved, ends in either collapse or triviality.

That was our era, a time of silence concerning carnality. There was silence everywhere about anything connected with that new word *sexuality*. There was silence in the schools, the churches, and the synagogues. There was silence at home, in the drawing rooms, and in the public squares. The newspapers were silent, as were the books. Clothing that covered everything from toe to chin also served as a covering for that word. Girls and young women were most often kept in complete ignorance about their sexuality from birth until marriage, and they could only vaguely sense such things. They went out of their homes only in the company of their mothers or some other adult relative. Every image of the intimate parts of the male body and every image of intimate relations was hidden from them. Some young women found out from their mothers only hours in advance what would happen on their wedding night. Chastity was an ideal because of the husband. Those young women who remained unmarried became the subject of scorn, and their virginity, the century's ideal, was turned into an embarrassment, as if it were unnatural, because there was no one to whom it would be given.

Such was our era, the era in which we grew up, but Sarah, Klara, and I knew much more than the majority of our peers. Occasionally, we would take a peek in some of Sarah's father's medical books. Sometimes we overheard something in Bertha's salon. Sometimes Klara passed on to us something she had learned from

Gustav, or from the women she helped find their way through life's vicissitudes. We also learned that that same era carried within it a different world from the one that was talked about openly and that could be seen in the course of a day. Behind the silence of sexuality hid insincerity and hypocrisy.

• • •

ONE DAY MY BROTHER DECIDED TO SHOW ME SOME OF THE things Sarah, Klara, and I had only heard about. Sigmund had just graduated and was already interning at the Vienna General Hospital. Sometimes I went to visit him, and during one of those visits my brother led me to a unit of the hospital that he said was secret and illegal. While leading me to this unit, he told me what choices a young unmarried woman had if she became pregnant and the man who got her pregnant did not want to marry her. I knew that most often the parents, because of their shame, threw these young women out of the house, and very soon thereafter their lives ended from hunger, cold, or sickness, even before the birth of the child. I knew that some who survived long enough to give birth left the child in an orphanage, and they worked the hardest jobs, and as a result their lives did not last long. I knew that there were those who were unable to endure the shame and, in order to preserve their family's honor, killed themselves without telling their closest kin that they were pregnant. I knew that some women sought out someone with a little knowledge who would give them bitter liquids to drink, after which their bodies rejected the fetus, and that sometimes they themselves died from the poison. Then Sigmund told me that the wealthiest people, with their influence and money, could skirt the law forbidding abortions.

At the Vienna General Hospital, there were surgeons who

spent some of their time performing an activity that was against the law but was nevertheless permitted for some people: they performed abortions on the daughters and mistresses of the wealthy. We were standing outside the secret unit when my brother told me that he himself had learned how it was done; he began to describe the procedure in detail, and, as I imagined the metal grabbing the fetus, I felt sick to my stomach and vomited.

When it was already growing dark, we went to the poorest section of Vienna. We proceeded through the semidarkness of the narrow alleys and barely squeezed past girls in tattered dresses, and men in equally tattered clothing who approached those girls with prematurely weathered faces, with makeup that served only to emphasize the coarseness, and with breath that smelled of alcohol. Some of the girls touched Sigmund, stated their price, and then ran after us, lowering the price until it came to about as much as one would pay for a piece of bread. In some of the decrepit houses, half-naked women stood in the windows and called to the men walking past.

We left that part of the city and entered one of the more elegant quarters. Sigmund pointed out the small hotels on the side streets and told me that middle-class men came here to visit prostitutes, and that in those same rooms young middle-class men met poor girlfriends whom they hid from families that would not allow them to see each other. He told me the people from the wealthiest class went to brothels housed in mansions, or else kept unsuccessful actresses and ballerinas. "Do not think there is a difference between the first, second, or third; what some do in the dirtiest rooms of nearly decrepit houses, others in hotels, and still others in mansions does not make them different," my brother said. "Only the façade varies. The insides of those who do it are the same. The coarse give vent to their impulses; we abstain. We abstain in order to maintain our integrity. We do not squander our health, our capacity for enjoyment, our strength. We are saving ourselves for something, even though we ourselves often do not know for what. Rather than spend ourselves so shallowly and basely in animal gratification, we abstain, and our abstinence allows our feelings to deepen, to become more refined."

That evening spent along the Vienna streets was intended to be a lesson for me. What my brother wanted was for me to see the animal in man that does not permit the union of the corporeal and the spiritual, and for me to be repulsed by it in the same way he was. That night, the thought of a corporeal union of Sigmund with some woman kept me awake; the horror of it had me tossing in bed. My heart recoiled at the thought that some woman, resembling those we had seen that evening along the narrow alleyways, would introduce him to that which is only corporeal and emptied of the soul, and in this way separate him from our shared dreams.

●　●　●

SOMETIMES I WOULD ASK MYSELF, WAS THE IMPETUS FOR MY suggesting to my brother that he meet Sarah the horror of the thought that he would seek bodily satisfaction in one of those alleyways if he did not encounter true love? The closeness between Sarah and my brother began at their first meeting, from the moment he approached her in her room, gently extending his hand, and she stood up, attempting to keep her balance. Many times afterward, I returned in my thoughts to that moment, that uncertainty not only in her behavior but also in his, the forced restraint in their glances, pierced with anticipation and curiosity, and that joyful unease, composed of happiness and timidity, that flickered across her frail face, and across his, which he had always striven to give an appearance of seriousness—a desire that had led him, already in the first years of his studies, to grow a beard. All their subsequent meetings held these nuances of that first meeting, that joy and that unease, that anticipation, that curiosity, that restraint, that uncertainty, all those things that mingled with their words yet remained unspoken. I was always beside them, as a witness to something that was happening behind the words, something they never told each other.

Sometimes I wanted to be a witness as well to what happened when they were not together, to what happened to them in the absence of the other, in their solitude. I wanted to be able to see the images that flickered in their dreams and to discern their thoughts; I wanted to know what they would say to each other if that restraint, that unease, that timidity, were to fall away. I wanted to see the movement of their bodies in the moment when desire overcame all that remained, making the skin of their bodies all that separated them.

Their worlds were composed of such different elements, but both he and she wanted so much to hear from the other about those differences. My brother spoke to her about his world, which extended from his home to the university, the library, the homes of his friends, and the hospitals, where, together with his colleagues, he was acquiring a practical knowledge of medicine. Sarah told him about her world, which ended at the threshold of her home, about the things she could see beyond the border of her world, that other world, which she could see through the window of her room: the street and the houses on the opposite side, and the trees beside the houses and the sky above them; part of that intangible world was also what she could see in her books. Sarah would ask Sigmund about himself, about his studies, about his friends, about what he wanted to do the next day, and in ten years, and he said he wanted to unravel the riddle of being human; he wanted to know how love and hate are born, what it was that created desire, how our thoughts are propelled. "Perhaps we do not need to know these things," Sarah said, as she ran the palms of her hands along her legs, along her dress that hid the metal braces.

After they became acquainted, I never spoke with Sarah about my brother, nor with my brother about Sarah; I only sensed how much they looked forward to Wednesday's arrival, the day when our peers gathered in Bertha's salon, but Sigmund and Sarah stayed a long while in Sarah's room, and I stayed with them, a witness to what they kept silent, and when we knew that the gathering in Bertha's salon was nearing an end, then he, she, and I would go to the upper floor, and we would greet the guests, and we would hear Bertha's gentle reproach that we had not honored them with our presence.

• • •

I SAW KLARA LESS AND LESS. SHE NO LONGER CAME TO THE hospital. She rarely visited Sarah. When Klara came to see me, my mother always found some unpleasant word for her, and she did not feel welcome. She was now helping out in homes where women who had been driven out by their husbands lived, and in homes for children without parents. Her brother was earning enough to support the entire family, and she no longer had to sell flowers in the city's cemeteries; now she dedicated herself to helping those who had been outcast and to enlightening them about their rights.

She went to factories and incited workers to strike for shorter hours and greater pay, but the factory owners paid people to beat her so ruthlessly that she lay unconscious for days, and then, when she was back on her feet, she went to the factories again and organized the workers, and again she was beaten. She went to the spinning mills and the weaving sheds, and she persuaded the workers to join her in the battle for the same rights as men—for the right to vote, the right for political action—but the police detained her; they sentenced her to solitary confinement until her brother begged for her release. Her photograph appeared in the newspapers connected with the word *anarchy*. She was conspicuous by her inconspicuousness: instead of the delicate hairstyles of that era, her hair was simply short; instead of dresses with lace, bows, artificial flowers, and ribbons, she was the first woman in

Vienna to wear trousers. So she was recognized on the streets, where she was pelted with coarse epithets and stones, and spat on. The more she fought for women's self-assurance, the less self-assurance she had. All the blows against her left their mark. She lost her penetrating gaze and her confident voice; her words trembled in her throat; her gaze did not rest on a single point, but seemed to flee from where she was looking; and her body no longer had its confident bearing—she hunched her shoulders, her head drawn down. She resembled a bird huddled in the rain.

Sometimes I took Klara with me when I went to visit my brother at the hospital, and she asked him how to help those women who were unjustly taken by force to the asylums. She told him that if a woman stood up for her rights in marriage her husband could report her as insane, and she would be placed behind bars; that if a sister sought property rights after her parents' death, her brothers could place her in an asylum. The madhouses, Klara told Sigmund, were filled with sane women. There was nothing easier than for a woman to be accused by her father, her husband, her brother, or her son of being a danger to herself or to society, and she would end up in a madhouse. She asked him for advice on how the situation could be changed, and he told her that nothing could be changed. She continued to go from one madhouse to another, to enter into discussions with the doctors. One of the doctors responded to her with Nietzsche's words: "If you gaze long into an abyss, the abyss also gazes into you."

Sarah and I knew where Klara had been by the look in her eyes. There was always something maternal in her gaze when she came from the institution she herself had taken a part in founding, an institution where women who had been driven out by their husbands were cared for. The law did not grant these women— regardless of why their husbands had driven them out—the right to take their children with them; that is, if their husbands had not thrown the children out with them. Klara helped them, but she did not idealize motherhood. She said that every mother's experience of motherhood was different, just as each person's life was different, no matter how similar it was to others.

Once, when we were sitting in the butterfly house, the large glass garden with tropical plants built beside the Auerbachs' house, where there were clouds of butterflies flying about, Klara said to us, "I have seen mothers who gave their lives for the lives of their children, and mothers who took the lives of their children. I have met women whose only thought in life was to become mothers, and women who became mothers not because they wanted to but because they had no other choice except to marry and have children."

"But most mothers take care of their children," Sarah said.

"That care is most often not a question of choice," said Klara. "Even the most dedicated mothers I know would share the care of their children with the fathers. Their desire to share that care is a sign not that a mother loves her child less but that she needs some time for herself as well. And the belief that only mothers should look after the children is imposed by the husbands, so that they can expropriate all their wives' free time."

"You are forgetting," Sarah offered, "that in families in which all the mother's time is devoted to the children and to the home the husband also has no free time, because he works from morning till dusk to support his family. That is a natural division that has existed since the beginning of the human race—men, as the stronger sex, were able to earn more, and the women stayed at home with the children."

"Today both men and women need to work, but they also need to share equally in the care of the children. But it doesn't happen that way; it is the women who stay at home with the children."

"That is the natural way. The mother is the one who carries the child before it is born; it is fed from her body both before it is born and after."

"But each person is different," Klara asserted. "Each mother is different. Even though every mother has carried her child in her womb, every mother has a different relationship with her child, and every individual mother-child relationship is different. The connection between the womb and the child is also a curious matter."

"Why?"

"There is something curious about it, even in animals," said Klara. Then she asked, "Tell me, which animals do you think are the most maternal?"

Sarah thought for a moment and then replied. "The females of animals like deer, animals with hooves. It is not just that I have heard they show concern for their young, but in the eyes of does, cows, antelopes—and not only in their eyes but in their movements as well—there is something maternal."

"Well, I have heard the majority of such animals will reject their newborn if they do not lick it immediately after giving birth, if they do not mark it with their saliva, the sign that says specifically, 'This is mine, this is me.' The newborn will tug at the mother, beg to suckle, but she will turn roughly away, condemning it to die of starvation. Perhaps this explains the secret of the bond between mother and child. The mother sees the child as a part of herself, and when she does not view it that way she condemns it to death. A mother's love toward her child is love toward a part of herself. A form of self-love."

I waded into the conversation. "The sacrifice some mothers make for their children is not, then, a sacrifice, because what they are doing, they are doing for themselves, for something they experience as a part of themselves?"

"I don't know," Klara said. "Every destiny is its own story. At present, it is most important for us to fight for equality between men and women. They assure us that this is not possible, that men must always rule, but there was an era when women ruled. We do not need a new matriarchy, simply equality."

"Why not a new matriarchy?" Sarah smiled.

"Because justice is possible only when there is equality," Klara argued. "And when someone rules, in order to maintain that power, he also oppresses. While it is the men now, at one time, in the age of matriarchy, it was the women. When women ruled, they, the mothers, made child sacrifice obligatory. Every firstborn son was killed. They cut off the newborn's head, drowned it in water or burned it in fire, threw it to the dogs or the swine. The mothers created that unwritten law. When the patriarchy began, the fathers continued the custom. Embedded within it was the hatred of those who ruled toward those who would rule after them, and the fear of those who ruled of the loss of their power. The biblical story of Abraham and Isaac was first a story about a father sacrificing his son. Much later, the killing of the firstborn was replaced by a symbolic sacrifice, by circumcision. Then the story of Abraham and Isaac was also changed."

"If the killing of the firstborn was an unwritten law," offered Sarah, "then surely some parents experienced it as coercion. Surely some of those who were forced to kill their firstborn child suffered."

"By all means," said Klara. "That is why I said that no single destiny resembles any other."

We never asked Klara whether she wanted to become a mother. Sarah and I sometimes spoke about motherhood, and once she said to me, "The doctors tell me that my illness will not prevent me from becoming a mother," and she ran her hands along the metal on her legs. Klara always spoke about motherhood as something that happened to others, and as something she both could and should help with if a mother found herself in distress. She never suggested that she herself wanted to become a mother. Once, when she was telling us how a child in the orphanage where she helped out from time to time had called her Mama,

I seemed to detect from something in her voice that she was touched, some hint of desire.

That day in the butterfly house, when Klara, Sarah, and I spoke about motherhood, Sarah pointed at two butterflies flying through the air, conjoined, conceiving their offspring.

• • •

SIGMUND KNEW HOW MUCH SARAH LOVED POETRY, AND ON
one visit he brought her a just-published translation of poems by
Adam Mickiewicz. Before she opened the book, Sarah caressed
the cover, which depicted a fall landscape, and remarked that she
had not been to a park in years. "Then let's go to the Augarten,"
my brother said, and Sarah closed the book and set it down on
her bed.

The Auerbachs' coach took us to the park. My brother supported Sarah under her right arm, and I under her left. It was an
exuberant spring. We moved through a tangle of sights burning
with color, through a symphony of the sounds of nature, through
a sea of smells. Every few steps, Sarah begged us to stop, not because it was difficult for her to walk but because she wanted to
look at something along the path, something to which we paid no
attention because it was part of what we saw every day: a mother
and child sitting on a bench, throwing crumbs to the pigeons; a
painter standing beside his easel, painting a birch tree; a young
woman leading an old blind woman by the hand and telling her
about the world stretching out around them; two children digging
in the ground with their hands while their father read a newspaper, paying no attention to their search for worms; a young man

reclining as if in an armchair on the branch of an enormous oak tree, whistling softly; some young boys playing with a ball.

"So much happiness in one place," said Sarah.

"I am not sure all these people are happy at this moment," my brother said.

"Maybe happiness, like sin, is in the eye of the beholder," said Sarah.

"Happiness is a short-lived phenomenon. It is the fulfillment of some pent-up desire or need," my brother said.

"I would not call that happiness. I would call such a fulfillment of desires or needs *satisfaction*."

"Then what would happiness be?" my brother asked.

"I don't know," said Sarah. "I think happiness is one of those things for which there is no definition. It is something you simply feel."

We slowly reached the part of the park in which Vienna's first kindergarten was located. We sat down on a bench beside the fence and watched the children playing on the swings. A woman came out of the kindergarten courtyard, leading a child by the hand.

"That is happiness," said Sarah, looking toward the woman and her child.

"Parenthood?" my brother asked. Sarah nodded. My brother continued: "I do not see parenthood as the attainment of happiness, but as a part of reproduction, and reproduction as a part of the process of evolution and natural selection."

"And not as a part of your own life, something that will be a part of your own existence?"

"My existence is also a part of the process of evolution and natural selection. Only the strong survive in this world; that is the law of the survival of the fittest. Those who are quicker and stronger have a greater capacity for survival."

"Which means that the world is created for the aggressive," said Sarah, and she stood up from the bench, signaling to us with her hand that she wanted to walk without assistance. She reached the kindergarten fence and held on to the bars.

"That is only a superficial impression," my brother said. "But such survival is a part of the great evolution, of the advancement of animal species. And also of the human race. New generations can be stronger, faster, more adaptable than their parents, and they pass those traits on to their heirs, who are then able to advance further. Over the course of many generations, those improved traits become more articulated in the context of one animal species, and which species will survive and which will disappear depends on the development of those traits. The weak ones will vanish; that is the law of this world. We humans originated as part of the process of natural selection; we developed from lower forms of life. So that is how I view parenthood—as part of the great evolutionary process."

"I view it in an entirely different manner," said Sarah, and she turned toward the children who were playing in the courtyard. "To carry a new life for months beneath one's heart, and then to bring that new life into the world, and to see how that new life arrives, dazed, shocked by its expulsion from the womb and its encounter with a world that cannot but be unknown to it, because what it does know, it only senses; to see and feel how much I am needed by that new life, how it needs the food flowing from my breast; to observe how experience accumulates in its eyes, and to see the first hope and first disappointment of that new life; to see how that life becomes independent, how it no longer needs me, how that life that came forth from my life leaves me and embarks on the creation of a new life. That is what parenthood is for me."

One child separated from the others and walked right up to

the fence, bent down, picked a dandelion, and handed it to Sarah through the bars.

Before she died, Sarah found that dandelion pressed between the pages of the book Sigmund had given her. But that day in the park she held the dandelion in one hand, and with the other she reached out to stroke the child, yet before she could touch his head she stumbled, and once again took hold of the fence.

· · ·

MY BROTHER BECAME ACQUAINTED WITH MARTHA BERNAYS on his twenty-sixth birthday. The following month, he moved into a small room in the Vienna General Hospital, where he was already employed, and a month later, on the day Martha turned twenty-one, she and Sigmund became engaged.

One afternoon at the end of that summer, Sarah asked me, "Why doesn't Sigmund visit anymore?"

Until then, I had not spoken of Martha Bernays in front of Sarah. As I explained to her why Sigmund no longer visited, Sarah looked at her fingers, and then she put her hand under the pillow on her bed and pulled out the book my brother had given her several months earlier. I knew her habit of dreaming atop the books she loved the most.

Sarah slowly bent down, and although she was sitting, I thought she would fall over, that she would tumble onto the floor. But she grabbed the hem of her dress and raised it above her ankles, above her knees, above her thighs. Her thin legs, encased in the metal braces supporting her, looked fragile, like the stems of plants grown in dead shadow. Sarah began to free her legs from the braces; she opened them at her ankles, at her calves, her knees, above the knee, at her thighs, and then laid the braces on the floor. She rested her palms on the bed and raised herself up a little, attempting to stand and take a step, but her legs were not strong enough and she sat down, powerless, collapsing onto the bed. She tried again, and again her body returned to the bed as if it were toppling over. Yet again she raised herself, her lips trembling, her face contorted, tears welling in her eyes; she raised herself from the bed and toppled down again, and when she could no longer raise herself she bit her lip and cried, and struck her hands, now clenched into fists, along her powerless legs. I kneeled down beside her, took her hands, and she rested her face on my neck. I heard her sobs, her broken breathing, and I knew that the tears caused by her physical weakness were mixed with the tears caused by a different pain.

Then she became calm, took the book she had placed on the bed, and tucked it back under her pillow.

. . .

AFTER MY BROTHER MOVED OUT, HIS ROOM REMAINED EMPTY. Sometimes I went in and looked at the empty shelves where, until recently, his books and clothes used to be. Whenever my mother found me standing in the room that belonged to Sigmund, or sitting on his bed, she said he would be lucky if he had a little room like that for himself and Martha.

Part of my world disappeared with the appearance of Martha Bernays. My closeness to my brother disappeared; the world of our dreams disappeared before it had ever appeared; Venice disappeared; and the two of us together there disappeared. Sometimes, when I recalled how he greeted me before the appearance of Martha Bernays, the way he would run the tip of his index finger along my forehead, down to the tip of my nose, and across my lips, I raised my index finger, as if to point toward the sky, and then I ran it along my forehead, down the tip of my nose, and along my lips.

．　．　．

WHEN I WENT TO VISIT SARAH, MORE AND MORE OFTEN I found her in the butterfly house. Even her bed had been brought there, and throughout the day she napped in the glass garden. Sometimes I found her sleeping with butterflies covering her, and as she awoke and slowly shifted her body they floated off her like clouds. She spoke more often about the butterflies, about their metamorphosis from an egg to a caterpillar to a chrysalis and, finally, to a butterfly. She spoke about their hibernation, about their migrations in which they traversed thousands of miles, about the mimicry that helped them evade danger.

Once, I found her asleep in the glass garden, resting against a tree. When she awoke, she felt something scratching her head. Her hair was filled with caterpillars that had been crawling along the tree. I began to take them from her hair, managing to remove some, but some escaped through my fingers, releasing a slimy liquid that stuck to my skin and to Sarah's hair. In her hands, Sarah cradled the caterpillars I had managed to liberate, and she said, "One day they will turn into butterflies. One day they will no longer be crawling—they will fly." Then she cupped her other hand over them, as if protecting them from something. "Klara has not visited me for a long time."

"She leaves her house less and less," I said. "I went to visit her yesterday. She barely said a word."

"She loves to talk, but never about herself. She never speaks about how much her mother mistreated her when she was a child, nor about how much they mistreat her now in the prisons. I had a premonition that one day her strength will be broken."

"She was so strong, but now she is like a frightened bird."

"Promise me," she pleaded. "Promise me that you will not forget Klara. And help her if you can."

I promised, and she set the caterpillars in her lap.

Sarah had always been sickly, but we look on the illnesses of sickly people as part of their everyday life, and we rarely think that one of those illnesses must be their last. During the final weeks of Sarah's life, her imminent disappearance from this world was fully evident, but we all still believed her illness was something that would pass—all of us, that is, except her, though she never said so. I recognized her presentiment of death in the concern that some who, on seeing their end approach, have for those who will be left behind. I no longer remember how I detected her quiet concern for me, about what awaited me in my life, but I do remember that during each of my visits she mentioned Klara. "I beg you, do not forget Klara," she said to me. "And help her if you can."

After every meeting with Sarah, I thought about going to see Klara, but instead of going to visit her I returned home.

Whenever Sigmund came to our home, I said not a word about Sarah's illness, until the day it was evident she would soon no longer be in this world. My brother wanted to visit her with me. As he approached her, lying in bed with her hands clasping the book on her chest, it seemed to me that I saw the same thing I had seen during their first encounter, what I saw every time they met: that forced restraint, that subdued excitement, that anticipation. Again, I was here with them (they had never met alone; I was the eternal witness to the quavering in their words and the persistence of their silence; I closely observed each of their gestures, each facial expression, which disclosed many unspoken things), but now, when my brother sat down beside Sarah's bed, I lowered my gaze and only listened. I listened, but I did not hear anything except the weary tolling of their voices; somehow I could not make out their words. When my brother stood up from Sarah's bedside, I turned my gaze back upon them. Sarah had unclasped her hands from the book, and she handed it to my brother.

"You gave me this book that day we were walking in the park. We have not seen each other since, and I forgot to give it to Adolfina to return to you."

My brother hesitated. He had given her that book of poems by Mickiewicz, and now she was returning it to him as if he had merely lent it to her. While he stood staring at the book, the unpleasantness of that thought was expressed in the stiffness of his body, in the stiffness of his voice when he asked a completely ordinary and unnecessary question: "Were there any poems you especially liked?"

"The one about the young woman who, even years after his death, sees her beloved with the eyes of her soul and never stops talking to him."

My brother took the book, and from between its pages fell the dandelion that the child in the park had given her through the bars of the fence. The dandelion fell to her breast.

Sarah and I never saw each other again. Afterward, whenever I thought of her, I thought of the dandelion and of her hands receiving that fresh flower in the park, when a child handed it to her through the fence, of her hands raising the dried dandelion from her breast after it had fallen from between the poems of the book.

• • •

AFTER SARAH'S DEATH, I VISITED KLARA SEVERAL TIMES AT her home but was greeted by her mother's hostility. Klara was absent even when Klara was at home. I spoke to her, but I knew she could not hear what I was telling her. Her gaze drifted somewhere far, far beyond the wall she was staring at, and even when I touched her hand and asked, "Are you listening to me, Klara?" she remained absent. Only when I mentioned Sarah would she smile the smile of those who have made peace with the devastation their lives have become. When I saw how Klara was lost to a kind of emptiness, I recalled Sarah's words: "I beg you, do not forget Klara. And help her if you can." So I spoke to Klara about Sarah. I told her about the butterfly house, about the butterflies that landed on her body, about the poetry that Sarah read. I told her about so many things that had happened, told her these things as if they were happening now, and I said not a word about one thing alone: the thing that would prove that what I was telling her existed only in the past and in the memory of that past.

．　．　．

AFTER MY BROTHER HAD MOVED AWAY FROM HOME AND started spending all the time he was not with patients with Martha Bernays, after I had begun to meet Sarah only in my memories, after Klara had sunk into her oblivion, a feeling of abandonment, a sense that no one yearned for my presence any longer, made me vulnerable.

My mother often said to me, "Look at your sisters. Try to be at least a little like them. If you cannot be like them, try at least to resemble them a bit."

I looked at my sisters. During the previous summer, the four of them, without telling me they were planning it, had gone to take care of the children of German families who lived in Paris. They returned that fall, and in the course of just one season they had turned into beautiful young women with refined manners, French phrases accenting their coquettish speech, expressions on their faces that conveyed not confusion or humility but an easygoing modesty and joy of life. I was entranced by my sisters, by their gestures, their conversations. I always sat near them but never with them; I watched them, listened to them, felt happy for them. But aside from that happiness, I also felt something different, because I knew how distant I was from them, as distant from them as I had once been close to my mother.

My mother often gathered my sisters, finding some way not to

include me, and then they would sit for a long time in the kitchen.
At those times, I would sometimes walk a little way down the hall
and then return to my room, and in that short moment when I
approached the door dividing me from them I managed to hear a
small part of their conversation, the kind that most mothers had
with their daughters: what a daughter had to do in order to be a
good daughter, the ways in which one enters marriage, the re-
sponsibilities of wives toward their husbands and children. I
remained outside their world and their conversations, in which
they spoke about themselves as wives and mothers. I overheard
how they looked toward the future, while I looked to the past, and
it seemed to me that with marriage and motherhood, for which
they were preparing themselves, they were conquering time, that
through those things they were connecting themselves with the
entire line of mothers down to the first blood. But I felt I remained
far from that line.

My mother sensed my vulnerability, and she plunged her
hatred into it. Hatred cannot be understood completely, nor its
sources known, just as Sarah had once said of happiness that it
could not be defined—it could be only felt. Perhaps, like sin and
happiness, hate also exists only in the eye of the beholder. Sometimes I tried to make sense of my mother's hatred toward me. Perhaps I was something like a pit into which my mother could throw
her darkness. Perhaps, I thought, she hated in me my father, her
ancient husband, who was older even than her own father. Perhaps in her hatred toward me she extinguished her longing to
have a husband her own age even before that yearning had been
ignited. Perhaps her hate was an expression of that distant pain,
born of being forced to smother her girlish dreams prematurely,
to obey her ancient husband in silence, to live in poverty and give
birth and raise children in that poverty. Or perhaps, because of
my attachment to my brother, she hated me because she was powerless to hate the one who had separated her golden Siggie from

her. He was beginning a different life, building a new world in which we could be only incidental passersby, and had now chosen to be just a guest in our world. But if my mother had taken a dislike to Martha Bernays, there was nothing she could do to her, since poison directed at my brother's beloved would never reach her, would remain in my mother, and therefore she had chosen me.

That is how it seemed to me, though perhaps I was mistaken, as I tried to explain to myself the burden of my existence. Already in a child's first glimmers of consciousness there is a heavy sense of time, a vague premonition that our existence is formed of grains of sand that the wind disperses, and that it is only the sense of ourselves, of our *I*, that holds us intact, until the last small grain of sand—the last relic of life—is blown away, when our *I* will also be extinguished, and behind us all that will remain is the wind of time. From time to time, the wind blows so fiercely that it carries away not only the grain of sand but also parts of the *I* itself, and the *I* feels powerless—it feels the wind will carry it away along with the sand, that it will be extinguished before all the grains of sand allotted to it for a lifetime have blown away—and then the *I* seeks another *I*, some other *I*'s, to accompany it while the wind of time howls around it; it needs these other *I*'s as support for the survival not of its material substance but of what is most essential to that *I*.

My mother, by her glance, her word, her gesture, broke off a part of me, a part I would always lack, a part I would always seek. Throughout my life I felt I was lacking something, the way the *Venus de Milo* lacks arms. I lacked nothing in my outer appearance but something inside me, as if the arms of my soul were lacking, and that absence, that lack, that feeling of emptiness, made me helpless. Throughout my life I felt as though someone's gaze were destroying my existence, and, at the same time, I sought some being who would heal the brokenness of my *I*.

"COME SEE WHO HAS TURNED UP IN OUR CITY," my brother said to me one day while I was visiting him at the Vienna General Hospital. There, lying motionless on one of the beds in the room my brother had led me to, was a young man who had been pulled from the Danube the day before. As we approached him, he cracked open his eyes. Although years had passed, I recognized that look—those were the eyes that cried inside, and whose tears fell somewhere deep within him. They were the eyes of Rainer Richter. I had heard nothing about him all those years, but that afternoon he told me why he had returned.

He had not yet posed the question one asks on the threshold of maturity, "What will I grow up to be?," when his parents died one after the other—first his mother, then his father. Rainer opened the letters his father had kept; from one, he learned he had been adopted. He began to search for those who had conceived him, and his path led him back to Vienna, where those he had long believed to be his parents had lived when they adopted him. For him, the search for his parents was like heading down a hallway on whose left-hand wall was his past, which was already dead, on whose right-hand wall, behind a veil, were those who had discarded him at birth, and at the end of which, somewhere far in the distance, spread out the emptiness of his future.

His abandonment by those who had conceived him hurt more than the death of those who had raised him. "Why did they abandon me?" was the dark question that carried, like an echo, a demonic double: "Was it worth my being born at all?" His abandonment reverberated like a rejection of his existence. He searched for his origins, hoping to discover that some great tragedy had separated him from his parents; he surmised that they had died suddenly after his birth, or that they had lost him in some unfortunate circumstance and never could find him. But that other thought, that he was abandoned as a newborn because he was unwanted, caused him mortal pain, a pain that led him to jump into the Danube. Despair drove him, not thought or readiness. He had not set off to drown himself in the river, but he had abandoned himself to the water to carry him away to some different existence.

At the time I stood beside his hospital bed, Rainer was eighteen years old. After he returned from the hospital to his Vienna home on Schönlaterngasse, I left home every morning, saying I was going to read in the library, leaving behind my mother's rebuke that my peers stayed at home all day and went out with only their mothers, or an older family member, so as not to ruin their reputation in front of the matchmakers. At home, Rainer waited for me so he could fall asleep.

"I cannot fall asleep when I am alone," he told me the first time I encountered him after a sleepless night.

I watched him as he fell asleep, and I wanted to lie down beside him, but I remained sitting in the corner of the room with a book in my lap. I had told him that I read while he slept, when in fact I spent the hours focused on his face. Sometimes he moaned in his sleep, the way a sick person moans, and I would go near him to try to understand the words he was whispering. When he awoke, we would set off to the atelier of some painter or other to ask whether twenty years earlier he had been acquainted with the painter Friedrich Richter and his wife, but none of them had heard of them, so the motivating question, "Whom did they adopt their child from?," was left unspoken. Rainer also visited Dr. Auerbach, who had cured him of despair at one point in his childhood, but apparently Friedrich Richter had not told the doctor his son was adopted.

In the way Rainer's movements cut through the air, in the shadow of his glance, in the echo of his words, something resembling the flow of blood was discernible. Once, he recalled the words of Kierkegaard: "What is a poet? An unhappy man who conceals profound anguish in his heart but whose lips are so fashioned that when sighs and groans pass over them they sound like beautiful music." And then he added, "But I have only the pain, not the gift of poetry." And immediately he bit his lip to silence his despair.

Once, while we were walking along a street lined with wild chestnut trees, he said to me, "Everything is so full of life, but there are moments still when many things compel me to death. There are moments when I am afraid to go near the window—it beckons me to open it and jump out. Sharp objects call me to cut my body; pointed objects, for me to stab them into my heart. The river calls me to it, with the same rapidity and strength with which it flows. Everything is so alive, yet everything calls me to my death."

Even as he spoke these words, I could see from the expression on his face that he regretted what he was saying.

"No," I contradicted him. "Everything calls you to life. Even that dead house," I said, and pointed across the street.

We walked toward the house, whose residents had long since moved away. We entered through the broken door, and then moved through the rooms. We looked at the floor, where objects no longer needed were strewn about. Rainer went to one of the corners, bent down, reached out his hand, and picked up a needle threaded with red thread. He held the needle and thread between his line of vision and mine. I wanted Rainer to run the thread along the edges of my lips, but I did not say anything. He put the needle and thread back on the floor in the corner of the room.

We were at an age of innocence. His innocence and mine were like two soap bubbles that merge rather than burst on contact. When Rainer's eyes looked into mine, and mine into his, his glance did not descend along my neck, to my breasts, between my legs, nor did my glance fall on his neck, his chest, and below. Rather, the center of my eyes pressed into his and went beyond; the center of his eyes pushed behind my eyes; and then we sought and found beyond our bodies something warm and soft, what some call a *soul*. We waited for the day we would feel that unseen and untouched warmth and softness through the union of the hidden parts of our bodies as well. We were at an age of innocence when, through touch and sound, taste and smell and sight, one could sense things beyond the surface, when it seemed to us that blood flowed even through inanimate objects. We were at an age when we could not foresee that one day our senses would convince us only of our captivity in space and time, and not lead us to an awareness of something beyond. We were at an age of innocence when the soul is still soft clay and does not know that one day it will turn to stone or barren earth; we were at an age when the soul is clay that can easily be warmed by a kindred spirit, when it is possible for two to become one. We were at an age of innocence when a shy look and a secretly expressed longing make our souls erupt under the delicate and tender wrap of our bodies, an age when the soul and the body are still bound into one, an age when excitement does not know it will someday turn into indifference or a simple urge to satisfy bodily needs, and that when one manages to infuse oneself with passion there is neither the capability nor the desire to turn that moment of pleasure into a brief eternity.

I did not go to Rainer's on Sundays, because the library was closed then, and I did not know what pretext I could use at home. One Monday morning, I found Rainer lying in bed with a piece of paper in the palm of his hand. He said that, the day before, he had met a gallery owner who had been a good friend of the person who had called himself his father, the person who had raised him. He told Rainer what he knew. She was a young girl named Gertrude, who was fifteen years old when she gave birth to him, and at that time, more than eighteen years ago, had lived on the street whose name Rainer had written down on the piece of paper he held in his hand. As we stepped across the threshold of the house to which he had been brought eighteen years ago by those who had adopted him, and as we set off toward the house in which his mother had separated from him, Rainer took my hand in his, the one that held the scrap of paper, and said, "Ever since my childhood ended, up until I came here, sometimes when I closed my eyes I glimpsed a bodiless female. She had no name, she did not even have a face; she was a being of light that flickered before my closed eyes. She was bodiless, yet still all my longing poured into her, because I knew that somewhere in this world she had her own bodily form. And my heart was restless with the thought that if I wanted my life to be called a life I must leave my parents' home and search for her, but I did not know whether I would find her. When my parents died and I learned I had been adopted, I set off on a different quest. When I met you, I realized my search for those who had conceived me had led me to the embodiment of that female being who had appeared to me for years. That female being must have been created from the traces of our childhood meetings. I did not tell you, because I knew that first I needed to complete the quest to learn about my birth. But now, when only a short time separates me from discovering that answer, the dreamed-for existence I have waited so long to attain is beginning for me."

Our heads drew near each other's. I felt his breath on my face and my chest beating wildly, as was his. Our chests touched before our lips did. We were so close that it seemed to me the whole world consisted solely of Rainer's eyes. He closed his eyes for a moment, seeking that bodiless female being he had found there at the time he separated from his childhood. Then he opened his eyes and smiled, finding me in front of him; he closed his eyes again and opened them again, as if wanting to confirm the affinity between that faceless being, woven from the light flickering before his closed eyes, and me. Our lips touched, and then I closed my eyes, and in the sweet touch of our tongues I felt something like a promise that the sweetness would last forever. At that moment, if someone had told us this was our final moment on earth, and that later no trace of us would remain, it would not have pulled us from our rapture, because we believed that what was between us, what made the two of us one, was eternal, and that if our material being were taken from us we would continue where the forces of nature and the laws of decay and transience have no power, and where the human soul is stronger than all the heavenly bodies, because they are condemned one day, millions of years after their creation, to burn out, whereas the soul in which our rapture and yearning were interwoven would last even after not a single particle of dust from all the matter in the universe remained.

As we walked through the city, Rainer checked the scrap of paper on which were written the names of the streets we needed to travel in order to reach the house where his mother lived. "We are getting close," he said when we entered that part of the city known to me from the outing with my brother when he wanted to show me what the depths of Vienna looked like. The streets were sleepy after the work of Sunday night. We reached the street we were seeking. Several boys were kicking around some scattered garbage. A drunk was rolling about on the sidewalk. An old woman was sitting on the stoop of a small house, singing a song about

luckless love. Two children were throwing two broken broom-
sticks high into the air, catching them before they hit the ground
and then throwing them skyward again. Rainer asked them if they
happened to know where a woman by the name of Gertrude lived.
One of the children pointed to a house where clothes were hanging in the windows in place of curtains. We knocked on the door.
The children told us not to wait but just to go in. The door was
open. In a small corridor that smelled of mold, one of the doors
was ajar. We went into the room and looked at the damp walls. A
woman walked in, leaning on a cane. She looked at us and said,
"This is no room for a wedding night. What are you looking for?"

"I am looking for Gertrude," Rainer said. "I do not know her
last name."

"What's Gertrude to you?" asked the woman, hissing the
words through her gap-toothed jaws, and running her fingers, like
a comb, through the sparse straight hairs on her balding head.

"I want to speak with her," Rainer said.

The woman pointed to the chairs beside the table, and we sat
down.

"I am Gertrude."

"Then I have made a mistake," said Rainer. "You must have
the same name as the woman I am looking for. She is about thirty-
three years old."

"Yes," said the woman, as she poked her tongue through the
gaps where her front teeth were missing. "I am thirty-three." Then
she sat down on the bed opposite us. "And it looks to me like I can
guess why you're looking for me. You look like someone I haven't
seen for a long time, but when I knew him he was your age."

The mother was looking at her son; she knew she was right,
because he said not a word. She stretched her hand out to him. It
was a slow movement; perhaps she wanted to caress him. Then,
before she touched him, she turned her hand toward herself and
just as slowly brought it close to her face, but before her hand

touched her face she dropped it into her lap, onto her shabby dress.

"I wasn't expecting you," his mother continued. "And you were certainly not expecting me to be . . . like this."

Rainer was silent.

"So, you are silent," she continued. "Everything a mother needed to tell you, some other woman told you. What you want to know—who I am and what I am—is unnecessary. I have often wondered what I would say to you if you turned up one day. But everything I would say to you would be an excuse. I was raised by humble and honest parents. I was barely fifteen years old when I got pregnant. I was a young girl who knew nothing about the facts of life. In our yard I had seen roosters mount hens, at the neighbors' I had seen a ewe give birth to a lamb, but there are many ways in which a human life is different from the lives of birds and animals. Different, and yet the same. Your father was handsome, and everything that happened between us took place in the neighbors' stable. Before I got pregnant, all I knew about him was that he had come to our town, really more like a village, a few months before to fix the wheels on the horse carts. When I told him I was pregnant, I found out a bit more about him. He not only fixed things; he also stole things. He was a thief who traveled from town to town, so he wouldn't get caught. And then he set off for another town. Yes, my parents were humble and honest, and on account of that humility and honesty they kicked me out of the house. They wanted to save my sisters' honor, and they knew that no one would want to marry them if word got out that I was pregnant. They gave me a little money and sent me off to a distant relative here in Vienna, and I never saw them, my sisters, or your father again." She looked down at her hands. "The people who adopted you seemed to me like good people. They told me they didn't have any children, they told me they had lived awhile in the city but were now getting ready to return home. They wanted to go back with a child. You were barely a year old then." She ran her hand along the bed she was sitting on. "I gave birth to you on this bed."

Rainer looked at the bed. I suspected that for the past eighteen years this woman had earned her living on that bed. Her pinched face, her gap-toothed mouth, her thinning hair, could probably still deceive a drunk or two in the darkness of the evening alleyways.

"Well, that's it—that is what I planned to say to you if you ever came. I have been repeating those selfsame words to myself all these eighteen years. This is the first time I have ever said them out loud," she concluded, and turned her head toward the cracked mirror on the wall and half smiled at her reflection. Then she turned to Rainer.

Rainer stood up.

"As for you," the woman who had given birth to him asked, "did you think of anything to say to me while you were looking for me?"

Rainer headed for the door; I set off after him.

"Some questions are better left unasked. Some answers better not given," his mother said. He no longer looked at her. She followed us to the exit of the dilapidated house. I heard her footsteps behind us even in the narrow alley. I heard her footsteps and the striking of the stick she was leaning on. I looked at Rainer's steps. The sound of her footsteps stopped; his steps continued. As we turned into another small street at the corner, I looked around and saw Rainer's mother standing beside the wall of the house, and passing the fingers of her right hand across her face.

That afternoon, Rainer decided to leave Vienna. The answer to the question he had repeated aloud, "Who am I?," shook him to the core. My assurances—that he was who he was, that his *I* was not dependent on the person who had given birth to him or the fact that he had been cast aside after his birth—were useless. "Who am I?" Rainer repeated with eyes closed, with eyes pointed toward the mirror, with eyes staring at me. He believed that if he went as far as possible from the city in which so many things conspired to convince him that he did not know who he was, then he would manage to find the core of his *I*.

．　．　．

AFTER RAINER LEFT, I WENT TO SCHÖNLATERNGASSE EVERY
day. I knocked on the door of his Vienna home, but there was no
one to open it. The line of hope that sustained my waiting for his
return was cut off by the fear that woke me every morning, the
fear that did not sleep and that tormented my dreams. I believed
Rainer that he would return, but I feared that his despair would
cast him into a nothingness from which he would be unable to
fulfill his promise. Sometimes, when my fear conjured the thought
that he would take his life, I wanted to ask my brother for money
so I could go find the estate near Munich where Rainer had grown
up and where he most likely was now, but I knew that in order for
him to make peace with himself, to find an answer to the question
"Who am I?," he needed to be alone. That is why, when he left the
city, he did not take my address, nor did he give me his, and so
even by letter we could not tell each other how we were or what
we were doing.

My mother sensed my fear, although she did not know where
it came from. My fear, born of Rainer's despair, revealed itself in
the way my body cut through the air as I moved, in the echo of my
words, in the shadow of my glance. And my mother picked up the
traces of my fear; she plunged her words into my vulnerability.

She told me I would be alone my whole life, I would drown in my solitude, I would remain unmarried and be an embarrassment to the family. I said not a word, and I thought of Rainer. My anxiety about whether he would return and my belief in his promise to return battled inside me.

. . .

ONE MORNING, A YEAR AFTER RAINER LEFT, AS I WAS approaching his home I saw him standing at the window.

Our two worlds were again one, and we filled our joined world with our daydreams. Rainer wanted us both to study philosophy at the University of Vienna; with him, I wanted to fulfill the dream I had had at one time with my brother Sigmund: to live together in Venice.

Then we crossed the distance that seems immeasurable to the innocent, the distance between the contemplation of the sexual act and the uniting of two bodies. Our glances shyly explored our nakedness, and we searched each other's eyes—I his, he mine—and then our glances fell to the floor, out of shame, out of confusion, out of fear. Everything was for the first time, the glance at a naked body, those few steps to the bed, made with such tentativeness as if we had just learned to walk, the drawing together of our bodies, and the way they completely entwined, and our breathing, which was as strong as at birth.

One day he said to me, "I want to visit my mother."

I waited a long time for him to express that wish again, and later I reminded him of it.

"I am afraid," he told me.

Then we talked about his fear and about many other things; we spent days in which, just as we explored our bodies, just as we searched our bodies, discovering the source of so much love for precisely that body, we also searched each other's souls: we wanted to know what pain meant and what pleasure meant for each other. We asked each other and we asked again and again what love was, and infidelity.

We were in those years of inexperience when one still thinks with the heart, when one believes unquestioningly in the ideas written down by the philosophers, when one feels as one's own the sweetness of verses sprung forth from happiness, the bitterness of poems wrung from despair. We were in those years when words are born not of emptiness but of the essence of one's being. We were in the years of inexperience, unencumbered by the deathly triviality of life, and so we could speak naively about elevated things, things experience discards because they are as useless and unnecessary as a patch of sky.

We asked ourselves what we were now, but also considered what we had been, because we knew that all layers exist within a person, that in the present there are glimmers of everything that has been important at one time and that has become not a stunted relic of the past but a source of light that brightens one's countenance. We told each other about our past. I told him about myself, about my mother and my brother, about Sarah and Klara. Rainer recalled the moments with those who had loved him as their own son.

Then I reminded him of his desire to meet his mother again. He evaded my reminder, recalling a fear he had had since childhood, when he was afraid he would lose his parents. Everything seemed to portend such a loss; perhaps fear had nested in him because of some hazy memory of his first year of life, when he had been abandoned by his mother, and this fear, that he would lose everyone he loved, persisted.

"What if I lose you, too?" he asked. "What if it is my fate to lose the people I love the most? What if you reject me, the way my mother rejected me?"

"I will always be with you," I told him. "But now let's go visit your mother."

Rainer shook his head.

•　•　•

WHEN RAINER SHOOK HIS HEAD, I WAS REMINDED THAT THERE was also someone expecting me. I recalled the words Sarah had said to me at our last meetings: "Do not forget Klara. And help her if you can."

I visited Klara less and less. During those visits, while she and I sat opposite each other, Gustav would break the silence. He always talked about the same things: how his mother had spewed rage at his sister when she was just a girl; how Klara was beaten for organizing protests for the rights of women, children, and workers; how gradually her courage and spirit became imprisoned in her empty world. I knew these things, and I saw how Klara tormented herself by closing herself in, but I listened attentively to Gustav, because I felt he needed to talk in order to ease himself a little of his suffering.

Sometimes, when she emerged from her passivity, Klara ran away from home. The police would find her lying on a bench, sitting propped against a tree, leaning out over the railings of a bridge. When she was returned home, Gustav would ask, "Why did you run away?" And she always answered the same way: "I am not at home here." Gustav then decided to place Klara in the psychiatric clinic the Nest. When I first visited her there, I saw in her look, in the movement of her body, in her voice, that slowly her confidence was returning.

"I have finally found my home," she told me.

I became acquainted with the head of the Nest, Dr. Goethe. He explained that directness was the new method for treating madness. While he was explaining this, a patient came up and spat in his face. He carefully wiped away the spit with a handkerchief and continued: "Patients with mental disturbances loathe their healer; they see in him a God who punishes them, a tyrant who does not allow them to create their world, but I do not interrupt their outbursts. I listen to them when they curse or insult me, as I would someone outside the Nest. And when faced with their absurdities I tell them it is foolishness. Yes, that is exactly what I tell them."

"Yes." Klara smiled. "That is the word Dr. Goethe uses most often: *foolishness.*"

"You see," said Dr. Goethe, "directness is a first step toward creating a true relationship between patients and their doctors."

As in all madhouses (Dr. Goethe resisted the fashion to call madhouses *psychiatric clinics*), classification was the first principle of the Nest: men and women were segregated. There was a wing for tranquil patients, another for the helpless, who needed constant care, a third for manic patients, who needed to be bound or placed under constant supervision if they were not too dangerous, and a fourth wing—for the senile. Only some of them ever met: in the large dining halls, in the Great Hall, in which Dr. Goethe gave lectures, or when they walked the grounds. Here, as elsewhere, the rich and the poor were separated; those whose families paid large sums had their own rooms or were housed two to a room. Klara had her own room, and Dr. Goethe persuaded me to go there to do crafts with her. He believed that work could cure madness, or, at least, help to cure it. The only ones at the Nest who did not work were the senile, the paralyzed, and those who lay motionless in their beds. Not only did Dr. Goethe consider work a cure; it was also a way to fill the Nest's coffers, because there were many peo-

ple there for whom no one paid. Those whose stay was paid for by
their relatives did simple jobs: embroidery, sewing, knitting, rug
making; the men's section made artificial flowers out of paper and
wooden figures. The others did the more strenuous jobs: they laun-
dered clothes and bedding, they made buttons and shoes. . . .

"You are welcome to visit our shop by the exit," Dr. Goethe
told me. "Everything there has been made by our dear patients:
socks and shawls, nightgowns and dresses, handkerchiefs and tow-
els, wooden crafts." Then he continued telling me about life at the
Nest. "Wake-up is at six. First everything that was disturbed during
the night is cleaned up under the supervision of the nurses, and
that is not as simple a task as it might initially seem. For example,
someone defecated in the middle of the room, someone wedged
his pillow between the window bars, a third spread his blanket in
the middle of the room, a fourth hid everyone's slippers under his
mattress. . . . Then the doctors visit the patients. After that, we go
to breakfast; we have six dining halls in total, completely adequate
to hold our patients. Then we begin our work, up until lunchtime.
After lunch, we have a short rest, and then we work again, since, as
I said, work created the man and will make a man again out of the
one who avoids responsibility. That is how it is: to be mad is to
avoid the responsibility of being a person. Then we go to dinner,
and afterward we have a little social time before bed."

While we were walking along the hospital corridor, a woman
approached Dr. Goethe, fell to her knees, and begged him to
let her go home. He simply walked around her, and the woman
continued to scream until attendants arrived and carried her off
somewhere. Dr. Goethe noted how upset I was by what I had seen,
and he said, "Ah, do not look at everything so blackly! You should
look at even the most terrible things with at least a little irony. You
know what my grandfather Johann said about irony: 'It is that little
grain of salt that alone renders the dish palatable.' "

"But this is not lunch; it's life," I said.

"All the more so," said Dr. Goethe. "Without irony, life would be bland. And frighteningly unbearable."

We continued walking along the corridors. From time to time, Dr. Goethe would open a door enough for me to peek inside. The whole time he noted my horrified expression and looked for ways to calm me.

"Things are perfect here. Do you know how it is at the Salpêtrière, in Paris? They sleep on mattresses on the floor. They lock up the patients and do not allow them outside. The patients do their business in the middle of their rooms, and there is excrement on the floor and the walls. Though there is not too much excrement, because they feed them just enough to keep them alive, and even if they gave them sufficient food, why amid that stench would they eat more than just enough to stay alive? The excrement is cleaned from the rooms once a week. The doctors make their rounds only to determine which patients need to be restrained and to untie those who have now become exhausted from rage. And that is how it is in Paris! But here, on the beautiful blue Danube"— and through his lips he whistled a few bars of the waltz—"there is no need to tell you, you can see for yourself. You should count yourself fortunate that your friend went mad in Vienna."

"Klara is not mad," I told him. "Klara just needs time to come to herself."

"Well, what do you think madness is? Something monstrous? No, madness is a condition in which people are not themselves. And here we apply the best methods to help the patients come to themselves. Do you know how they treat them in Paris? With fear! They think that if they pour great quantities of cold water on them, if they beat them, if they threaten to cut out the tongues of those who scream, that it will bring their minds back. Yes, yes, that is how it is in Paris, but here, on the beautiful blue Danube . . ." Again he whistled a few bars of the waltz. I wanted to tell him I knew that even in Paris they no longer treated patients the way he was describing, that it was precisely the methods Dr. Pinel had introduced decades before in the Salpêtrière that he himself now preached here, but I said not a word and continued to listen. "Here we treat patients through conversation, with the aim of getting at what is tormenting them. We converse with them about what they want to talk about, which is usually nonsense, but, in the end, out of all that nonsense they will also reach some wise conclusions. I am not saying all of them, but some will be fortunate enough to return to normal."

While we were walking along the bars of the fence toward the exit, Klara said to me, "Yes, some of us will be fortunate enough to return to normal. All that's needed is time."

I passed through the gates, and as I moved down the street I turned around several times. There was Klara, still standing behind the bars.

• • •

TIME PASSED, AND A CHILL SETTLED BETWEEN RAINER AND me. When our bodies intertwined, his related to mine as toward something mechanical; when he looked at me, it was as if he were looking at something lifeless. And I no longer recognized his voice. A suspicion was awakening in me, something like what we feel when we dress in a fine garment and a needle unexpectedly pricks our body. Rainer was studying philosophy at the time, and at first I attributed the change to his dedication to his studies.

One afternoon, he said to me, "It is time for you to leave. My classes are beginning."

"I can accompany you to the university," I told him.

"No," he said. "I beg you to leave. I need to go alone."

He pushed me toward the door. He had not been tender with me in a long time, but now, for the first time, he was rude.

Some dark shadow in me told me that he was not going anywhere. I knew that he was waiting. I did not go far from his house. Upon reaching the spot where the road curves, I waited. Not much time passed before a young woman approached the house. The door opened, and she went inside. I wanted to be there, too, and to be hurt by what I would see. I remained where I was, leaning against the wall of a building. I dug at the wall with my nails. I do not know how long I stood like this, and when the young woman left, I wanted to go to Rainer's house. But I set off for home.

The following day I told him what I had seen. He did not deny anything, and when I fell before him weeping, the pain trampling my dignity, he did not try to comfort me. I raised my arms, touched his fingers, seeking some kind of hope and support, but his fingers remained limp. As I knelt there on the floor, I raised my head and stared into his eyes. I could not recognize his look, a look that had been like that for some time, foreign and altered, but now, for the first time, I grasped the true reason for the change.

"It is time for you to go," Rainer said, looking at his watch.

I got up from the floor and left.

I had not reached the end of the street when the young woman appeared and went into Rainer's house. I waited a long time, and when she came out I ran after her. Hearing the hurried footsteps, she turned around. She had a frightened expression, probably expecting me to do something to her. When I was just a step away, she covered her face with her hands, as if to protect herself.

"I want to talk to you about Rainer Richter," I said to her.

She lowered her hands.

"Who are you?" she asked.

I only repeated, "I want to talk to you about Rainer."

"What do you want to know about Rainer?"

"I know everything about him. Or almost everything. It is only your presence in his life that I do not know enough about."

"Ah, you must be . . ." she said, and from the expression on her face, with the nonchalant gesture of her hand, it was clear that Rainer had mentioned me.

"I want to know something more about you. And I want to know what you want from Rainer."

"Why do you want to torture yourself?"

"I just want to know," I said.

"Only someone who wants to torture herself would want to know what you are asking me to tell you. If you had even the slightest self-respect, you would forget that Rainer exists."

I wanted to tell her that once certain events have happened to us, we cannot forget the people who were connected with them. But she had already turned and headed off in her own direction. I did not go after her. I turned back to Rainer's house, but I did not knock on his door.

Walking slowly, I made my way home. I looked at the happy faces of the people on the streets and recognized my own face in the unhappy ones with downturned mouths. I watched as the bag an old woman was carrying ripped, spilling apples to the ground. As she bent down to gather them, some tough kids ran up and snatched them. A young man and a young woman seated on a bench looked lovingly at each other. A child wandering away from his parents came up to me, bit off half of the chocolate bar he held in his hand, and offered the other half to me. There are moments when even the sweetest things are bitter.

I arrived home. My father looked at me and smiled; for a long time he had been losing his vision.

"Our daughter is becoming happier and happier," my mother said to Father.

I went into my room. It belonged to me alone. My parents and I were the only ones remaining in the house. Right after Sigmund went to live in the hospital, Anna had gotten married, and she and her husband had left to live in America. Then Paulina and Marie got married and moved with their husbands to Berlin. The year Rosa got married, Alexander also moved out of the house. I remained alone with my parents, alone with myself, and I no longer had anyone to share my pain with, not even within my room, because in conversation with those closest to me I never shared my troubles.

I lay down on my bed. I turned my head to the wall.

For several days I did not go to Rainer's, and then when we saw each other he said, "You should not have tried to speak with her."

"I had to. I thought that if she let me speak with her I could make her leave you."

"She asked me to force you to leave. Do not come here any longer."

"I cannot not come."

"Forget that I exist."

"I cannot," I said.

"If you had the slightest bit of dignity, you would forget about me," he said.

"It is not a question of dignity but of love."

"What you call love is self-degradation and self-torture. Leave and do not come here again."

I told him that I would not come again, yet while I was going home I already wanted to return to him.

Rainer became for me a constantly present absence. He was not beside me, but he was more present than I was. I forgot about myself. I walked along the streets, I crossed the bridges, I stared into the river. Sometimes I lifted my gaze skyward. I sat on a bench. In the evening, I roused myself and looked into the darkness. I did all these things, yet I was absent; Rainer was always there. The thought that he was whispering words of tenderness to a young woman, the thought of their bodies conjoined, their assumptions about their future, a future that Rainer and I had sometimes dreamed about, eternal love, family, a home in Venice—these things were in me more than I was in myself.

But within me I still had a flicker of hope that Rainer would return to how he had been before, and all that had passed in the interim, all the disappointments and pains, would be carried away as if by a flood, and our souls would regain their purity and move toward maturity. And so I went again to Rainer's, and there his coldness awaited me, and the reminder of my promise that I would never come again. I left his house, yet a part of me remained there, like a shadow on the floor.

Years before that, when I was a frightened young girl, despairing of my mother's hatred, I believed that one day a hand would appear that would lead me to another existence. Sometimes I even dreamed of that hand, and in my dream I stretched my hand toward it, and my hand would strike the wall and I would awaken. At that time, I eased my despair with the belief that my suffering would end the day I found that other hand, when my hand and someone else's hand joined and set off through life together. And then I gave my hand to Rainer. When his hand no longer needed support, that same hand pushed me into despair as if into a vacuum, where with equal speed, with equal slowness, fall feather and lead, blood and soul. In that vacuum, all the despair one has lived through exists layer inside layer. New hurts cause all past hurts to ache; the despair of my childhood aches through my current despair. Had I not despaired as a child, Rainer's unfaithfulness would have been only a short-lived pain; I could have turned my back on it and then moved on. But now this new pain cut open the old wound. Rainer's unfaithfulness brought back that young girl who, at the beginning of her memories—those memories she called her life—had pain, something like blood dripping from a hidden wound. She was not the woman I was now but the girl I once was, whose wound continued to bleed inside me even in those moments of my life when I did not sense it, the girl who compelled me every morning, even before I was fully awake, to go to Rainer's and, with a feeling of guilt, beg him to let me into his house. That long-ago pain drove me to ask him where the Rainer was who was once afraid he would lose me just as he had lost those who had adopted him, the Rainer who was afraid I would reject him just as he had been rejected by those who had conceived him. I asked, he said nothing, and when the questions turned to weeping or accusations he forced me to leave.

One morning, one of those mornings when I begged Rainer to let me into his house so that I could beg or accuse, he told me that the love affair between him and the young woman had ended.

"That means we can be together again," I said.

"That means I am leaving Vienna," said Rainer.

"Then I want to come with you." I touched his shoulder with my fingers. "Wherever you go."

"I do not know where I am going. Maybe to Venice."

Venice had been our dream ever since our age of innocence.

"I will go with you to Venice," I said.

He removed my fingers from his shoulder.

"You may go wherever you wish. But not with me. You were born to be a stone, a stumbling block for those you deceive yourself that you love. You cannot love. Those who truly love do not overburden with their pain those who have stopped loving them. You want only to bring unhappiness. To yourself, and to those you deceive that you love them." I stretched my fingers out toward his shoulder once more, but he pushed them away before I could touch him, and added, "I never want to see you again."

I wanted to hurt him. In a few words, I wanted to inflict on him as much pain as he had inflicted on me during these past months. I said to him, "You are the same as your father. Not the one who raised you but that thief who, as soon as he heard he had conceived you, ran away from the one into whose womb he had sown his seed. You are the same as your mother. Not the one who raised you, who taught you to play the piano and who taught you to love poetry. You are the same as the one whose blood you carry, and who, had she not given you up for adoption, would have tossed you out to die in the street, so that you did not bother her when her customers lay between her legs. You used to ask yourself, 'Who am I?' Now you know the answer. You are the fruit of a thief and a whore. That is who you are."

Rainer slowly sat down on the bed. He put his elbows on his knees, leaned his forehead on his palms. I drew near him and apologized, but he did not say anything. I heard his breathing. I sat down next to him, and I begged him to say anything at all, even the coarsest word. He said nothing. We sat like this a long time, one next to the other, without words. Evening came, but he did not move from that spot. I stood up and told him I would come again the next day. The following day I did not find him at home. Nor was he there for days afterward. Then one of the neighbors told me that Rainer had moved away.

. . .

ONE NIGHT, WHEN I AWOKE AND THE TRACES OF MY DREAM
had me believing that Rainer was in bed beside me, I felt for the
first time how my heart, my womb, and that place between my legs
were beating together as one. Until then, that sweet pain and that
bitter yearning to bring forth a new life had been unknown to me.
I got up from bed and stood in front of the mirror. I slowly slipped
out of my nightgown and dropped it to the floor. The moon cast
its light on my body. I placed my hands on my belly, as if to cradle
the life within it, although my womb was empty.

Awake, I waited for the morning, and then I went to visit Klara
at the Nest. We recalled the conversation about motherhood that
she had had with Sarah. Then we went to the shop that sold things
made by the residents of the Nest. I passed the display cases. My
fingers touched the decorations made of wood, paper, and metal,
the clothing and household furnishings. An item would linger in
my hand, and I would put it into my bag. When I went to pay, and
I emptied out my bag, Klara said to me, "You want to become a
mother."

I looked at what I had taken, and in front of me lay a baby
bonnet, a small cape, tiny shoes the size of a finger.

When I got home, I put these things into a suitcase in the cupboard in my room. From time to time I would pull the suitcase
out, take the objects from it, and lay them on my bed.

Years passed, but I did not forget Rainer, and my love and hate toward him hurt me in equal measure. I often went to his house. If it was daylight, I knocked on the door; if it was dark, I looked to see whether there was light behind the curtains. But it was empty there, just as it was inside me. I felt love and hate tearing me apart, and both were leading me to despair, because they had nowhere to go: I was absent from the life of the one they were directed at, while he was more present in mine than I was myself.

I went less and less often to see Klara, and one time I told her, "I want very much to see you, but I am afraid to come here." I did not tell her what I was afraid of, but she sensed I was afraid not of what I saw there but of what I carried inside me.

Years passed, and one October day my father died. Afterward, whenever my mother saw me in the morning, instead of responding to my wishing her a beautiful day, she would tell me that another empty day awaited me. In the evening, when I wished her a good night, she told me how she pitied me because of my empty bed. Between morning and night she shared from the Jewish holy books a bit of wisdom, which perhaps she had invented: that a woman without offspring is not a human being. And to that wisdom she added, "Your life is meaningless."

MY BROTHER, after he married Martha, opened a practice in his home, and he worked there with patients who had psychiatric problems. I begged him to let me move in with him, but he explained that they did not have enough money or enough space, because every year another child was born: first Matilda, then Martin, then Oliver, Ernst, Sophie, and finally Anna. All the same, every time we were left alone at least for a moment—and it was rare to be left alone for longer than a few moments—I would beg him to let me live in their home. I begged him until the day he told me that Minna, his wife's sister, was moving in.

The years passed, and I felt I was not myself. When I got up in the morning, part of me remained in bed. Perhaps it was because I wanted to free myself from my very self, from that part that ached with despair, but the despair continued to ache, no matter how much I divided myself. That destructive pain became my only biography. In the uniformity of the everyday, the same banalities would repeat, and I did not notice how the years rolled by. Even my dreams resembled one another. Once, I dreamed that my home was flooded. Water was pouring in from everywhere. "Is this the Flood?" I asked myself in my dream. I wanted to flee, but a child's cry could be heard from between the walls. "My children are in there! Someone has walled them in," I told myself in my dream. I scratched the wall, I tore at the wall, the wall tore at my nails. The water was rushing in with greater and greater force; it covered my head and was drowning me. But even underwater I could hear a child's cry from between the walls.

. . .

I AVOIDED LOOKING IN MIRRORS, BUT WHENEVER I LOOKED at a certain print by Dürer, it seemed as though I were looking at myself. The woman in the engraving, caught at an instant when she is peering into the nothingness, has wings, but she is not an angel; she is an allegory for melancholy. Her head is inclined, and were it not supported by her hand, clenched in a fist, it would fall to her breast. Her other hand, placed in her lap, is relaxed and holds a pair of compasses. My head also leaned, but fell to my breast. One hand, clenched into a fist as if to protect itself from pain, could not support itself and fell to my lap; the other hand relaxed, because I knew I would not save myself from sinking by grasping at straws.

The face of Dürer's Melancholia is sunk in shadow, and from out of that shadow the whites of her eyes glitter, and her gaze is fixed on some absence. In the background glitters the sea, like the whites of Melancholia's eyes, and in the sky, with its wondrous glow, there is a comet that will soon disappear, and once again Melancholia's world will sink into gloom. Somewhere near that great watery expanse, a city is just visible, but Melancholia is separated here, alone. I, too, was peering into an absence, my sky empty, gloom enveloping me. Around me was desolation, and those who were closest to me were separated by an unbridgeable eternity, one that Zeno alone could explain.

In the engraving, Melancholia employs several things for salvation from her pain. Behind her hangs a square talisman on
which sixteen numbers are inscribed; it is to attract Jupiter's healing powers, which can overpower the sorrow that Saturn brings.
Beside the talisman is an hourglass, and above the talisman a bell,
and also a scale. Half the sand in the hourglass has streamed
through, the balances of the scale are in repose, and the bell is
still, although at any moment it could toll the final hour. Or perhaps time has stopped, and the sand in the hourglass will stop,
neither here nor there, and the pans of the scale, balanced, demonstrate that everything is already the same, without meaning,
and the bell has no reason to strike.

Melancholia sits in front of her unfinished building, tools all
around her; she is seated and looks as if she has rejected everything,
as if something tells her that construction will never be completed.
A ladder leans against the building, and on the ground beside the
lower rungs lies a stone block—is Melancholia to mount it, then
climb the ladder to the building? But the stone block is unwrought.
Melancholia is surrounded by many tools and implements for
carpentry and stonecutting, but everything is in repose; she
knows that nothing will be completed, she knows that everything
is pointless. It is pointless even to make all the things of this world.
Meaninglessness has entered everything. That building behind
Melancholia is, in fact, her life, the life that will—no matter how it
is lived, no matter what is built—remain unfinished, be lived in
vain. Is the scale beside Melancholia there only because it is needed for measuring weights for construction, or is it also a symbol of
constant weighing, constant measuring, constant vacillation?

To live or not to live? That is the question in the engraving, in
the face drowned in darkness, the whites of the eyes glittering. In
Dürer's engraving, Melancholia has wings, but no one would
think she had ever flown with them; they are not even an adorn-

ment. Perhaps she has wings solely to hinder her steps as she walks, to weigh her down, to remind her that she could have flown but that now it is too late.

"To live or not to live?"—the question that Dürer's Melancholia seems to ask herself—became a question of my own existence. I tried to avoid it, the question that some shadow in me asked, just as I avoided looking in mirrors. My home was itself a kind of mirror, a shadow of the shadow asking me the question that weighed existence and nonexistence, and because of this, even when the cold seeped into one's bones, even when the wind blew so strongly that one's eyes had to close, I wandered the streets, lingered on bridges, walked into a synagogue or church, sat on a bench, and in doing these things I aired out my soul as if it were a fabric that had absorbed a bitter smell. In my wanderings through the city, my gaze would sometimes fall on a large plate of glass, or on the surface of the river, or on a puddle, and, without meaning to, I would come eye to eye with my face, its gaze peering into an absence. And no matter how much I silenced my inner shadow, no matter how much I turned my gaze toward the light that should have destroyed the shadow's existence, it constantly asked its question: To live or not to live?

One afternoon, when I had returned home from a meandering walk through the city, my mother said to me sarcastically, "There is a jovial young man looking for you. He asked to wait here. We spent some time together in your room, but he's not exactly talkative."

I went into my room. There on my bed sat Rainer.

"I'm back," he said.

He stood up. I went near him. We touched our heads together; our temples touched. Blood pulsing against blood. I heard his tired breathing.

"I have come back, but I do not know why. . . ." he said.

Slowly, I separated my head from his. His look had changed; in his eyes I now saw an emptiness, and that emptiness stared back at me. He was thirty-four years old, one year older than his mother was when we met her that Monday morning in that neglected quarter of Vienna, and he resembled her, not in his looks—she had told him, years ago, that she recognized him because he looked like his father—but in the way he had aged: his hair was thinning, his teeth were worn down, his bones warped, his fingers strangely twisted and gnarled. We sat down on my bed. He told me that all that remained of everything his adopted parents had left him was the house in Vienna on Schönlaterngasse. Everything else had gone to drink and gambling, or, more precisely, everything had gone to gambling while drinking.

We held hands. At one time we had held each other like this, and beyond the life of our bodies we had felt the tenderness of our souls. Later, we had grown to feel nothing. But now, interwoven with our bodies, prematurely foreshadowing old age, there, though chilled and more fragile than tender, our souls were present once again, and we felt the vague tremors of our spirit.

We left the apartment under the derisive send-off of my mother's gaze. We said nothing until we reached Rainer's house. It looked abandoned, even though nothing had changed. Everything was in its place, but the years of no air and the layers of dust gave the interior a different appearance and a certain deadness. Our footsteps left traces in the dust on the floor. Rainer pulled back one of the curtains, and a cloud of dust swirled out. As I wiped the dust off the mirrors with my fingers and the palms of my hands, I heard Rainer say as he walked about the room, "I know you think I returned to find comfort. I am not looking for comfort. Those who still have life in them seek comfort. Everything inside me is dead. There is no longer anything that could restore life to me. Forgive me, but not even your love could do that—your love, which sustained me at a time when I was on the precipice. Now, even a precipice from which I could fall does not exist. Now nothing exists for me. Neither struggle nor pleasure. I struggled with the thought that I had been rejected. I never struggled for your love. It was a gift to me. Perhaps that is why I rejected it, for we value a gift only if we have earned it. Then I set out to conquer love. I did not know that love was not a prize and could not be won. I lost the prize, and then set off in search of pleasures. I did not enjoy them, but destroyed myself through them. Each experience was more insipid than the last; the most intense pleasures lost their taste. I lost all my ideals. And, with them, I lost myself. Now everything is meaningless. Both life and death. That is why I am saying I did not come back for comfort. There is no comfort for me. I do not know why I came back."

I wiped off the last mirror, and in the reflection I saw Rainer standing behind me. I turned toward him. As we kissed, we could taste the dust that clung to our lips. When he drew his lips apart from mine, he said, "I used to ask, 'Who am I?' and I hoped that through questioning I would find a reason for my existence, something that connected me to everything in the universe, a stage that everyone who poses that question must reach. I used to ask, 'Who am I?' and now I know: I am nothing."

The following day, I spoke with my brother. He agreed to see Rainer in his office, but after several sessions he told me, "There is no one who can help him. He does not want to be freed from his torment. His problem is simple. Deep inside him is buried the trauma he experienced when he was a year old and his mother gave him to others. But he does not want to solve his problem. He enjoys it."

"He does not enjoy it," I said. "He is suffering."

"Enjoyment, suffering, they are the same. It is called *enjoyment of negative pleasure*," my brother told me.

————

MY MOTHER LEFT for several months to visit the spas at Bad Gastein, and I left to live with Rainer. The first morning I woke in his house he said to me, "I dreamed that I was building a house. I was building a house downward, not upward. I wasn't building it, I was digging it. I asked myself whether this was going to be a house for me or a pit. I dug, and dug, and dug. I was amazed at how quickly my hands were digging, as if they were swallowing the earth. I looked up to see what kind of house I had excavated. And there above me I could see barely a ray of light. The sky was a small point. I continued to dig, because I could not return to the surface. I continued to dig until the last ray of light disappeared, in order to forget what I had done."

Sometimes we looked together at portraits of him made by the man who had been like a father to him.

"These are all that will remain of me," said Rainer, gathering the portraits. "And they, too, will one day turn to dust. But I am no longer connected to them. At one time there was a thread connecting this child, this boy, and me. There was a thread linking us, one soul through time. Many things would fall away, and new things would appear, things unknown until that moment, yet my soul's spark stayed the same. Now I have nothing in common with any of them. Now I am no one. Now it will be best if I turn as quickly as possible into nothing."

I told him that his soul's thread, the thread that binds him from the moment of his birth until this moment, could not be cut. I told him that despair prevented him from seeing that thread, but he shook his head and said it was not despair that prevented him from seeing it but the way he himself had changed that had cut the thread.

There was no longer passion or pleasure in his body when we made love. He seemed to use lovemaking merely to attempt to push away his despair, and so his despair became even more present in our bodies when they were conjoined. Still, I continued to feel my heart, my womb, and between my legs beating as one; I felt that sweet pain and that bitter yearning to create a new life.

"I want us to have a child," I told Rainer one morning.

"So that we can throw it into the senselessness of existence?"

Several weeks later, I was sick to my stomach and vomited. I felt nauseated the following days as well, and I had another, much stronger reason to think I was carrying a new life within me. I went to the doctor, and after he examined me he confirmed it: "You have reason to be happy. You are pregnant!"

While walking the streets, I felt how happiness inhaled and exhaled with me.

"You are very happy," Rainer said when he saw me. "I would like very much to be able to join in that happiness, but my despair is stronger than my desire."

"You should be happy, too," I told him. "Do you want to become a father?"

"I have already told you: I do not want to create a life that will fall into the meaninglessness of its existence immediately upon its birth."

"Why must its existence be meaningless? It's up to us how our child will experience his existence."

Rainer did not respond. And then, when I had gotten up from the bed and gone to the window and was pulling aside the curtains, I heard him say, "I want to see my mother."

As we had many years earlier, we set off to find his mother. We reached her street and entered the house. In the hallway, a girl was taking money from a hunchbacked old man, who, a bit embarrassed, quickly left the house. The girl looked at me and Rainer.

"I want to see Gertrude," Rainer said.

"Gertrude?"

"Yes," said Rainer, and, uninvited, he went into the room where he had been born. "I met her right here, fifteen years ago."

"Gertrude is dead," the girl said. "It's been a few years. It was wintertime. She died from hunger or cold, one or the other. It's common for those of us in this line of work to die from that. We buried her as most of us are buried—not in a grave but in the pit where the homeless and the poor are buried. Just don't think it was a poor funeral. Even emperors would envy a funeral like that. All of us who do this work gathered. Hundreds of us girls and women were there around the pit. Our tears mixed with the snow-flakes melting on our faces."

Rainer slowly approached the bed where, years before, his mother had sat while telling him that this was where she had given birth to him. He sat down on the bed and ran his fingers along the dirty cloth.

"So why are you looking for Gertrude?" the girl asked.

Rainer stood up from the bed and thanked the girl, and we left the house.

While we walked, he looked at the ground. Then he said, "I could have done something for her. Even many years ago, I could have done something for her."

I wanted to tell him not to blame himself, but I knew that words would be little comfort.

As we passed the Karl Theater, we saw the large poster in front announcing performances of several classical tragedies. On the wall of the theater, someone had written in charcoal a line from Pindar: "Man is a dream of a shadow."

We said not a word until we reached the Danube Canal. Rainer thought of that line and said, "That man continues to be only a dream of a shadow is what sustains our tragic sense from the very origins of the human race up to the present. Kierkegaard once said that, despite all the changes in the world, the tragic has remained essentially unchanged, just as crying has remained nat-ural to man—although I do not believe the tragic is always con-nected with tears. At the base of human existence is the question of the meaning of life. Whoever reaches that base will, at least for

a moment, come face to face with the meaninglessness of existence and with the tragic. There are people who peacefully and
quietly experience their existence as tragic. The tragic consists in
the actual experience of one's life as meaningless, not in the way
that experience is expressed."

I did not want him to be consumed by such dark thoughts,
and so I said, "I would like us to go somewhere. For a few days. Do
you remember how we once dreamed of living in Venice?"

He nodded and swallowed. He stopped a moment, and then
we continued walking along the quay. It looked as if he also
wanted to start a different conversation, but the bitter sediment
gathered in him did not let him speak of something else. He
seemed to be struggling with himself, and I wanted to pull his
thoughts from that struggle, but I knew that confrontation was not
a cure for his pain. So I pointed to the shadow that a tree on the
quay cast on the water.

"Do you remember how we played with the shadows of our
fingers when we were children?"

"Man is a dream of a shadow," said Rainer.

I said not a word.

"Will you remember me for the good things?" he asked me.

"Why are you speaking like that? Nothing has ended."

"You cannot remember me for the good things. I not only
disregarded the life of the woman who gave birth to me, I not
only destroyed my own life, I destroyed your life as well."

"Do not talk like that."

"You remained alone because of me."

"I am not alone. You are with me."

"I no longer exist. Will you remember me for the good
things?"

"There is no reason to remember you. I will be with you."

"For the good things," he said with a pleading voice.

He put his right hand into his pocket and pulled out a red

patch. Many years earlier, when we were children, I had torn off that small pocket and given it to him at our parting so that he would remember me. Now he scrunched that red patch, the size of a child's heart, into the palm of my hand. Then our palms separated, and he took a step. And another step. And another step, toward the river. I saw his last step before he fell into the water and it swept him away.

I ran along the quay. I pleaded for help and watched his body disappear. Then I felt a weariness that pulled me away from my pain and toward unconsciousness.

• • •

THE RIVER CAST THE BODY UP AT THE EXIT FROM THE CITY.
I was brought to the hospital by people who saw me running along
the quay, pleading for help, falling to my knees, pounding the
palms of my hands on the quay, and falling into unconsciousness.

I lay in the hospital bed and looked at my bloodied palms. A
quiet madness saved me temporarily from the pain. I spoke with
Rainer, and in those moments he was still alive to me. That is how
I survived. "You will return," I told him. "Everything is past, your
eternal search and eternal loss of self, your cruelty toward me and
my desire to return that cruelty to you, all the pain, everything is
past. Your question to life—Who am I?—has been answered with
your death—You are nothing!—and with the way you confronted
death eye to eye and your desire to fall into it. You will return,
Rainer," I told him. "The river is only a great purgatory. Do you
hear me, Rainer? It is only a sailing away. I will be waiting for you
at the end of the river, Rainer. I will be waiting there where it flows
out into another existence. I know that you are here, Rainer. Here
is my hand. Look at my hand, Rainer. Everything will be fine,
believe me. When you finish your voyage, when you come out of
the river, you will just need to change your clothes. You will need
to put on new clothes, and everything will be fine. Believe me,
Rainer, believe me, as I believe in myself. Here is my hand, Rainer.

Grab hold of my hand, and I will pull you out, and then we will set off toward a different existence."

I spoke those words to myself, my eyes closed, and I stretched my hand toward Rainer, but my hand struck the wall. I opened my eyes. All around me were hospital beds.

I returned to reality and felt fear. Young women my age, when they were unmarried and became pregnant, often killed themselves to preserve the family from shame; or, rejected by their families, they left home and worked as prostitutes; or they secretly obtained abortions.

I lay in the hospital bed, my hands on my belly, and looked up at the white ceiling. I recalled the words of the prophet Jeremiah: "Cursed be the day wherein I was born: let not the day wherein my mother bare me be blessed." I lay in the hospital bed with my hands on my belly, and I looked up at the white ceiling. And then I closed my eyes. I tossed in the bed and cursed. I cursed the moment of my birth; I cursed my mother, who had not pressed her legs together to crush the small bloody head that had barely come out of her. I cursed my mother's womb, which had held me for nine months, that it had not become my grave. I cursed my father's seed, and his desire to approach my mother during the night of my conception. I cursed that night of conception. I cursed the first day of the first people, and their first passion. My despair had turned into physical pain. I tossed in my bed and cursed. I had no other cure for the pain. But the pain continued, as if it were stripping the flesh from my bones, and even my bones ached with despair. I could not breathe. I cursed my breathing as well, and that unstoppable need to inhale and exhale—if my breathing were to cease, I told myself, my suffering would cease. Then I thought the pain would not cease. I thought my despair would last forever. I did not yet know that I was separating from them—the pain, the despair.

When I left the hospital, I went, we—the child in me and I—went to the Danube Canal, where Rainer had disappeared. I stood there a long time, staring into the water. I bent down and dipped one hand into the water. The other I held to my belly. Thus our threesome bid farewell to one another.

That evening, I called Sigmund. He said he had a little time the next day, and that we could talk while he visited "The Mother and the Son of God," an exhibit at the Kunsthistorisches Museum for which hundreds of paintings representing the Virgin Mary and Jesus had been brought from around the world.

We stood a long time in front of Giovanni Bellini's *Madonna and Child* and *Crucifixion*, brought from the Correr Museum in Venice. We observed how the Virgin Mary holds the young Jesus. Sadness flickers on the child's face. His half-closed eyes look out with the gaze not of a child but of someone who has seen much more than childhood. It is a look directed not in front of him but toward some great pain, some terrible loss, as if the child senses his destiny, and his separation from the one who stands behind him so peacefully and protectively at that moment, and who, many years later, beside the Cross, will be in despair herself, because she will be unable to do anything to prevent her separation from him, her loss. That pain descends even onto the child's lips, and in the gesture of his hands; he has placed one high on his chest, above his heart, and with the little fingers of his other hand he holds his mother's finger, and seems to point downward with his index finger. His mother cannot see her child's sad disquiet; she is looking toward some other place, somewhere far away. The point at which her gaze is directed is somewhere beyond the painting. She protects him completely; the child is leaning his back on her arm, with one shoulder against her left breast, just above her heart. Although the mother cannot see the disquiet in her child, perhaps she senses it. Perhaps she, too, knows what will be, but she knows it must be that way. She knows this is how it should be, and in this reconciliation she is calm. Her look directed toward the horizon outside the painting is perhaps a look into some other reality, where everything is preserved, where everything that was, everything that is, and everything that will be acquires its true meaning.

Then we looked at *Crucifixion*, at the face of Jesus, which holds only resignation at the horror; at the face of his mother, filled with horrid despair. Resignation and despair, just as in that other painting, *Madonna and Child*, only now resignation is filled with horror, the resignation of Jesus at the moment of his expiring, and his mother, standing by the Cross, is in despair, her hands folded, her head bowed, her gaze blind to everything around her except the pain in her soul, her eyes that seem wasted to their hollows, and in their place despair alone remains.

We looked at these two paintings for a long time, and then I said that all the theologians and philosophers I had read, and who had written on this theme, agreed that with the appearance of Christianity, and the concepts of salvation and resurrection, the tragic disappears. They asserted that in Christianity the tragic is destroyed. Either those who suffer have sinned and are punished with suffering or those who suffer without fault will be rewarded in the afterlife, and theirs will be the kingdom of heaven. These philosophers and theologians are convinced that the concepts of salvation and immortality negate the tragic.

"However," I said to my brother, "look at this painting. Isn't the tragic strongest here, in that moment when the mother sees her son dying?" My brother said nothing. I stretched my hand toward *Crucifixion*, toward the eyes of the mother standing beside her dying son, toward the crucified body expiring before the eyes of the one who gave birth to him. "Do salvation and resurrection destroy the tragic, or are they only consolation?" I asked, while continuing to hold out my hand toward the mother and son. "There is no justice in this world. No single punishment can correct an injustice, because what is past cannot be changed, and those to whom injustice was done remain with their loss. But even if justice were attained in some other world, for what was lost in this one, if in some other world those who had been injured had returned to them what they had lost here, that is not a return of their life's fulfillment; it is only consolation. What is lost at a certain moment can never again be compensated, because what is lost was needed at the moment it disappeared. So even if our existence continues in some other world after our death in this one, our existence in that other world will be only a consolation. In the material world, everything is a great injustice, and since we do not know whether we will go on after this life to exist in some other reality, in some consolatory existence, our only comfort in this world is its beauty."

My brother smiled. "Although it is not a precise statement, it sounds beautiful: Beauty is our only comfort in this world."

I moved my hand away from the man bleeding on the Cross, and away from his mother, who looked inconsolably at him, but my brother continued looking at that beauty, at that comfort.

"I am carrying a child," I said. "Rainer's." My brother looked away from the painting, but he did not look at me. "Rainer is dead." I ran my hands across my belly. "Someone needs to take this fetus from me." My brother said not a word, and he looked at the floor in front of him. "I want you to do it."

"Do what?"

"Take the fetus from me."

"I can't."

"You know how."

"I know how. But I cannot." He said that he would find a good doctor, and a nurse who would look after me as long as I needed help. "We need to hurry. The day after tomorrow, I leave for Venice."

"Venice." I remembered how Rainer and I dreamed of living in Venice. "I do not want to go there."

"To Venice?"

"I do not want to go to the hospital. I do not want to lose this child in the secret unit for abortions. I want it"—and when I said the word "it," I felt something pain me in my womb—"I want it done on my bed."

THE FOLLOWING DAY I lay on my bed with legs spread. In the corner of the room, Dr. Kraus was preparing the instruments. Next to him, providing assistance, was Frau Grubach, the nurse. My brother sat on the bed beside me. He sensed my fear.

"Don't be afraid," he said to me, and he put the palm of his right hand on my left temple. His palm was trembling. "Everything will be fine."

"Fine? Perhaps it will be fine, but not everything," I said. "After this, there will be nothing."

"No," said my brother, and he ran the palm of his hand from my sweaty forehead to the crown of my head. "Everything will be the same as it is now."

"That is the most terrible." I took his hand between the palms of my hands. "For everything to be the same as it is now." I lowered my hands and his to my belly. Motherhood is the giving of a new life, but for me it was something more than that; it was a continuation of an existence that had ended. "Everything will be the same, and everything will be nothing."

"Don't talk like that," my brother said, and he lifted his hand from my stomach. My two hands grabbed his and held it over my eyes. "Everything will be fine."

The doctor asked Sigmund to leave. Frau Grubach was standing above my head, holding a cloth soaked in a bitter liquid to make me fall asleep. My brother made our secret greeting from the time when I was a girl: with his index finger he touched my forehead, then my nose, then my lips. I wanted to return the greeting, but I only pursed my lips and closed my eyes tightly. I felt my brother stand up from the bed, and then I felt the bitter cloth on my mouth and nose. While I sank slowly into unconsciousness, there appeared before my closed eyes a memory from long ago: At a time when many things in the world still had no name, my brother gave me something sharp and said, "Knife."

HOURS LATER, while I was regaining consciousness, the first thing I felt was the pain in my womb. Slowly, slowly, I brought my fingers to my stomach. I opened my eyes, and everything before me shimmered; I could barely make out the contours around me. I did not know where I was, or who I was. And the first thing I remembered was my brother's name.

"Sigmund," I said as loudly as I could, whispering.

"Your brother is in the next room," said a female voice through the haze. It was the voice of the nurse who was to stay with me as long as I needed help. "Should I call him?"

I nodded.

A short time later, the door opened. I could see a bit better, although still indistinctly. I saw that it was my brother Sigmund. He approached the bed and sat down beside me. He placed the palms of his hands over my hands.

"You are fine now," he said.

"I can never be fine again," I said. I turned my head to the wall. I saw there a trace of blood. My brother saw my gaze pause.

"That is due to Dr. Kraus's carelessness," he said.

That bloody trace on the wall was all that remained of my unborn child.

We said nothing. Then I said to him, "It is time for you to go."

"I will stay here tonight."

"You need to leave."

"I am leaving tomorrow."

"You need to get ready."

"I am ready."

I felt the delirium slowly passing, and in its place I was over-whelmed as I sank into bitter pain, and then I said, "I beg you, go."

I made our secret greeting from the time when we were chil-dren: I stretched out my hand, and with my fingers I touched his forehead, then his nose, then his beard. My vision was cloudy, and I could not see whether there were tears in his eyes. He bent down and kissed my forehead. I turned my head toward the wall, toward the bloody trace, and he hastened to leave the room.

I SPENT THOSE DAYS in confusion because of my awareness that I could not feel pain, as if, along with the fetus, the part of my soul that could suffer had been removed.

When my mother returned from Bad Gastein, she noticed the bloody trace on the wall by my bed, but she said nothing. She suggested we visit Sigmund, who had just returned with his family from the Vienna Woods, where he had spent the remainder of his vacation after his trip to Venice. I told her to go alone, and I no longer went with her to those shared lunches. When my brother came, as always, to visit her on Sunday mornings, I left the house before he arrived.

Our mother's birthday was approaching, and the family had decided we would all gather in our home. I spent days getting the apartment ready, and I prepared the food. On the evening of the eighteenth of August, guests began to arrive. For the first time in many years, Anna had come from America with her family, and Paulina and Marie from Berlin with their families. Rosa sat with her hands crossed on her belly—she was pregnant. We were still waiting for Sigmund and Alexander to arrive in order for the cel-ebration to begin. My mother's grandchildren played around her.

I listened to their happy voices, and I wanted to say something, too, but I stood by the door and remained silent.

"There is nothing more beautiful for a mother than to see her children happy," said our mother, stroking her grandchildren's heads. "Of course, Adolfina remained single." Then she turned toward me. "I told you that you would be alone. I saw that you did not know what you needed to do in your life. I gave you advice, but you did not listen. Now look. Look at their happiness. But your life is one big emptiness."

Anna, my brother Sigmund's youngest daughter, who could still barely walk, came up to me and threw herself at my feet. I took her in my arms and brought her close to my face. She laughed and happily struck my cheeks with her little palms.

Then my mother said those words that she had forgotten for years but had said to me at the beginning of my life: "It would have been better if I had never given birth to you."

At the beginning of my life there was pain. Like the quiet dripping of blood from a hidden wound. Drop by drop. And now, when again I heard those words that long ago had opened that first wound, I felt all the blood that flowed from it, and from all the later wounds.

I slowly set Anna on the floor and went to my room. I opened the cupboard, which held the suitcase with infant's clothes. I opened it and took out everything that was inside: the knitted cap, the little mittens, the tiny shoes the size of a finger, the little cape. I left those things in the cupboard and filled the suitcase with my clothes. Then I closed it, took it with me, and left the room. The little girl was still waiting for me in the hallway, and she started toward me again. I set off toward the other door, then opened it and went out. As I went down the stairs I heard the little one rapping her little palms on the door.

When I entered Klara's room with my suitcase, she was not surprised. She only asked me, "Has the fear gone?"

I nodded.

I picked up my suitcase. We opened it as if we were unswaddling a baby, and we took out my things and placed them in the small cupboard by the bed.

When I opened my eyes the first morning that I awoke at the Nest, I heard Klara's voice: "How was your night?"

I turned toward her. She was lying on the bed by the opposite wall of the room.

"Fine," I said, and placed my hand on my chest.

"Does something in your chest hurt?" she asked. I said nothing. "It is life that is hurting you," she said. "But that, too, shall pass."

No one before had given any indication of having noticed my pain, the thing that since my childhood had ached so much that it seemed to tear my heart from my chest. Although neither that pain nor the invisible wound it had opened existed any longer, Klara noticed the traces of them that remained.

In the afternoon Klara went to the knitting room, where she had to spend her working hours that day. I did not feel well, and I was lying on my bed when one of the nurses on duty entered the room.

"Someone wants to see you," she said.

As soon as the nurse moved from the doorway, my brother entered the room.

"Dr. Goethe told me you were here," he said.

"Yes, I am here."

I invited him to sit on my bed. I stood up, took the pillow in my hands, and sat down on one side of the bed, and my brother sat on the other side.

"Why did you leave home?" he asked. I did not know how to answer him. "You could at least have said where you were going." I said not a word. "But that is not important now. You are going home today."

"I can never return there."

"You have no other place to go. That is your only home. Even if you do not want to go back, you must."

I said nothing.

He looked at me a long time, then said with authority, "You are coming with me."

"I am staying," I said.

ALL NORMAL PEOPLE ARE NORMAL IN THE same way; each mad person is mad in his own way.

THE PSYCHIATRIC CLINIC the Nest was located in the very heart of Vienna, and yet it was cut off from the rest of the world.

At night, cries break the silence of the large sleeping rooms. These are the cries of those condemned to share their madness with the madness of others. The nights stream into one another and flow into years, and among those who cry out are others who remain mute, who yearn for quiet, who want only a small piece of this earth in which to safely tuck their heads and sleep through the night. At night they breathe quickly, or they weep, or they pray, even though they do not know to whom to direct their prayers, since they had renounced God long ago, after he had renounced them. Or else they simply breathe slowly, and through that inhalation and exhalation they gently push away some pain lodged in their chests, a clump that has wrapped around the question of why they exist at all if they exist like this, and they are happy as long as that clump enfolds the thought, because stripped bare, without that surrounding clump, the thought would be unbearable. Finally, they are overwhelmed with exhaustion from trying to cope with the noises. The whistles and shouts of the Nest increasingly seem to come from a distance, and they are no longer human voices but a sound created by the pangs of human pain, turned to rage, banging the gong of fate.

In other bedrooms, with only two women or two men, happiness and misfortune wind together in a knot.

In the course of a single day, a girl counts her toes, an old woman tries threading string through the eye of a needle, an old man talks in the corner, a young man trembles in fear at the right sleeve of his shirt, a woman . . . a man . . . In the course of a day and in the wakeful hours of the night, all those at the Nest do something that cuts them off from others, leaving them in their own worlds, separate, alone.

Every night, before falling asleep, a woman gazes for a long time into the darkness and then whispers, "World, good night."

MY BROTHER WROTE THAT each person remains "a child of his epoch, even with regard to his most personal traits." One could say even that each individual madness is a child of his epoch, but also that the most personal traits of madness are the same in all epochs.

MADNESS ORIGINATED AT the same time as the human race. Perhaps the first person, the one who first said "I," experienced his *I* breaking apart. Later, in mankind's early childhood, members of the community looked on those who were different the way one regards with wonder something for which there is no ready explanation, the way one observes the wonder of the sun moving from one edge of the sky to the other, or a flash of lightning.

Aeons passed, and man began trying to explain things: thunder was the heavenly spear of an angry god, the sun was a god who traversed the sky, and madness was the result of being possessed by divine or demonic forces. Did these people, the possessed, flee from their homes and crawl into animal dens, unaware that the wild beast crouched inside would tear them apart? During the hunt, rather than hurling their spears at their prey, did they set their weapons on the ground and bow to the hunted animal? Did they throw stones at the sun, thinking they could extinguish it? In all primitive societies, the cure was the same for anyone believed to be possessed by demonic forces: small holes were drilled in their heads to release the demon. The bodies of those who did not survive the exorcism were thrown a distance from the human dwellings, lest the demon enter another person in the community.

Aeons passed, and man began to explain things differently: lightning was the result of clouds striking each other, the sun was a heavenly body that revolved about the earth, but madness was still the result of being possessed by divine or demonic forces. In the Bible, madness is a punishment for disobedience to God. This is how one is punished according to the Old Testament: "The Lord shall smite thee with madness, and blindness, and astonishment of heart." In the New Testament, madness is understood as possession by evil forces that must be driven from the one they have possessed. In other religions as well, madness results when one has fallen under the influence of dark forces, a consequence of the battle between God and Satan.

But there have been others who sought a different cause for madness. At a time when his compatriots and contemporaries explained madness in terms of the influence of the goddess Hera, or of Aries, the god of war, Hippocrates wrote that it is neither the forces of light nor those of darkness that induce madness but our brain alone that makes us "mad or delirious, brings us dread and fear." Several centuries later, Aretaeus of Cappadocia, in his work *On the Causes and Symptoms of Acute Diseases*, writes: "A patient may believe himself to be a sparrow, a cock, or an earthen vase; another may think himself a god, an orator, or an actor, and carry a stalk of straw believing it to be the scepter of the world. Some cry like an infant and demand to be carried, or they believe they are a grain of mustard and constantly tremble in fear that they will be eaten by a hen." The Cappadocian researcher of illnesses posited melancholia and mania as the two poles of madness: "The melancholic isolates himself, he is afraid of being persecuted and imprisoned, he torments himself with superstitious ideas, he hates his life," he "curses life and wishes for death." Those who are possessed not by melancholia but by mania, however, are in an uncontrolled fury, agitation, or exhilaration, and under these conditions may feel inspired to great deeds that they have no basis for performing, or else they might kill someone for no real reason. Sometimes the two poles of madness appear in the same person: "Some patients after a bout of melancholy have an attack of mania" yet again, while someone who was euphoric due to mania is overtaken by melancholia, so that "he becomes, at the end of the attack, languid, sad, taciturn, he complains that he fears for his future, he feels ashamed." And then the circle turns again in a constant cycle of melancholia and mania.

Centuries passed, and it became clear that the sun does not orbit the earth; rather, the earth orbits the sun, and explanations were sought for natural phenomena. Yet divine intermediaries continued to declare the mad to be possessed by the Devil, and executing God's will, they determined whether they would be healed by prayers or sent on a pilgrimage to a holy place that could heal them. If, however, it was determined that it was not possession but a voluntary pact with the Devil, the punishment was to be burned at the stake or hanged or drowned.

When the Age of Reason began in Europe, the insane were viewed not only as sinners who had fallen under the sway of demonic powers but also as dangerous beings, or beings who could not contribute to society and whose existence hindered its functioning. Yet even then, one of the explanations for madness was God. During the Renaissance, madness was understood as a consequence of three basic sins: madness of the imagination, whereby a person believed he was someone or something he was not; madness as a curse from God; and madness as a result of great passion. At that time, every large city had a prison for the insane. There they were not treated but punished; madness was considered not an illness but a crime. Those whom society considered normal needed to erect a barrier between themselves and those they declared to be mad. The rulers of coastal cities bribed sailors to gather up those thought mad, and then the boats sailed off with the unfortunates lashed to the decks. If they survived thirst and hunger, if they had not been defeated by the wind or the cold, they were secretly unloaded at the first harbor, and if that was impossible they were tossed in some desolate place or thrown into the water.

In the seventeenth century, Reginald Scot, Edward Jordan, and Thomas Willis asserted in their studies that madness was neither a pact with Satan nor possession by him but an illness of the nerves and the mind, yet the conviction that the eclipse of the mind was provoked by forces of darkness would continue to be held even by intellectuals. At the end of the seventeenth century, Ernst Wedel, a professor of medicine at the University of Jena, explained to his students the ways in which the Devil manifested himself in people through madness. But it was too late. John Locke had already declared that religion, too, must be rational, and Thomas Hobbes had explained madness as an error in thinking provoked by a defect in the workings of the body. In spite of their works, the sanatoriums for the insane continued to resemble torture chambers for criminals. In the two most renowned asylums, the Salpêtrière and the Bicêtre in Paris, the sick were kept like animals. Some were even kept in underground cells with chains around their necks, and as punishment were confined to pillories. If some lout on the outside wanted to observe them and enjoy their torture, the guards granted that pleasure for a bit of money, and sometimes even struck the unfortunates with whips, as if it were some sort of circus performance.

In the nineteenth century, religion and penal institutions finally handed the insane over to psychiatry. Madness was no longer a sin against God or a crime but a barren existence, a failed life, a lost opportunity. That which a human being receives but once—his life—he destroys by his madness, because even though he lives it, he lives it to no constructive end. A life of madness is a mistake, a failed investment, of nature and of God.

ALL THE WINDOWS of the rooms at the Nest looked out onto the grounds in the middle of the hospital. The grounds were covered with soft grass and crisscrossed with pathways, with benches set along them. In several areas, clusters of trees called to mind a stage set representing a forest. Toward evening, when dusk fell, Klara and I would stand by the window and watch it grow dark.

AT THE NEST there were people who were as afraid of darkness as of death.

WHEN WE SENSED QUIET set in, Klara and I would immediately stop talking, no matter how important the conversation we were having. We loved the quiet all the more because it was such a rarity at the Nest. Hans and Johann lived in the room above us. One walked with slow and heavy steps, as if he had hooves instead of feet; the other walked quickly and decisively. In the room next to ours, Krista talked loudly to herself nonstop, most often accusing herself of something. In the room on the other side of ours, Beata and Herta often giggled feverishly. Occasionally they banged their heads or their fists on the wall. Dull blows like forgotten pain. Yelps, howling, weeping, and laughter, clangs, squeals, and blows reached us from other rooms near ours. Quiet was such a rarity that we yearned for it, and in those moments when it set in we fell silent, perhaps without thinking. We stopped our conversation, not deliberately, in order to enjoy the quiet; rather, words escaped us, as when a miracle occurs.

THE HUMAN RACE HAS always sensed—and, being unable to prove whether it is truth or self-deception, will ever only sense—the feeling that at the very core of a human being glimmers an incorporeal light, something that may continue to burn even after the body has died. That light consists of a large number of rays, each of which is one of the essential human traits. People, then, owing to the similarity of the rays they carry within them, form human-constellations. Countless people are a part of each of these constellations; each person belongs to as many constellations as the number of rays that constitute his light. Countless people are connected in each constellation even when they do not know one another, even when they will never see one another. In order to be a part of the same human-constellation, it is important not to be close to, or even to live at the same time as, the others in that constellation, but to carry, in one's incorporeal light, the ray characteristic of that constellation. Some of these rays are traits of madness. The constellations that madness creates are interwoven with the other human-constellations, because they share the same people, and yet it appears that each of these constellations of madness sparkles in a separate sky, alone.

THE NIGHTSTANDS BESIDE THE beds at the Nest held the most
varied souvenirs of past lives.

On her nightstand, our neighbor Krista kept a lock of hair
from her daughter's first haircut, and the first tooth she lost.
Whenever someone went into her room, during the course of
their conversation Krista's gaze would turn toward the small table,
and, forgetting the countless times she had said it before, she
would say, "This is my little Lotte," and she would pick up the
lock of hair and the baby tooth and hold them in the palms of her
hands, looking at them the way children look at a sliver of broken
glass, as though it were some kind of precious object.

Everything imaginable was on the nightstands at the Nest:
pieces of brick, photographs, postcards written in faded ink, bird
feathers, the legs of chairs, pillowcases, scraps of curtains, torn-off
pockets, buttons, small mirrors, pebbles, carved pieces of wood,
shoelaces, hatbands, diapers, beads, the hands, feet, bodies, and
heads of dolls, and here and there a complete doll. . . .

On some tables the objects were arranged with care, sometimes in a strictly determined order, while on others they were
scattered, chaotic. By the chaos or the order on a nightstand, by the
manner in which the objects were arranged or scattered, by that
remarkable geometry of order or chaos, one could read the geometry of someone's past, something that those who lay beside those
tables and who had lived those lives with wondrous geometry
could not, or did not know how to, put into words.

On Klara's nightstand was a sketch that no one would imagine had been drawn by her brother: a woman, her back turned,
poised on the edge of something.

My nightstand was empty. There were many empty nightstands at the Nest.

AT THE END of the east wing of the hospital building, there was a small library. There some of us quickly paged through books from the first page to the last, and then from the last to the first. Some, from the time they sat down to the time they stood up, did not turn a single page but looked at a letter or a period, a comma, an exclamation point, or a question mark. Some of us read.

SOMETIMES KLARA WOULD PICK UP the sketch that lay on the table beside her bed—the sketch, drawn on a small piece of paper that her brother happened to have in his pocket during one of his visits. Gustav had a habit of keeping his hands in his pockets while he talked, and at the end of the conversation he would suddenly take them out, and then pencils, pieces of chalk, erasers, coins would fall from his pockets. During one visit, as he pulled his hands from his pockets a rumpled piece of paper fell to the floor. Since then, Klara kept that sketch on her nightstand; sometimes she held it in her hands and stared at it. There, on that small piece of paper, a woman stands on the edge of something, her back turned. Beyond the edge stretches a void. Once, after staring at the drawing a long time, Klara said, "I ask myself whether this woman is looking into the abyss or whether she is standing on the edge with her eyes closed."

ON AFTERNOONS WHEN THE WEATHER was fine, we would go outside to walk the grounds. If someone had a good enough reason, he could remain in the hospital building. Sometimes I stayed in my room because of stomach pains or a headache. I would stand by the window and study the others who were outdoors. Some ran about the grass like children; others sat on benches and talked; a third group argued; some stood alone, pensive, or laughing, or tearful, or indifferent. The window framed the world below, keeping me separate in some other world, from where I could observe myself.

ONCE, WHILE LOOKING OUT from behind the window, I noticed a man leading two children by the hand approach one of the women walking by herself on the grounds. When she noticed him she stopped stone-cold, and that somehow froze her three visitors as well. Her husband said something, pointed to the children, and rested the palms of his hands on their heads for several moments. He paused as he spoke, probably expecting her to say something. She stood unmoving, as I looked at her from behind. I could not see the expression on her face, nor did I know whether she was even able to say anything. The expression on her husband's face showed that he was continually failing to extract a single word. At one moment, his face showed that he had given up. Then he took a step toward her and hugged her, and her hands made a barely perceptible motion, as if she were attempting to return his embrace. The children drew nearer. The two of them hugged her, clasping her around the waist. She did not bend down, or did not succeed in bending down. The husband and the children set off toward the Nest's exit; before they passed through the gates, they turned back toward the woman, raised their arms, and waved. She raised her arm as if it were a heavy object; she made a barely perceptible motion that resembled a wave, and then slowly lowered her arm beside her body. One of the children separated from the husband and took two steps in the woman's direction, two steps that could have turned into a run, but then stopped suddenly. The child turned back and joined the other child and the grown-up, and out they went through the gate. For a long time, the woman remained standing stock-still. Although she was standing there on the hospital grounds, I had a feeling that she was standing on the edge of some abyss. I tried to imagine her face but couldn't. I asked myself whether she was looking into the abyss or standing on the edge with her eyes closed.

THE LIFE OF KRISTA, our neighbor at the Nest, turned upside down in an instant. This happened just before they brought her to the Nest. Perhaps it was the death of her husband, but when madness is in question one can never be sure. All at once, she stopped recognizing the people around her. She looked at her parents as if she were looking at a wall. She looked at her little daughter, born several months earlier, as if she were looking at an object. When Krista was brought to the Nest, something immediately revived in her. She began to move, to eat, and to bathe herself, to walk the grounds, and to weave during the work hours. But when her parents and her little daughter came to visit it was as if some part of her past returned, and her whole body stiffened. Then, after they left, she cried for her daughter, and begged for her to be brought back to her. Once, when her parents learned what would happen when they headed home after their visits, they took Krista home, and she spent several weeks with them, completely impassive. So they returned her to the Nest, and as soon as they had left, Krista stirred and began to moan for her little daughter.

Her loud moans of despair lasted for hours after those visits. We would go into her room and assure her that we would bring her little daughter to her, but it was as if she were incapable of hearing us. At the moment the falsehood touched her consciousness, Krista would simply nod, fall silent, and life would continue.

AT A TIME WHEN people still believed the earth was as flat as a dinner plate, when people trembled before the Last Judgment, feared hell, and hoped in heaven, it was customary in every city for the mad folk to be locked in cages from time to time and brought to the town square. There all the city's inhabitants are gathered: the municipal dignitaries and the craftsmen, the clergymen and the soldiers, the fine ladies and the washerwomen, the children and the old folk, the physicians and the fishermen, the honest folk and the thieves. They wait in anticipation for the grand festivity, which begins when the cages are opened and those imprisoned come out. Their exit is greeted by the delighted cries of the crowd; they step from their cages with their strange looks, their incomprehensible mutterings, their tattered clothing. The guardians of the city, in a wide circle around them, make sure they remain in a tight cluster; the guardians stand with their legs spread, getting down as low as possible so as not to block anyone's view. Everyone looks at the mad folk, and they look back at the people gathered in the square, and at themselves and at one another. Someone from the crowd—clergyman or thief, it's all the same—tosses out some insult or other. Some of the mad ones reply, while others remain in their rapture with their saints, or in their confusion as to why they have found themselves before so many eyes. And the crowd waits. A child picks up several small stones, bends down between the spread legs of one of the guards, and begins to throw. A woman who greedily chews her fingers is struck in the forehead. Another stone strikes the leg of an old man, who tries to warn the others by chirping like a sparrow. The third stone misses its target; it falls somewhere among the mad people. The woman stops chewing her fingers and begins to scream in panic. The old man stops chirping like a sparrow and begins to yell at the assembled throng. And the other mad folk become agitated; some join in the old man's howling at the crowd; others begin to run in place; a third group rolls over on the ground; someone laughs with a sound like the shriek of a bird; someone scratches himself from head to toe and back again. The gathered crowd is excited by the view, by the tu-

mult, the writhing, by the rage and despair of the insane. One of
the madmen stands with arms outstretched and begs to be crucified. "Crucify him! Crucify him!" shouts the crowd. Someone
calls out that he is the god of the sun and that all he needs to do is
blow and the sun will burn out. "Can you extinguish the sun by
peeing on it?" shouts a voice from the crowd, and the man drops
his pants, urinates into the air, toward the sun, and pisses all over
himself. The crowd roars with amusement. "Where is my baby?
Where is my baby?" screams a woman in the mad cluster. Some
in the crowd tell others that the madwoman's child died at birth,
but others say she never had a child but told everyone she was pregnant. "Where is my baby?" wails the woman, and someone from
that happy crowd who is enjoying the show takes off his shirt,
quickly rolls it up, and throws it to her. "Here is your child!" he
calls to her. "My baby! My baby!" cries the woman, hugging the
bundle to her breast. She hugs it and does not stop her joyful ex-
clamations: "My baby is back! My baby is back!" Everyone delights
in the spectacle: the municipal dignitaries and the craftsmen, the
clergymen and the soldiers, the fine ladies and the washerwomen,
the children and the old folk, the physicians and the fishermen,
the honest folk and the thieves. Now comes the most enjoyable
part. The guardians begin to flick their whips, and, as if driving
livestock, they herd the mad people toward the gates of the city.
The crowd steps along after them, some in the throng bend down,
take a stone, and hurl it at those being snapped by the whips, who
scream from the blows, try to run away, and make strange acro-
batic movements in response to the lash of the whip. Finally, they
arrive at the exit through the fortifications surrounding the city.
The gates open. The guards give the final cracks of their whips and
then call out, "And now you are free!" and let them pass through
the gates. And they run away, not knowing that behind them the
city gates will close and they will be left beyond the fortification,
not knowing that in this way the cities, every few years, drive out

the insane. Some of them continue circling the fortifications for a while. A few will even manage to push their way back in, but others wander a long time in the trackless terrain, across the fields, along the rivers. The woman who was greedily chewing her fingers will freeze to death that same winter. The old man who whistled like a sparrow will be ripped apart by a wolf. The young man who, even while walking, scratched himself from head to toe and back will reach the fortified walls of another city, and will want to enter, but he will be killed by a knight who just days before had won his beloved in a chivalric contest and dedicated to her a song whose rhymes told of his love. The woman who had sought her baby will be raped by highway brigands, who will take her with them and later abandon her, and she will die in her sleep, beside a tree, hugging the bundle of rags, her child.

DORA'S CHILDREN WERE CONSTANTLY with her at the Nest. She told them stories, fed them, took them on walks, lulled them to sleep. Dora's children were constantly with her, even though no one but she could see them. At mealtimes, at her table in the dining hall, she asked us not to sit at the places next to her because she needed to seat her children there, and she fed them piling up invisible food with invisible spoons that she then placed in their invisible mouths, scolding those who refused to eat. When we went outdoors, she taught her children to play children's games, and she played with them. She played with the invisible around her; with the invisible she tossed a ball, threw pebbles into a circle; she jumped and hopped together with the invisible. In the Nest's library, she opened books in front of the invisible and taught her children to read. Before tucking them into bed, she told them stories, and as soon as she awoke she awakened them, too. Some said that Dora had never had children. Nonetheless, her children were always with her.

WHEN MY SISTER ROSA came to visit me for the first time, we sat on my bed. She kept rubbing her large belly, caressing it.

"Two more months," she said when I asked when she would become a mother.

AT THE NEST THERE were rooms from which the mad inhabitants never left. Those were rooms in which tens of bodies lay lifeless, or fought like animals against the straps and chains that bound them. This second group we termed "dangerous." Dr. Goethe sometimes allowed us to go into these rooms, where the residents lay motionless or thrashed about. We looked at their pensive heads, frantic heads, dreadful heads, terror-stricken heads. They looked at us with their tired eyes, empty eyes, eyes filled with fear, rapture, insane joy, unfounded hate and unfounded love, eyes filled with disgust and delight; they pursed their lips in silence, thrust them out in wonder, letting escape some barely audible word; they blessed or cursed; they shouted in pain and in joy.

WE CALLED THE ROOM where they brought the inhabitants of the Nest who were expected to die soon the dying room. One day Klara brought me to that long room that smelled of death. A smell of raw, disintegrating flesh, of excrement, of sweat, and, in the middle of that stench, of bodies tossing on the eve of death, and bodies stiffly awaiting it. Several of the dying, laid out on mattresses on the floor, agonized with yet one more breath. It was cold, but it seemed that something was vaporizing in that dark room. Looking at those whom death was approaching, I thought that in death, everyone was different and everyone was the same. Everyone let go of his spirit by exhaling, but each one exhaled in his own way.

KLARA SAID TO ME, "I will never forget the first death I saw here. During lunch in the dining hall, Regina's head dropped down beside a bowl of soup, as though she were dropping off to sleep."

WHEN SOMEONE at the Nest died, the news spread from one end of the hospital to the other; everyone passed it along in his normal voice, mumbling or speaking loudly, quietly or screaming, quickly as though trying to keep up with his thoughts or slowly as though wanting to let his thoughts disperse.

OFTEN, DURING THE TIME reserved for rest outside on the hospital grounds, Heinrich's mother would come to the Nest. At that time, Heinrich was almost motionless, because his mind could not tell his body to move. He spent days in bed, except during the rest hour outside, when the orderlies would set him upright and push him, and he would move like some kind of machine, making choppy steps as long as someone pushed him. So they pushed him along the corridors to the exit, brought him to one of the benches, then pressed down on his shoulders, and he sat down. Everything in his movements was somehow mechanical. While he sat, he stared at a single point, and continued staring at it even when his mother came. His mother would sit beside him, place her hand on his hand, and speak to him with such warmth and composure that one could not imagine she knew her son's condition. In those moments she spent with her son, there was wonderful life in the old woman's eyes, and in her lips as she spoke, and in the movements of the hand that did not rest on her son's hand but tenderly and freely waved through the air, in time with the lilt of her words. She looked at her son, and it was as if she were look-

ing into a face as animated as her own. But Heinrich stared without moving his pupils, as if there were nothing around him, as if
he, too, were not there. Later, when it came time for us to return
to our rooms, the orderlies grasped Heinrich under his arms, and
he raised himself up, and then, with their hands prodding his
back, he stepped with choppy, mechanical movements. When he
disappeared into the building, his mother stood; already her face
had completely transformed (as if some misfortune had suddenly
descended on her—not some new misfortune she has just learned
of but a long-standing one that no longer arouses horror but is carried with an anguished resignation), and with tired eyes, and
equally tired movements, she made her way to the Nest's exit.

SOMETIMES MY BROTHER VISITED ME at the Nest. Dr. Goethe
was always happy when his colleague Dr. Freud appeared; they
would converse a long time, and their conversations often turned
into minor disagreements. I did not take part in their discussions.
I heard only the tone and inflection of their voices, watched their
facial expressions, noted the gestures they made with their hands.

Once, Dr. Goethe came up with the idea that we should hold
a grand carnival at the Nest. The carnival was going to brighten
us up, and visitors would contribute money to the hospital. We
spent weeks preparing for the great event. The only ones excluded
were the violent, the manic, the nymphomaniacs, and those lying
motionless in their beds.

"But why can't I take part in the carnival?" Augustina protested, licking her lips.

"Because we have decided that nymphomaniacs will remain
locked in their rooms during the carnival," said Dr. Goethe.

"That is not fair," Augustina grumbled. "Not fair."

We lived those weeks for the carnival; we waited for it, not the
way you do an event lasting a single evening, but as though for

each of us it would begin a new existence. The doctors allowed us to decide for ourselves what kinds of costumes we would wear, and we sewed them together. We spoke about the costumes, and we sewed them as if we were making ourselves new bodies.

"There," said Karl, stroking the large hat he had just completed. "I will regain my kingdom once again." Karl, who believed he was Napoléon.

Everyone selected clothing according to his imagined, or desired, existence. For those who believed they were someone or something the external world did not recognize—such as Thomas, who, in addition to scant clothing, had requested that he be allowed to carry a large cross on his back; or Ulrike, who requested real diamonds for her diadem; or Joachim, who insisted on Werther's yellow trousers and blue overcoat—their clothes were the beginning of full acknowledgment of an existence that, in some fashion, they had already attained in their unreality. Others, who wanted not to be something else in this world but to be what they were in some other world, constructed clothing to protect themselves here in this world. They made armor, or fashioned wire into chain mail that resembled cages. They prepared costumes that they needed in order to help them defeat this world, costumes that transformed them into dangerous animals or creatures from some bestiary. They made clothes that would enable them to escape this world, they made wings so that they could fly away, or they sewed clothing that was not clothing but a fabric that covered a moving wall, a box, a stone.

Every day I went to the room where the costumes were being readied. One day, while I was watching the others measuring, cutting, sewing, Dr. Goethe asked me, "Why haven't you begun to get ready for the carnival?"

"I simply don't know what to dress up as," I told him.

"Ah," said Dr. Goethe. "The carnival is not about dressing up but about transformation. The question is not 'What do I want to dress up as?' but 'What do I want to be transformed into? What do I want to become, so as to be not what I do not want to be but what I am?' That is the question."

"What do I want to become," I said, not as if asking a question but as if saying I do not want to become anything. "I do not want to become anything," I said.

"But at one time, surely, you wanted to become something, something that you were not at that moment," said Dr. Goethe.

Then I saw a long piece of fabric that had been tossed aside. I rolled it up and placed it by my left breast, cradling it in my arms the way one holds a nursing baby.

"All right," I said. "I will be a mother. At the carnival."

THE WHOLE CITY had been invited to the carnival at the Nest, and the spacious grounds were too small to accommodate all who wanted to come.

"All the tickets have been sold," said Dr. Goethe, rubbing his hands in satisfaction a week before the event. "Your brothers are also coming," he added, turning first to Klara then to me.

"Let them come," said Klara. "I will stay in my room that night."

On the night of the carnival, the grounds of the Nest were overflowing. The crowd had gathered in a circle around the central area and was pushing to see the people in feathered costumes, people with clown hats and large fish tails, people with clothes steeped in color, red as blood, people with the wings of angels and butterflies and birds, people hidden in large eggs with openings for their eyes, people under long blue sheets representing a river, people with trumpets announcing the apocalypse, people who rolled around on a red sheet and burned in the eternal fire, people who lay on a blue sheet and enjoyed heavenly peace, and one man with a cross on his back, who looked up toward the darkness and called out, "Lord, Lord, why hast thou forsaken me?" Everywhere there were lanterns, torches, and several large fires whose flames rose up toward the dark sky. My eyes searched for my brother but could not find him. Someone tugged my sleeve. I turned. It was Gustav.

"Klara is in the room," I told him.

"I will visit her later," said Gustav. "Right now I need to finish some very important business," and he winked at me, then set off toward the bushes at the edge of the park with a young woman he surely had met in the crowd.

I continued to search the crowd for my brother. When I had given up and headed toward the tables placed by the entrance to the hospital building, where several nurses sold drinks and food, I saw Sigmund setting down an empty glass, handing over money, and taking a full glass. I went over to him.

"I see you are enjoying yourself," I said.

He smiled.

"Would you like some schnapps?" he asked, pointing to his glass.

"Alcohol is permitted to the guests, not to us."

"I can get some for myself, but you can drink it."

"You know I don't drink."

"I don't drink, either," he said. "I do not know why now . . ."

We climbed the stairs at the entrance to the hospital building, and from there we had a good look at what was happening in the central area of the grounds. Scores of people were riding atop an enormous fish made from pillows sewn together and calling out, "We are flying! *Flyyyyiinnnng!*" In one spot, an old woman held up a small glass slipper and asked, "Now where is the prince to see that this slipper fits as if cast for my little foot?" In another spot, entranced, an old woman and an old man with enormous butterfly wings were stamping now on one leg, now on the other.

"This is like the theater," said my brother.

"Or the circus," I said.

"Yes. Like in the Middle Ages. When the municipal leaders gathered the city's mad people together in the square, and the crowd turned them into something like a circus performance. And then they were driven out of the city, the fortified gates closing behind them."

"I think the majority of people here would have nothing against being driven from the Nest after the carnival. The only ones left would be me, Klara, and a few others."

"Which proves this is not the place for you."

"Or that it is the only place for us," I said. "But why did you come like this?"

"Like what?"

"Without a mask. You see that even the visitors have come in costumes."

"Only some of them."

"But you need to change your clothes."

"You know I do not like such things," he said.

"You do not like alcohol, either, but still you are drinking this evening."

He went down the stairs and over to the tables, paid, and handed the empty glass to one of the nurses, who filled it up again.

"Come," I said, "come and change." And I led him right up to the entrance to the hospital building. I told the guards that my brother had to change, and they let us inside.

We went to the Great Hall, where costumes we had borrowed from the Burgtheater were scattered about, unused, because everyone had wanted to devise his own.

"Here," I said. "This is for you."

"You know I never like to appear foolish," said my brother, holding the costume in his hands.

"I know," I said. "That is exactly why I am changing you into a fool. For one night at least you can give up your mask of seriousness."

"It's too late. It has long since fused with my face."

"Come," I said. "Get dressed." And I turned to the wall so that I would not see Dr. Freud in his underwear.

After a short time, he said, "I'm ready."

I turned around and had to laugh. The rose-colored pants fit his legs tightly, the shirt was a wild array of colors, and above that serious face with a beard and glasses rose a cap with two orange-colored points topped with green pompons.

"I really am a fool, aren't I?"

I did not answer; I only laughed.

"What about you? You haven't changed either!"

"For me it's easy," I said. I took a shirt from the scattered clothes, rolled it up, and tucked it under my dress and over my stomach. I placed my hands on my dress, supporting the rumpled shirt, and said, "So now we are both what we need to be."

My brother looked at my hands and how they held my belly.

"And now," I told him, "I will show you the common rooms. This room here, which today is serving as our changing room, is the Great Hall, where Dr. Goethe sometimes lectures. He explains madness to us. He thinks this will help us understand ourselves."

"Does he continue to use the word *madness*?"

"Yes. He says it is better, and he is right."

"But medical ethics has been searching a long time for different terminology."

"Dr. Goethe says that if he calls madness *psychosis*, if we mad people are called *patients*, if a madhouse is called a *psychiatric clinic*, if he terms our madness and foolishness *symptoms*, then a distance is created between us and him. I do not know why he must not have distance, but it is nice for us. When one of us is

angry at Dr. Goethe, he can even shout at him, insult him, and
Dr. Goethe does not punish us for that. We are like his friends."

"You do not need to be friends. There has to be distance.
That is one of the foundations of the doctor–patient relationship;
it is a precondition for healing."

"But who said anything about healing? After all, no one here
is sick; everyone here simply lives in his own world." I straightened
the glasses on his nose, which had turned a bit red from the alcohol. "Come so I can show you the other rooms," I said, and we left
the hall and hurried along the corridor. "This is the library. You
see, it is small, but it has lovely books, and there are enough even
for those who will stay here for the rest of their lives." Then we set
off back down the corridor, and we reached the dining hall. "This
is where we eat." Then I took him to the workrooms, to the one in
which objects were made of wood, and to the sewing room, the
weaving room, and the room where we embroidered and knitted.
"Klara and I taught Dr. Goethe how to knit."

"And does he?"

"Sometimes."

I took him to the last room that I wanted to show him.

"And here is where people die," I told him, cracking open the
door. My brother knew what he would see inside, and he did not
want to enter. "Please, come in, you are welcome here." I entered
first, and he followed. There, as always, it smelled of death, of raw,
disintegrating flesh, of excrement, of sweat, and, in the middle of
that stench, of bodies tossing on the eve of death, and bodies stiffly
awaiting it. Several of the dying, laid out on mattresses on the
floor, agonized with yet one more breath. "In life everyone is different, while in death everyone is different and everyone is the
same. Everyone lets go of his spirit by exhaling, but each exhales
in his own way."

"A little water . . . a little water," begged an old man dying on
a mat under the window. The on-duty nurse was handing out

drinks at the carnival, and there was no one to give water to the dying.

I took my hands from the bundled shirt I was holding against my stomach under my dress so that I could take the bottle of water from the table, and I poured several drops into the pleading mouth. The old man thanked me. As I was returning the bottle to the table, the shirt, no longer supported, slipped from under my dress and fell to the floor. I bent down, picked it up, bundled it up again, and placed it by my left breast, cradling it in my arms the way one holds a nursing baby. My brother watched me.

"Let's go," I said, and we exited the room that smelled of death.

We went out of the hospital, stood at the top of the entrance stairs, and looked toward the grounds, where the guests and residents of the Nest had become intermingled. They danced, they sang, they created quite a commotion, chasing one another, conversing, or arguing.

"Sometimes I recall those words of yours," my brother said.

"Which words?"

"That beauty is comfort in this world."

"Look how much beauty there is around us. Which means how much comfort. And that, in turn, means how much pain, because comfort always appears for a reason."

"Yes," my brother said, "how much beauty."

We went down the stairs and walked over to the tables. My brother was already drunk—his face was red, his movements quicker than usual, and he spoke with the warmth in his voice that he had had when he was a young man, and I a child.

"I have had enough to drink," he said, and paid them to refill his empty glass. Then we moved away from the tables where they were serving drinks. "I think of you often," he said.

"Often," I repeated.

"And do you also think . . ."

"Of what?"

"Of the world outside here . . ."

"No," I said. "Ever since I got here, it is as if nothing outside these walls exists."

He took a sip, his hand or his mouth trembled, and the rest of his drink spilled to the ground.

"Yet another reason for yet another glass," he said, and he set off back toward the tables. On his way there, he stumbled. I wanted to go to him, but as he straightened up he signaled to me to stay and wait for him. He paid, they poured him a drink, and he came back to me.

"I promise this is my last glass," he said. I smiled. "Yes," he continued. "There are so many things I want to tell you, but I do not know whether you want to hear them, and I do not know whether there is a reason to tell you. . . ."

"What things?"

"About our mother, about me and Martha, about the children, about Minna. About our sisters. About the city. About everything . . . You have been here for years. . . . There are so many things I want to tell you, but I do not know whether you want to hear them, and I do not know whether there is a reason to tell you. . . ." He spoke with his eyes fixed on the ground. Then he looked me in the eyes. "Do you have anything you want to tell me?"

"I do not know whether you want me to tell you something. I do not know what you want me to tell you."

"Everything," he said.

"Everything," I repeated. "But what I have to tell somehow does not exist in words. It exists only in images, and even those are merging one into another.

We said nothing.

"Does something hurt you?" he asked. I had heard his voice tremble only a few times in my life.

"What should be hurting me?"

"Something from the past."

"No," I said. "It is as if nothing ever was before. As if life began the moment I got here. Or ended at that moment."

He raised the glass of schnapps to his mouth, but rather than put it to his lips he brought his index finger to his teeth and bit it. Then he drank the schnapps. The glass fell to the ground. His whole body was shaking. He took my hand in his hands and kissed my palm. Then he hugged me, pressing my head to his chest with his hands, and he said, "O my sister . . . O my sister . . ." as if by stating our kinship he was stating my whole fate, everything he knew and everything he did not know, and he cried between each utterance of our relationship; he lamented what was expressed in that utterance, "O my sister." He kissed me on the forehead. I remembered how in our childhood he would kiss me on the forehead secretly somehow, when our mother was not around, because she scoffed at such tenderness. It seemed to me that I was not breathing, it seemed to me that I did not feel anything, only the touch of his lips on the crown of my head, the warmth of his breath that smelled of alcohol, and the firmness of his hands pressing my head to his chest.

"Oh, what passion!" Suddenly, Augustina's voice could be heard near us.

I felt the pressure of my brother's hands slacken. I straightened my head and moved away from him.

"Sir, I need a little tenderness, too," shrieked Augustina, while my brother wiped his tears. "Give me a little tenderness, too, sir." She went up to him and grabbed him between the legs.

"Didn't we say nymphomaniacs were to stay in their rooms?" Hilda the nurse was calling from somewhere. My brother was pushing Augustina away, and then the orderlies came and led her away. "And make sure the other nymphomaniacs are locked up tight!" Hilda called after them.

People with wings, people with dragons' heads, people with

fish-scaled clothing, danced, forming a circle around us. My brother staggered and then vomited. I held his head up, placing my palm on his forehead. Dr. Goethe appeared from somewhere.

"When I said alcohol would be served only to visitors, I did not imagine they would drink more than the mad people would if they were allowed to drink!" Dr. Goethe said. My brother wiped the vomit from around his mouth with a handkerchief. "As for the choice of costume, I can only praise you," Dr. Goethe went on. "It looks cut to your measure," he said, grabbing the pompons on the cap perched on my brother's head. "But it is time for you to return to your false clothing and go home."

We went into the Great Hall. My brother began to change his clothes, and I turned to the wall and listened to the conversation between Dr. Goethe and Dr. Freud.

"You know," said Dr. Goethe, "I respect your efforts to come to a new understanding of human beings, but the very method in which you carry out your so-called psychoanalysis—your patients lying on a couch while they natter on about something, and you watch them, but they cannot see you . . . that is a bit of a fraud."

"What do you mean, a *fraud*?" my brother said angrily. "My patients do not natter on while lying on the couch in my office. I prompt them to talk about their problems through free association, through spontaneous conversation, so that I can reach beyond the symptoms of their illness to their childhood traumas, which, together with their primary instincts, are buried in their subconscious, and in this way I can come to a true understanding of their illnesses and to the treatment of the disorders that arise in the processes of feeling, thinking, and behaving. Because I have listened to my patients attentively, I have come to important conclusions about the way a human being functions. With my discovery of the subconscious, and the explanation that it is precisely the part hidden and unknown to us that determines our thoughts, feelings, and actions, I am on a path to change the world. This will be the third great revolution—after those of Copernicus and Darwin—in human understanding of the world and of themselves. Copernicus showed the human race that it was not the center of the universe; Darwin, that it derives not from God but from an ape; and I, that a person is not who he thinks he is."

"You are lying. A greater revolution for humanity than these three theories put together came with the invention of the toilet bowl. Until several decades ago, people emptied the contents of their bowels into chamber pots and then threw those same contents out the window, occasionally onto the head of some chance passerby. Some homeowners had toilets in their courtyards. But in 1863, several years after Darwin had informed the world of his theories on the origin of species and natural selection, Thomas Crapper patented a bowl for the toilet bucket. So what if we know the earth revolves around the sun? So what if we know we are not the center of the universe? So what if we know we are descended from apes? So what if we are conscious that we are almost completely unconscious? That will not change anything. But the bowl for the toilet bucket . . . Is it really necessary for me to explain to you how greatly that changed people's lives?"

"Even if you are correct about the discoveries of Copernicus and Darwin, with my discoveries it will be different, because my theories discuss what is most essential in man. Copernicus's theory describes the relationship between man and the cosmos; Darwin's theory, the origin of the human race. But my theory speaks about what a human being is in relation to himself and to other people, as well as about the source of every human thought and emotion. Therefore, in contrast to the theories of Darwin and Copernicus, mine will be applicable."

"All the more frightening," said Dr. Goethe. "Think what will happen when some people understand your theories incorrectly, and adopt them incorrectly. And just consider that not all your theories will be correct, and in that incorrect form people will use them to help themselves. I tell you, Dr. Freud, the bowl for the toilet is the greatest invention since the discovery of the wheel."

I imagined my brother had finished changing, so I turned around. He was already in his suit.

"Perhaps the toilet bowl is the greatest human invention since the wheel, but only from the point of view of technology. Psychoanalysis is something much greater, something more essential. Its very name tells you that, from *psyche, soul*—" my brother explained drunkenly, but Dr. Goethe, smiling, interrupted him.

"The bowl very effectively cleans the excrement from the toilet bucket, my dear colleague, but I am not convinced that your psychoanalysis can clean the excrement from the human soul." Then he extended a hand to Sigmund. "On your head you still have this hat, which suits neither your attire nor your work," he said, removing the hat with the green pompons from my brother's head. "Go now. I will see you home, and there in your warm marriage bed you will be able to dream peacefully—it is all the same whether consciously or unconsciously." Uttering these last words, he turned to me, winked, and continued, "You know, your brother recently published a book about dreams, about some sort of Oedipal complexes, about parricide and mother-desire, about the conscious and the unconscious. Yet he cannot tolerate a few sips of alcohol."

The two doctors set off toward the hospital exit, and I went to my room. Klara was standing by the window, looking out over the hospital grounds. As soon as she heard my steps, without turning around she said, "How happy it is."

I lay down on my bed, set the shirt rolled up like a newborn beside me, and sank my head into the pillow.

"This revelry, I see, is going to last awhile. Why didn't you stay?" she asked.

I did not answer. I heard her walk toward me, felt her sitting beside me on the bed, stroking my head to comfort me, but I cried inconsolably on that night filled with beauty. I had not cried in years; from my eyes not a single tear had fallen since the day my child was taken from my womb, and now I cried inconsolably. Klara lay down beside me on the bed and hugged me. I felt myself lost in pain and in dream, or was it unconsciousness, and I heard Klara's voice comforting me: "It will pass. . . . It will pass."

MY BROTHER VISITED ME again several weeks after the carnival. We sat face to face, barely uttering a word, as was usual when he came to my room. Before he left for home I asked him, "Do you remember the fairy tale about the bird that you told me when we were children?"

"What fairy tale?"

"The one about the bird that pierced its breast and tore out its heart after the bird it loved flew off and never returned."

"I did not tell you such a fairy tale."

"Try to remember," I told him. "You told it to me."

"There is no such fairy tale," my brother said.

"If there is no such fairy tale, then you made it up."

"If I had made it up, I would remember it."

"But I remember you telling it to me."

"You made it up yourself, and you told it to yourself."

WHENEVER MY BROTHER LEFT for home after his short visits, I would lie in my bed, draw the blanket over me, propping it up with my fingers a foot above my head, and look into the white sky.

"TO DENY A PEOPLE the man whom it praises as the greatest of its sons is not a deed to be undertaken lightheartedly—especially by one belonging to that people." That is how *Moses and Monotheism* begins, and with that sentence my brother expressed the aim of the entire work: to take Moses away from his people and to prove that Moses was not a Jew. Not only did he proclaim Moses "a distinguished Egyptian, perhaps a prince, priest, or high official," he even described the Jews of that era as the opposite of Moses: "culturally inferior immigrants." Why, he asked, would such a distinguished person leave his country together with these "culturally inferior immigrants"?

Moses, my brother found, was an adherent of the first monotheistic religion, established by the pharaoh Akhenaton, who forbade polytheism, threatened death to those who prayed to the gods they had believed in for millennia, and declared Aton the one true God. Seventeen years after introducing this new religion, the pharaoh died. The former priests, humiliated during Akhenaton's reign, now with the passion of vindictiveness and fanatical revenge, commanded the people, who had never forgotten the old gods, to demolish the new temples, and they forbade monotheism, bringing back the old, polytheistic religion.

Moses, whom my brother supposed had been close to the pharaoh Akhenaton, could not renounce his devotion to the god Aton, and so forged a plan "of founding a new empire, of finding a new people, to whom he could give the religion that Egypt disdained." Thus, according to *Moses and Monotheism,* the Jews were chosen not by God but by the Egyptian Moses: "These he chose to be his new people," and set off with them in search of the Holy Land.

But these people could not relinquish their old beliefs, their Semitic polytheism; everyone who rejected the faith in this new god was, on Moses' command, punished by his close supporters. So, my brother claimed, Moses did not die of old age, as it says in the Bible; rather, "The Egyptian Moses was killed by the Jews, and the religion he instituted abandoned." What happened to them later, after they killed the one who had chosen them for his people and who had promised them that they were a people chosen by God? They later "united with tribes nearly related to them, in the country bordering on Palestine, the Sinai Peninsula, and Arabia, and . . . there, in a fertile spot called Qades, they accepted, under the influence of the Arabian Midianites . . . the worship of the volcano-god Yahweh."

According to my brother, the cult of Yahweh was spread among the Egyptians by a Midianite shepherd with the same name as the Egyptian leader, Moses. But this one, this second Moses, preached a God who was the complete antithesis of Aton: Yahweh was venerated by the Arab tribe of Midianites as "an uncanny, bloodthirsty demon who walks by night and shuns the light of day." Although "the Egyptian Moses never was in Qades and had never heard the name of Yahweh whereas the Midianite Moses never set foot in Egypt and knew nothing of Aton," they stayed in memory as one person, because "the Mosaic religion we know only in its final form as it was fixed by Jewish priests in the time after the Exile about eight hundred years later," by which time the two men named Moses had already been fused into a single person, and Aton and Yahweh into a single God, as different in their essences as day is to night, precisely because He is two gods in one.

Moses and Monotheism contains both a denial—Moses is not a Jew—and a condemnation—the Jews killed Moses. It expresses both revulsion toward and vengeance against his own people. But why? For my brother, being a Jew was a part of his destiny, something that had been imparted to him at birth, something that was not of his own choosing. Where there was no choice, in his blood, he was a Jew. Where a choice could be made, he had chosen German culture: he wanted to belong to it in the same way that he felt the fruits of that culture belonged to him. Before the end of his life he said, "My language is German. My culture, my achievements are German. I considered myself intellectually to be a German, until I noticed the growth of anti-Semitic prejudices in Germany and in German Austria. Since then, I prefer to call myself a Jew." He said it just like that: "I prefer to call myself a Jew," and not "I am a Jew." When he was asked, "What is left in you that is Jewish, when you have abandoned everything that you had in common with your people—religion and national feeling, tradition and customs?" he answered, "The most essential thing." He never said what that was, but it was understood: his blood, the thing he could not change, and he felt a kind of shame toward it.

At the end of *Moses and Monotheism*, my brother also blamed the Jews for the sufferings they have endured throughout the millennia. Patricide, he asserted, is at the very beginning of religious belief. Religion, at its origin, is an attempt to expiate the sin committed by the sons who killed their own father in the battle for dominance and then glorified him as their divine ancestor. Christianity, my brother maintained, is an admission of this murder: with the killing of Christ, the human race confesses the killing of its own father. Christianity was created by the Jews and disseminated by the Jews, but "only a part of the Jewish people accepted the new doctrine. Those who refused to do so are still called Jews. Through this decision they are still more sharply separated from the rest of the world than they were before. They had to suffer the reproach . . . that they had murdered God. . . . Through this they have, so to speak, shouldered a tragic guilt; they have been made to suffer severely for it." And so the Jews became guilty of their own suffering; my brother found justification for each crime against them. He would do this at a time when his people would need support, when the blood flowing through our veins would quake with the same horror that shook our ancestors.

THROUGHOUT HIS LIFE, my brother tried to prove in his works that the essence of the human race is guilt: everyone was guilty because everyone was once a child, and in the competition for its mother's love, every child desires the death of its adversary, its father. That is what my brother Sigmund said. He blamed the most innocent; the most innocent and the most helpless carried this primordial sin. He accused those who had just entered into life of desiring the death of those who had given them that life. In addition to this guilt, present in every human being, he took another upon himself: he maintained he remembered that when he was only one and a half years old, he had wished for the death of his newborn brother, Julius, who died six months later. So my brother was also Cain, and God's words pertained to him: "What have you done? Listen! Your brother's blood cries out to me from the ground!" And he was Noah, the one who, before the Flood, had gathered into the ark his family and "every wild animal according to its kind, all livestock according to their kinds, every creature that moves along the ground according to its kind and every bird according to its kind, everything with wings." But for the four of us sisters there was no room on our brother's list. He was Oedipus, he was Cain, and he was Noah, but in those desires that he did not wish to acknowledge to himself he wanted to be a prophet, and so he took Moses away from the Jews. My brother wanted to be unique, autonomous, self-made; and that is how he imagined the one proclaimed by his people to be what he himself wanted to be. Just as Moses had led a people to freedom, to the Promised Land, Sigmund wanted to lead the human race to freedom from the *I*, to free humans from the fetters of repression and the dark abysses of the unconscious. It was as if my brother were crying out from every page of his book about Moses, "Neither he nor I am a Jew. Like him, I am a self-made leader and prophet!"

THE HUMAN FATES at the Nest wove wondrous, often invisible nets. Sometimes in the dining hall there would be a woman who had poisoned her husband, eating side by side with a man whose wife had swung an ax but had not managed to strike him. A girl plucked blades of grass as she walked the hospital grounds, and then scattered them around her; an old woman, before falling asleep, imagined herself pulling up the grass in front of her home and scattering it. Here were people who could not fall asleep, and people who lay as if in eternal sleep. Here were people who were afraid to fall asleep, and people afraid of waking. A young man was brought to the Nest because he kept telling everyone that he had no head, while another young man was brought because he tried to convince others that they had no heads. In the small library, a man clutched his head and shouted, "The words are flying from the pages! The words are flying from the pages!" He would shout repeatedly until the other readers protested, and the orderlies would take him to his room. A woman moved her head left and right whenever someone spoke to her, because it seemed to her that the words were flying toward her and could plunge into her forehead. There were people who contorted their faces, altered their voices, and presented themselves as devils; they offered to buy souls, they announced apocalypses, they warned that the coming of the kingdom of darkness was at hand. There were people who sought salvation from demonic forces, not from those who claimed to be such forces but from those who were for the rest of us invisible demonic beings. They spat into the air, they ran from the air, they struck at the air, they threatened the air, they screamed in fright while looking at the air. Whenever the orderlies told us that our time for walking the grounds was over and that we had to return to our rooms, a girl would lie on the ground and hug the nearest tree, and until they managed to pry her loose she would put up a long fight, screaming, "I am this tree's dream! If you pull me from this tree, it will stop dreaming of me and I won't exist!"

Another girl sometimes repeated, "My dreams have leaves and branches, my dreams have a trunk and bark, my dreams have flowers and roots. . . . My dreams are trees, or perhaps the trees are my dreams."

The human fates at the Nest wove wondrous, often invisible nets.

IT WAS ALMOST NEVER QUIET in our room. In the room above ours, Hans and Johann paced; one walked with slow and heavy steps, the other quickly and decisively. From out of the rooms next to ours came self-accusations, feverish giggling, head-banging, fists and feet against the walls. Even when those nearby sounds subsided, through the windowpane the din from other rooms at the Nest reached us.

Sometimes Klara's voice woke me during the night: "Wake up—it's quiet!" And sometimes when I woke up, if no sound reached us—and that was a rarity—I said to Klara, "Wake up—it's quiet!" We had agreed to wake each other whenever a moment of silence could be captured. Then we lay in the darkness, silently in the quiet, but as soon as we heard the first noise or the first shout we would again close our eyes and try to fall asleep.

KLARA AND I WERE AMONG those who were allowed to leave the hospital sphere and, in groups, accompanied by the orderlies, walk about the city. Neither she nor I ever wanted to leave the Nest, however, so we remained with those who were forbidden to go outside the psychiatric clinic. There were those who begged Dr. Goethe to allow them to leave the Nest for just a few minutes. They clasped their hands and fell on their knees in front of him, but he did not give in, even though some of those who begged him were peaceful and would do no harm outside the hospital, nor would they run away. Dr. Goethe explained to them that going into the city would have an ill effect on their psychiatric health. So they waited at the doors to the Nest for the return of those who were allowed to go out; they waited for them with the expressions of those who await news from a far-off country, and they begged them to tell about the city, about the people, about everything that began just steps from where they slept.

GUSTAV VISITED KLARA on the first Wednesday of each month. At one of their meetings he said to her, "Mama has died." Klara said not a word. "Do you want to come home?" Klara continued to say nothing. "Home," said Gustav.

"No," said Klara.

WHEN HELLISH SCREAMS SPREAD through the Nest, when those cries fed one another, encouraged one another, strengthened one another, it seemed to me that we had been thrown into some unknown, frightening world, yet also a place where we were protected by the walls of our room. Sometimes, when hellish screams spread through the Nest, when those cries fed one another, encouraged one another, strengthened one other, Klara would say, "Our room is like a womb."

On the first Saturday of each month, Dr. Goethe held lectures for us in the Great Hall. He explained madness; he was certain that his lectures were another way to provoke change in some of us, but we sneered at him, shot crumpled papers at him, made noises to confuse him while he spoke. Yet he continued to expound on madness.

"But what is normality?" Klara asked him at one of those lectures.

"Normality . . . ?" Dr. Goethe was confused for only a second.

"Normality means to function in accord with the laws of the world in which we live."

"But if we follow your logic on madness, one could also say that normality is nothing but a respect for established norms."

"BUT WHAT IS MADNESS?" I asked Klara before we fell asleep.

If I asked my brother, he would tell me that madness arises when the human *I* unconsciously creates a new internal and external world simultaneously, that the new world is constructed according to the desires of the unconscious, and that the reason for the split from the external world is the serious and apparently unbearable conflict between reality and one's desires.

Klara said nothing. The following day she proposed to Dr. Goethe that, on the first Saturday of each month, instead of us listening to him lecture, we would speak about our illnesses. Several times thereafter we gathered in the Great Hall, and Dr. Goethe asked what madness was for us, and we spoke.

We said, "To be mad is the same as being in danger. You try to call for help, but nothing comes out of your mouth; your throat tenses, your tongue, your lips. Everything is useless. There are people near the person in danger, but their backs are turned, and they do not realize what is happening, because they and the person in danger are looking in different directions, toward different landscapes, toward different skies. Yes, we look toward different skies."

"Madness is an oar that strikes the wall instead of water, and it strikes the wall, and strikes, and strikes, and strikes. . . ."

"Madness is moving but standing still."

"Madness is a door without a knob."

"Madness is when you see that something is green, but everyone assures you that it is red."

"Madness is when everyone waits for you to speak, and they demand that you speak, and you talk and talk and talk, but no one hears you. Your mouth does not obey you; it stays closed while you talk, talk, talk, and everyone says you are mad, because they demand that you talk and you are silent, silent, silent. They do not hear you talk, talk, talk."

"A doll that is not fully alive."

"A dream dripping into your eye. An eye dripping into a dream."

Dr. Goethe kept repeating, "What you are saying is ordinary foolishness."

Klara once said to him, "Those of us who are mad say an endless amount of nonsense, an endless string of disorganized, unconnected, irrelevant things, and in the middle of all of them we will put some of the things that are most important to us and see whether others notice the difference."

FEW OF US CAME to those meetings in the Nest's Great Hall. The only ones were those who felt compelled by our madness—either always or from time to time—to discuss philosophical topics. At those meetings we looked like people at once thirsty for conversation and coerced into conversation, as if some nagging force inside us did not give us peace and we wanted to purge ourselves of it with words. Very often, we discussed why normality and madness were like two different worlds.

"It is misunderstanding that separates normality from madness," Dr. Goethe once said. "Madness does not understand normality; normality does not understand madness."

"No," said Klara. "Madness does not understand itself, and normality does not understand itself. And what separates normality from madness is fear. Normality fears madness, and madness fears normality. If madness were to accept normality's reality, it would perceive the unrealities it has created, and they would disappear, and, with their disappearance, the madness itself would disappear. If normality were to peer carefully into madness, it would perceive unbearable truths not only about madness but also about itself, and then its façade would crack, its armor would disappear, and out would come all the abnormalities that what calls itself normality carries within itself, and, in place of that destroyed normality, madness would then rule. For both madness and normality, to confront the other means death."

THERE WAS A CERTAIN GIRL at the Nest everyone called the Good Soul, because she asked everyone, "Do you need anything?" When we walked the grounds, she gathered flowers, or tore blades of grass, or broke branches from trees, and then she looked for people with despair on their faces and handed them the flowers, the blades of grass, the branches.

WHEN MY SISTER ROSA came to visit me after the death of her husband, we sat a long time on my bed. She held a picture of her children, Hermann and Cecilia.

"Now I am living only for them," she said several times in the course of our conversation, whenever her gaze fell on the photograph.

ERIKA WAS DEVOTED to her family. Wherever she went, she brought her closest family with her. Sometimes Erika begged the nurses to let her leave her room in order to come to the room where Klara and I lived. As soon as she entered, she would sit on one of the beds, take from her pocket a piece of cloth, and place it on her knees. She would untie the cloth and show us what was inside: several small twigs. She would take them out and run her fingers along them in a kind of caress.

"This is my family. This is my mother, this is my father, this is my husband, and these are our children," she would say, separating the twigs. "We are a happy family."

She moved the twigs, one after another, on the cloth a little longer, then tied them up and returned her family to her pocket.

She always carried the cloth with her, and often during meals, or rest periods out on the lawn, or at work in the sewing room, she would take it out of her pocket and arrange the twigs on it. One day, she did not have her piece of cloth; either she had lost it or someone had stolen it. She mourned a great deal for her twigs; the doctors tied several twigs in a cloth and gave them to her. She unfolded the cloth, ran her fingers along the twigs, and said, "This is not my family."

SOMETIMES DURING OUR AFTERNOON walks, Krista would approach Dr. Goethe and say to him, "I want to go home."

"Where is home?" Dr. Goethe wanted to confuse her with the question.

"Home is home."

"Here is home," Dr. Goethe told her.

"No," said Krista. "Home is where my little daughter is."

Dr. Goethe said nothing.

"I want to be where my little daughter is."

"Fine. We will let you. Just complete your walk around the grounds and we will let you go."

And that would calm Krista. She would be quiet for a day or two, and then ask to go home again.

SOMETIMES KRISTA'S PARENTS visited her. During those visits she would disappear. When her parents were beside her, she could neither speak nor see. Her gaze was fixed on a point, as if there, where her eyes looked, something immobile swallowed her gaze, swallowed her very self. Her parents tried calling to her, but she stayed fixed on that point. A few times, Krista's parents brought her little daughter with them. The little girl carried notebooks from school with her, or a drawing or two. She would spread them out in front of her, tell her mother what was in the drawings, read to her from her notebooks, but Krista remained as if swallowed up by the thing that drew her gaze but that no one else could see. Then her little daughter would fall silent, gather her drawings, and close her notebooks. She would look back and forth, from her grandmother and grandfather to her mother. No one said a word. From time to time, the daughter looked in the direction where Krista looked; she knew there was something there that only her mother saw, something they could not see but only imagine—the something her mother was focused on, that swallowed her. Then her grandmother or grandfather would stand up and say, "Let's go. . . ." The parents touched Krista's hands in parting, the little daughter threw herself around her neck and hugged her, but her mother remained frozen. And then they left. After these visits, Krista would remain seated, stiff, for a long time. Then, all of a sudden, she would return to the world, always in the same way: she would begin to roll on the bed, growl, kick, strike with her hands, throw herself against the wall. The orderlies knew what she would do at the end of these visits, and even before she regained consciousness they had bound her, and then, bound, she would cry out, "I want to go home. I want to be with my daughter. Do you hear me? I want to go home. Let me go home!"

Her lament echoed through the hallways.

"Why don't you let her go home?" Klara once asked Dr. Goethe.

"She feels bad only when her daughter comes here. The little one has to disappear for her. Disappear forever."

Krista's little girl stopped coming. Perhaps Dr. Goethe had asked this of her parents. And they, the old people, came less and less often.

From time to time, Krista would stop Klara outside.

"I will tell you a secret," she would say. "I will tell you a secret, but do not tell anyone."

"I will not tell anyone," Klara promised.

"They are going to let me out of the Nest. They are going to let me go home. Forever."

"They will let you go," Klara would tell her, in the same confidential tone.

"They really will let me go," and she repeated this as a sort of solace, as when a child repeats a lie, not to believe it through constant repetition but in order not to think about the truth.

A YOUNG WOMAN whose name I did not know shook her shoulders and waved her arms as if they were wings, and gazed up toward the hospital roof.

"There is my home. There is my nest," she repeated.

We walked by without reacting, because her daily attempts and her words had become routine for us. Every day she tried to get to her home, to her nest.

MANY OF THOSE who had been brought to the Nest by force asked to be released. Some begged quietly, clasping their hands or falling to their knees before the doctors, others screamed pleadingly, some threatened. "I will send you all to hell," shouted those who believed they were gods, gods who had fallen to earth for only a short time. Those who were convinced that they were great warriors now imprisoned by their opponents threatened that as soon as they regained power—if they were not released with goodwill—they would take their revenge. And there were also those whose threats were simple: they would wring the doctors' necks or stab them with a knife.

Some lied to themselves and to others: "We are just passing through, you know, we are staying in this hotel for today only, but tomorrow . . ." And they pointed somewhere with their hands.

Pleas made during work hours, when the doctors worked alongside us, weaving, knitting, or making wooden objects, were especially intense. Then voices poured out in chorus across the room, begging to leave the Nest. A composition for human voices, with entreaties, complaints, assurances, reverberated between the walls; scores of voices intermingled in this composition, weaving various rhythms, tonalities, tempos, and among the intelligible words there also sounded indistinct murmurs and yelps, wondrous sounds—of chattering teeth, buzzing lips, of one voice repeating, of the imitation of sounds heard only in a dream or a nightmare—and somewhere beyond the words one sensed the fate of those who spoke, moaned, buzzed, clacked, murmured, yelped.

"Why don't you let those who want to, go home?" Klara asked Dr. Goethe one afternoon in the room where we were knitting.

"Because their place is not there, but here."

"How do you know their place is not there but here?"

"Because the law commands that those who have gone mad should be protected from their madness, and that normal people should be protected from the mad ones."

"If they have not broken any law and they do not want to be here, they have the right to be freed," Klara said. "Or does madness itself constitute breaking the law?"

"In madness itself there is the potential to do something illegal."

"Every human being has the potential to do something illegal. Why don't we just place the entire human race in prisons and madhouses?"

"Sometimes I think the fact that you are one of the few who have never sought to leave here is a result of your pleasure in making observations and finding errors. Errors exist everywhere. They have to exist, because no system is perfect. But this system of care for patients with mental illness is the best way possible."

"No. Freedom is the first condition for any type of care for anyone. But the majority of us feel like prisoners here."

"You must understand that those who are mad, wherever they are, feel imprisoned; perhaps the first step toward madness is the feeling that the world is a prison. The world, with its laws—I am thinking not solely of societal laws but of natural ones as well—is experienced as a prison; perhaps this is what leads to the creation of one's own world, with one's own laws, yet the feeling of imprisonment remains forever." A ball of wool rolled from Dr. Goethe's lap and fell to the floor. He leaned forward, retrieved it, sat down again, and, resuming his knitting, continued to talk. "But for you and your friend," he said, pointing to me, "it is easy. You are acting out half madness, half normality. What you call here a prison is really, for you, freedom from the prison you felt outside. I grasped that immediately. You are here as if on a long vacation. That is wonderful, really wonderful. Your brothers pay for your stay, you experience your freedom in this prison—as you call our hospital—as opposed to the constraint and coercion you felt outside, constraint and coercion far less than what the truly sick feel. Nonetheless, your constraint and coercion can be reduced to family conflict, not to some deep discord within yourselves. Yes, you really are here as if on a long vacation. And I respect that, I respect your choice, only I beg you, also respect my work and do not meddle in it," said Dr. Goethe, and he continued knitting a long black shawl.

ONE OF THE TREATMENT methods Dr. Goethe employed was like stamping upon the madness. He would gather twenty patients in one of the large rooms in the hospital, and he would begin a game with one of the patients in which he portrayed the madness as stupidity. Sometimes these games seemed good-natured and light, as when he asked someone who believed he was Casanova about his amorous adventures, or when he asked someone who insisted he was Napoléon about his military campaigns. At other times the games were torture, as when Dr. Goethe contradicted the claims of patients who spoke obsessively about those close to them whom they had lost, or when he persistently asked Hans—who struck his head against the wall whenever he heard the word *why*— "Why are you striking your head against the wall?" When the game turned into torture, Klara would ask Dr. Goethe, "Why are you doing this?"

Dr. Goethe (who stretched his arm in front of a patient aimlessly moving about the room, in order to block her path, but she bent down, circumventing the obstacle, and continued walking about the room) answered, "My goal is not to force someone to ask why I am doing this but why this patient reacts the way she does."

"How should she react?"

"She should stop when I block her path, and not squeeze under my arm. You should have noticed that. That is the goal—for some of those present here to notice that something is not right with her behavior."

"The only thing I noticed was that you were being aggressive with her," said Klara.

"No. I do not imagine this as a torture chamber but as a theater."

"Theater?"

"Yes, theater. Those who could grasp that she reacts incorrectly would, through that realization, enjoy something like a catharsis, which could help them out of their situation. This does not relate to you. You are in an excellent situation; I have long understood that you are here on a long vacation. I was thinking of the others," said Dr. Goethe, pointing to the others in the room. "Yes, were they to understand that she reacts incorrectly, that knowledge really could have a cathartic effect."

"All of us understand that you are behaving incorrectly, but that does not provoke a catharsis in us," said Klara.

"That is because your understanding is incorrect," said Dr. Goethe, and once again he stretched out his arm in front of the girl who was walking quickly about the room. "One of the basic characteristics of people who are mad is that they demonstrate, through their actions, intentions, and utterances, that they are leading a senseless existence, but they are not aware of it. Were they to comprehend the senselessness of their actions, intentions, and utterances, it is very possible they would break off this existence, which is caught in the trap of senselessness, and return to a sensible existence," said Dr. Goethe.

"Aren't all these senseless actions, intentions, utterances a result of the fact that those who are mad have understood that existence itself—whether reasonable or unreasonable—is senseless, and the only difference is the manner in which one expresses oneself, and they have decided to live that senselessness in an unreasonable manner, which is termed madness?" Klara asked him.

"I do not have an answer for such a question. Ask me a simple question," said Dr. Goethe, and he approached a young woman who was standing in the corner of the room. No one knew her name; we called her the Good Soul. "Now, this young woman here never resists aggression." Dr. Goethe took a needle from his pocket and poked the tip into the girl's forehead. She remained calm. She did not move even when Dr. Goethe approached her head with the needle, she remained calm even when the tip of the needle was poked into her forehead. "I am hurting her, but she does not defend herself; she doesn't even try to get out of harm's way. Do you understand? She is behaving unreasonably."

"The Good Soul is not behaving unreasonably; your actions are unreasonable," said Klara, and she continued to argue with Dr. Goethe.

While that argument went on, Max separated from the group of patients standing by the window, went over to the Good Soul, and removed the needle from her forehead.

THE LOVE BETWEEN the Good Soul and Max began the moment he stretched out his hand toward her forehead and removed the needle that had been stuck there. Their love—it was not *love*, because *love* is only what those in love call it, and the Good Soul and Max did not give any name to what was between them. It was as if they kept alive a quiet fire that warms the soul.

Max spent his working hours in the woodworking section of the Nest, and the Good Soul spent hers in the sewing room, and when they met during the time for outings on the grounds she would take out a small handkerchief, cloth, or apron, which she had tucked into her brassiere by her heart, and he would hand her a small horse, flower, or angel made of wood. He arranged the cloths, handkerchiefs, and aprons both underneath and on top of his pillow, and slept on them; the Good Soul arranged the little wooden horses, flowers, and angels on the nightstand by her bed. And then, people said, then the Good Soul whispered his name in her sleep. And Max, people said, Max tried to find out her name, but nobody knew it; she had been the Good Soul ever since she had come to the Nest.

Max and the Good Soul grew close to each other, the way the

sky and the earth draw close together at some distant point—they merge in the eye that looks toward them on the horizon, yet for them there is neither union nor separation. That spring, there were moments when all of us at the Nest forgot about our madness, moments when our madness forgot about us, and we thought about the Good Soul and Max, and we often uttered the word *love*.

"Love cannot begin here," Dr. Goethe said.

"What does this place lack so that love cannot begin here?" Klara asked him.

"I was not thinking of the place. The realization of love is not possible between those who are mad, because madness has a mortal fear of love. In madness, hate of others and love of others are equal dangers; both love and hate threaten the destruction of the mad person's *I*."

"But isn't that the most terrible?" said Klara. "Because the *I* that barely flickers desires so achingly to be loved. Something in the person whose *I* has been pulled apart tells him—even when he does not want to acknowledge it—that only love can save his *I*, but the fear of love is always stronger than this awareness, and so he shoves that knowledge into oblivion or conquers it with an even greater fear."

"In madness, love can arise only toward some imagined, dreamed-up person; love toward a real person, and that means a true and real love, is impossible, because for the other to be loved means for the mad person to be one with the other; but to be one with the other means to lose one's self. Therefore, some imagined other is loved, one who is a reflection of only a small fragment of that broken *I*. To love and to be loved is more dangerous for the mad person than to feel mortal hatred or to be mortally hated."

"But," I asked, "don't some who are mad have a despairing need to love and be loved, and isn't that need as strong as life or death? It is a need to dig out the madness and to return to life."

That spring, the spring in which the Good Soul and Max kept alive some quiet fire that warms the soul, lasted a whole lifetime for them. Max promised the Good Soul what he had once wanted life to promise him. He promised her the most ordinary things, things that people do not promise each other, because these things are a given in life and they see no need to desire them; there is no precedent for longing for such things, because such longing arises only when something is difficult to attain. We listened to Max as he promised her a shared bed in a room with a window that looked out onto a street bustling with people (how similar and how different from the windows that looked out onto the hospital grounds, where patients and doctors strolled), as he promised days in which they would teach their children to talk and be happy, as he promised how close their bodies would be before falling asleep and in sleep. He promised her absolutely ordinary things, so ordinary that people do not think to promise them to each other.

That spring, the spring in which the Good Soul and Max kept alive some quiet fire that warms the soul, lasted a whole lifetime for all of us at the Nest; it was as if all of us felt, after aeons of ice ages, that something once again warmed our souls. While we watched them outdoors, while we listened to their conversations and retold them to one another as we thought about what would happen to them, we forgot about our madness, and our madness forgot about us.

One cloudy spring afternoon, when we expected rain and remained in our beds instead of going outside, the Good Soul's brothers came to the Nest. Someone had told them things that were untrue about their sister, had described that tending of a quiet fire between her and Max as something different, as who knows what else. When they entered Dr. Goethe's office, the first thing they told him was that they had brought their sister to a psychiatric clinic not to whore around but for treatment, and they demanded he take them to her. They then went into the large room where, in two rows, fifty women lay in their beds. Although Dr. Goethe had begged them not to tell her that they were taking her home—he had told them to tell her they were taking her on an outing—the brothers told her she was going home forever.

"I want to stay here," said the Good Soul, scrunching up in her bed.

"*Here* no longer exists for you," one of the brothers shouted. He seized her by the shoulders and dragged her from the bed. "We are taking you home forever!"

The Good Soul stretched her hands toward the table by her bed and grabbed several small wooden horses, flowers, and angels, managing to shove them into the pockets of her nightgown before her brothers could carry her from the room.

One of the women in the Good Soul's room opened the window and shouted, "Hey! Everybody! They are taking the Good Soul away! Everybody! Come out and say goodbye to the Good Soul. The Good Soul is going. She is going forever!"

The windows of the Nest opened; we stood by the bars and watched as the door of the hospital opened and the two strong men led their sister away. She was in her nightgown and slippers; as she was jostled between her two brothers, little wooden horses, flowers, and angels fell from her pockets.

Then we heard Max's wail, protracted and anguished, like a moonlight lament. For a second the Good Soul's brothers stopped, and the Good Soul stopped between them, turning her head back toward the place she was moving away from. And Max's wailing stopped. We silently watched from behind the bars of our windows; we watched as the Good Soul moved farther away, turning her head toward those bars where Max stood. She walked like that, with her legs carrying her toward one side of the world, her eyes looking toward the other. And when she reached the exit, before passing through the gate out of the Nest, she pulled one hand from her brother's, raised it, and waved. She waved as people do when waving for the first time; she waved as people do when waving for the last time. Her brother grabbed her by the hand and led her out. Her body disappeared before our eyes.

That afternoon, everything drowned in a strange silence.

WE SPOKE ABOUT the Good Soul for days. We hoped she would appear, and then we forgot her. We remembered her only when we looked into Max's face, but we saw him less and less. He stayed in his bed, lying motionless for hours, days, weeks, biting the handkerchiefs, cloths, and aprons he had collected under his pillow.

"WAKE UP," I heard Klara say in the middle of the night. "It's quiet."

That was our agreement from my first days at the Nest—if one of us awoke at a moment of quiet, we would wake the other up as well. I got up. I went over to Klara. We stood by the open window. We looked into the darkness out toward the grounds. It was a summer night, and a warm muteness shimmered around us. I turned toward Klara. She had closed her eyes. I did the same, and I breathed in the calm. From a distant room a shriek was heard; it swept across the space and died away. Then feverish laughter was heard, joined by a dry weeping; clumping steps heavy like hooves began moving along the floor of the room above us; from a room beside us came blows against the wall; from the other side, grumbling; from somewhere else came indistinct words seeking help, words expressing thanks, words expressing indignation, words pleading for release into freedom; from somewhere else, human voices that sounded like the gurgle of water, like an animal's roar, like a bird's call, voices that sounded like wind through branches and voices that sounded like the strike of stone against stone.

Then, all at once, everything grew quiet again, as if something had smothered all those open throats. Quiet. And then all the voices thundered again, crying and giggling, shouts and roars, gurgling and buzzing, pleas and laments, thanks and curses.

Klara closed the window and said, "All normal people are normal in the same way; each mad person is mad in his own way."

"ALL NORMAL PEOPLE ARE NORMAL IN THE same way; each mad person is mad in his own way," Klara repeated, standing by the closed window. I had already covered myself with my blanket and was struggling to fall asleep.

"What is that thing over there?"

"What thing?"

"That . . . over there, by that tree," said Klara.

I stood up and drew near the window. Klara was pointing toward a thicket of trees.

"It's dark," I said. "I don't see anything."

"Something is hanging from one of the trees. Something or someone."

"You are imagining things."

"No," said Klara. "Something or someone is hanging there."

We stood by the window and looked into the darkness. The darkness began to lose its thickness; it was thinning, acquiring a pale rosiness.

"Someone is hanging there," I said.

That morning they lowered Max from a pine branch. No one knew how he had stolen from his room, or how he had left the building unnoticed. He had climbed the tree and tied the rope around his neck.

Later that day, Klara took from her nightstand and tucked into her pocket the scrap of paper on which her brother had drawn a woman, her back turned, standing on the edge of an abyss.

"I want to leave here," she told me. "When Gustav comes, I will leave. You will leave, too," she said.

From that moment, she spoke less and less. She kept silent the way people do when they are waiting for something, with a kind of tension. She did not repeat those words of departure, but by her silence I knew she was waiting to carry them out. And that is what happened when her brother appeared.

"I want to leave here," she told him.

"You want to return home?" asked Gustav.

"I want to leave here," she repeated.

"Fine," he said.

"Adolfina will also be leaving," Klara said.

We packed up the few things we had. I put mine into the small suitcase in which at one time I had kept the little clothes for the baby I never gave birth to, Klara put her things into her small suitcase, and then we left. The Nest was a half hour between the home Klara needed to return to and the home I needed to return to. We embraced each other, parted, and I continued on my way. I arrived at the building I had departed from years before, climbed the stairs, took the key from my bag. The lock was the same. I turned it twice. I opened the door and went inside. I stood in the foyer, and the odor was the same as before I left, that smell we had brought with us when we moved into this building, when I was eleven years old, and that remained even after Sigmund moved out, when I was twenty-one, after my sisters married and left home, after my brother Alexander moved away from home; that smell of our apartment remained even after my father died, when I was thirty-four years old, one year before I left for the Nest. It had stayed the same even without me these seven years. I slowly moved through all the rooms, and finally entered my room. On the wall by my bed there was still the trace of my unborn child. I bent toward the wall and rubbed my cheek along the faded bloody trace. Had I been able to cry, the blood would have combined with my tears; as it was, my dry cheek stroked the dry trace. I went into the kitchen. On the table lay the box of silverware. I sat down. With a cloth I began polishing the spoons, the forks, the knives. I heard the door creak. I picked up one of the knives. The door to the kitchen opened.

"You have come back." I heard my mother questioning and confirming at the same time.

"I have come back," I said, running the cloth along the knife.

My mother sat down beside me. She took the candle from the candleholder that stood in the middle of the table and began rolling it between her hands, like someone who has nothing to say, or who has so much to say that she does not know where to begin. I set down the knife, picked up another from the box, and ran the cloth across its blade.

"In the end, we need to learn to talk to each other," my mother said.

I continued to rub the knife, although it was already polished. My gaze fled to my mother's fingers still turning over the candle. The cloth slipped, and I ran my fingers down the knife blade instead of the cloth. My mother quickly got up, brought some alcohol, a bandage, and cotton, and bandaged my fingers. Then she sat down again at the table.

"We need to learn to talk to each other," my mother said. Then she lifted the candle again, sank her nails into it, and picked at it. Small pieces of wax fell to the floor. I looked into her face; I looked into that face for the first time in many years. She lifted her gaze, and we looked at each other, eye to eye. I bent my gaze toward my bandaged fingers. My mother bent down to gather the pieces of wax from the floor.

"How is Anna?" I asked.

"She is well," my mother said, straightening up and then sitting again at the table. "And Sigmund's other little ones are well, too." That is what she called the grandchildren she had from Sigmund, *Sigmund's little ones*, and it was only when she spoke of them that she called him *Sigmund* and not her usual *My Siggie*. She looked at the pieces of wax in the palm of her hand. "Do you want to see them?"

"Yes, I do," I said.

IT WAS NOT YET afternoon when we set off for Berggasse 19. In the way we walked beside each other, in the way we were silent, and in the way that from time to time we broke the silence with a few words, I felt for the first time how much I had changed in the course of the past years at the Nest. I also felt how much my mother had changed, as if an abyss had opened between our former lives and our current ones, swallowing our bitterness and hatred, leaving only blunt reconciliation and a thick silence.

At my brother's, it was Martha who greeted us. Anna appeared from behind the door.

"Your aunt has come to see you," her mother said to her. I went up to Anna, hugged her, and kissed her forehead. She pulled away from me, wiped the wet trace of my lips from her forehead, and ran from the room.

"Where is Sigmund?" I asked, turning toward Martha.

"In Venice. With my sister," Martha said.

In the years spent in the insane asylum, where my existence was an escape from reality, I had forgotten that not even once in my life had I been outside Vienna, forgotten that when I was a young woman Rainer and I had dreamed of living in Venice.

"They were in Venice a few years ago as well," said Martha. I remembered that that was the day after my child was taken from me. "I could not travel, because of the children, and so this time, as before, my sister went with him." Then she asked, "Will you stay for lunch?"

"No, thank you," I said.

WHILE MY MOTHER and I were returning home, I recalled the years of my childhood when I had grown apart from Sigmund, and when I went out only with her; we would walk side by side to the market, or to my father's store, and something in this return home reminded me of our earlier walks.

"I made a veal stew this morning," my mother said as we stepped across the threshold. "Let's have lunch."

"It is just enough for you," I said.

"We will divide what is for me," my mother said.

"I want to rest," I said.

We went into my bedroom. My mother walked over to the windows and drew the curtains.

"I changed the bedding regularly," she said. "I thought you might return any day. I kept everything else the same as when you left."

She looked toward the faded trace of blood on the wall. Then she left the room, closing the door behind her. I headed to the cupboard, where years before I had collected the clothes for the child I carried in my womb. I opened it, and there before me were the diapers, tiny shoes the size of a finger, a knitted baby bonnet, a baby's cape. I picked them up. They were exceedingly light, just as in those intervening years my soul had been lightened of its despair. I lifted them to my eyes one after another; they were moth-eaten; they looked like spiderwebs. I picked up the little bonnet. I got into bed. For a long time I looked at the frayed threads, I looked at the moth-eaten fabric, and then I slept.

MY BROTHER AND MINNA returned from Venice several days later. At Sunday dinner at their home, they spoke at length about their trip. I interrupted them with a banal remark: "So it really is as beautiful as everyone says."

"It really is," said Minna. "But I cannot describe it to you. You need to see it for yourself."

"There are some things that need to be seen at the appropriate time," I said. "Not too early and not too late. If you see them too early, or if you see them too late, it is worse than if you had not seen them at all, because even if you do not see them they live their life within you, helped by your imagination, or else you first dream them, and you give them life within you. And if you see them too early, or too late, it is like killing something inside you, something that had lived within you until that moment, or something that first had to be born within you."

"You continue to think fatalistically. Just like before you went to the psychiatric clinic," Minna said.

"No matter how I think, it is too late for me to move to Venice," I said.

"I did not say to move to Venice but to visit it," Minna said.

"Ah, but at one time I dreamed of moving to Venice."

Then the conversation set off in another direction. Minna tried to tell me about the successes my brother had attained while I was absent, things he had not mentioned when he visited me at the Nest; she spoke about his books that had forever changed people's understanding of the human race, about his work with his patients, about his university career, about the founding of the Psychoanalytic Association. I listened attentively. Minna spoke; the others ate.

My brother, despite his obligations, continued to visit our mother every Sunday morning, and we went to his place for Sunday dinner. Every morning, I went down the stairs to the exit of our building, walked to the end of the street, and then returned home. Each time I went out, I walked a bit farther. I walked aimlessly. During one of these strolls, I ran into Dr. Goethe. He asked me how I was getting on in my life after my departure from the Nest.

"Well, I walk," I told him.

I asked him about life at the Nest. He told me the Good Soul's brothers had brought their sister back to the Nest as soon as they learned of Max's death. The Good Soul either would not or could not believe Max was dead, and she spoke with him constantly, barely noticing the others. Seldom did she ask her question, "Do you need anything?" She looked into the emptiness; she asked questions of the emptiness; she gave answers to the emptiness; everywhere in that absence around her, Max was present. I knew that the Good Soul's battle against meaninglessness with the help of the most meaningless thing—conversation with the emptiness— was meant to give meaning to meaninglessness; the world has always been filled with people who look each other in the eye and carry on empty conversations.

When I met with Klara after leaving the Nest, I felt that life could have meaning. Since leaving, she had assumed the motherly care of fourteen children. While she lived at the Nest, her brother had become a father several times over. He had impregnated women who appeared ten years older than their true age and who cleaned his atelier, young women who modeled for his paintings, workers who returned from the factories, exhausted, late in the afternoon. The children Gustav fathered with these women were for him the fruit of a short act, completely finished, over and done with. "I do not worry about what I have consciously created," he told Klara, referring to his paintings, "let alone about something I was not even thinking I was creating, while I was doing something completely different." It was as if his children had no father, but they had two mothers—Klara took care of them as

if they were her own. All were male, all had different last names—
the names of their mothers—and all had the same given name:
Gustav. "My fourteen little Gustavs" is how Klara referred to them.

She raced from one end of the city to the other to help their
mothers. She brought the sickly Gustav, son of Elsa the seamstress,
from doctor to doctor; she took care of Gustav, son of the sickly
salesclerk Hannah, whenever she took ill; she raced to the Central
Vienna Prison to beg for the release of the oldest of the fourteen
Gustavs after he had become embroiled in a fight with another
boy his age and wounded him with a knife. Once a month, she
took money from her brother for the support of his sons and gave
it to their mothers. Three times a year, she made her way through
Vienna with all the Gustavs to buy them clothes. I saw her less and
less. She spoke about the fourteen little Gustavs only if I asked,
and only after she had asked how I was. But when I did ask her she
spoke of them with joy, with a kind of concealed pride, and with a
certain discomfort, as if to apologize for what she was saying. Then
she spoke about other things that made her happy. She asked me
whether I had heard that wives were now allowed to seek divorce
and to possess their own property in marriage. Had I learned that,
henceforth, women would have the right to vote? Did I know that
workers were now able to organize to fight for their rights? I met
her less and less; with each new child of her brother's she had less
time and one more household. With the years, our meetings were
reduced to a wave of the hand whenever I saw her racing along the
streets with several of her fourteen little Gustavs in tow.

In the summer of 1914, the Great War began and quickly
spread through Europe. The young men were mobilized; my sister Rosa's son was sent to the front in September, and several
months later Sigmund's sons were sent. Martin fought the war in
Russia, Ernst in Italy, and Oliver was a member of the military
engineering corps, building tunnels and military barracks in the
Carpathians. Lists of those who had recently perished on the bat-

tlefields were posted at the entrances to buildings; on the streets, we met war invalids. The war brought poverty: we had no soap, no fuel, no flour, no bread; we ate mostly potatoes and rice. Those who wanted to taste meat during those years caught squirrels in the parks or kept rabbits in their apartments. We had neither coal nor wood to burn, and in the winters we sat wrapped in blankets, with hats on our heads and mittens on our hands.

One of those winters during the war years was the coldest I remember; the cold kept us from sleeping at night, so my mother and I stayed awake in the darkness of the sitting room, stamping our feet on the floor and rubbing the palms of our hands together to get warm. We spoke a few words, and then, when night had passed, when the morning had passed, and when the approaching afternoon had softened the cold a little, we went to our rooms and slept. Sometimes there was some news that cheered us, such as when a telegram arrived informing us that Sophie, who three years previously had married the photographer Max Halberstadt and gone to live with him in Hamburg, had given birth to a son. This was my brother's first grandson, and they named him Ernst. One evening several days later, Sigmund told me that Hermann, our sister Rosa's son, had died with a hundred other soldiers when several grenades had been thrown into their trench and exploded. Their bodies had been scattered, the corpses intermingled—severed arms, legs, heads—and rather than being buried in a grave, they were left there in the trench.

When I went to see Rosa the following day, I found her curled in bed, her head resting on her daughter Cecilia's shoulder. It seemed as though, in less than a day, she appeared diminished, as if all the energy she needed to look after her son had left her body with his death. "Now I am living only for Cecilia," she said. "If it weren't for her, I would not live a moment longer." And then she began to moan, as if slowly tearing old fabric.

During those war years, I slept at Rosa's from time to time.

Sometimes while we talked, we walked about the apartment, circling the rooms, the hallway, the balconies. On these long walks in that enclosed space, the only room we did not enter was Hermann's, where he had slept until he went off to war. Only once did Rosa crack open the door, and before closing it she said, "I always think he will return. That is why I keep his clothes, and I leave the things in his room the way he had them arranged when he left. When I sit by the window at night, I hear footsteps, and I recognize in them the sound of his steps; I get up and open the window, but there is no one in the street. Sometimes his laugh wakes me from my sleep; I go and open the door. His room is empty, but it smells the way it smelled when he was a young boy after I bathed him. When I eat, I think he is hungry. Had his body been brought back, it would have been different. How can I believe he died in a trench with a hundred other soldiers?"

At the end of the war, during one of our family gatherings in his home, Sigmund read aloud a telegram that had just arrived with the news that his sons would soon be returning from the front, and I thought of Rosa but did not dare look at her. I thought of her those days when I saw mothers on the streets embracing their sons returning in columns from the front.

The first spring after the war, I met Johanna Klimt. A year earlier I had heard that Gustav had died, but I did not go to the funeral; I did not go to see Klara, nor did I contact her.

"After his stroke, my brother lay motionless a whole month before he died," said Johanna. "Klara spent those thirty days at his bedside. Then, several weeks after his death, his two oldest sons died, one after the other, on the front. After that, Klara just sat in the corner of the room, not saying anything, not answering our questions. I brought the Gustavs to her, because she had taken such good care of them, and I thought concern for someone would return her to this world. But she stayed in some other world. That is why I decided to return her to the psychiatric clinic. Now I am taking care of the Gustavs: I visit their homes where they live with their mothers; when they are sick, I take them to the doctor; once a month, I bring them money from their father's estate. But I know I cannot care for them the way Klara did. The mothers of the Gustavs say, "Your sister was the best mother in the world," and the Gustavs agree. They constantly beg me to take them to the Nest to visit their aunt, but I refuse. "That is no place for children."

Johanna set off for her home, and I for mine. Then I changed my mind, and I headed to the Nest. On my way there, I imagined Gustav lying on his bed after the stroke, unconscious, and Klara sitting beside him; she knows he is going, and for the first time she looks at him—seeing him not as her brother and protector but as her child—and she tries to wake him from that which is not sleep, and from which he will never return. She speaks to him, and it is no longer the voice of the sister who begged him to protect her from their mother; it is now a mother's voice trying to comfort her child in his mute pain, a mother's voice, different from their mother's voice, a voice with which Klara tries to assure him that everything will be fine, that this will pass, not realizing that this is her way of reassuring herself. And when she learns about the loss of the two oldest young Gustavs she cannot reassure even herself.

"Do you want to see Klara now?" Dr. Goethe asked when I entered his office at the Nest.

"I will see her when I come with her Gustavs," I said.

I was there with the twelve of them one week later. Dr. Goethe told us that Klara had been placed in another room.

"Why isn't she in the room she spent years in?" I asked, but Dr. Goethe only waved his hand.

We walked along the corridors. From some of the rooms, heads popped out—pensive heads, frantic heads, dreadful heads, terror-stricken heads; they looked at us with their tired eyes, their empty eyes, their eyes filled with fear, rapture, insane joy, unfounded hate, and unfounded love, eyes filled with disgust and delight.

They pursed their lips in silence; they thrust them out in wonder; through them they emitted some barely audible word. They blessed or threatened; they shouted in pain and in joy. Several of the Gustavs were quite frightened. The youngest, four-year-old Gustav, held me firmly by the hand and clung to me, hobbling me as we walked.

In the bedroom Dr. Goethe took us to, there were ten women lying on the beds. Some were motionless; others tossed in their beds, mumbling; one of the women's arms and legs were bound. At the end of the room, in the corner, lay Klara on one of the beds in a white nightgown. She was huddled up—legs curled, knees to her chin, and heels by her bottom. She had folded her arms and pressed them to her chest, and she was staring at the wall. The twelve Gustavs and I stood by her bed. Then the oldest of the brothers sat down beside her.

"Auntie Klara," said the oldest, seventeen-year-old Gustav.

Neither the name nor the familiar voice moved her. She continued to breathe uniformly, staring at the wall.

"We've come to see you," he continued. "We are all here."

Klara did not move.

The youngest Gustav came up close to his aunt and stroked her hair. He was too short to see her face turned to the wall. The oldest of the brothers, the one sitting on the bed, placed his hand on hers. Her hands were closed in fists. Not clenched, just closed into fists.

A woman who was lying on the other side of the room began to shriek. Her shrieking impelled the other women to howl, to cry, to laugh. One of them threatened to set everyone on fire. Klara alone remained silent. Her silence was louder than all the surrounding shouts.

The oldest of the brothers turned to Dr. Goethe.

"Isn't it too loud for her in here? Everyone is screaming, but she is silent."

Dr. Goethe wrote "No" in the air with his index finger, and then he repeated that "No" out loud several times and continued:

"She was alone in a room until just recently. In the same room she had lived in for years. But when she was placed in that room a few months ago she did not say a word. So last week we transferred her here. Surely the quiet of the room where she was alone was killing her even more. She needs provocation. I think these cries will drive her to speak."

"These cries will drive her to drown in silence forever," said the oldest Gustav.

"You are mistaken," said Dr. Goethe.

"It is not important whether I am mistaken. It is important that you stop torturing her by keeping her here amid this squalling."

"I do not think she is being tortured here. Look at her face. When we brought her here from her peaceful room, her face was alarmed. In that room, Klara was silent and motionless, as she is now, but her face was set in an indescribable grimace. Now it radiates serenity."

Indeed, Klara's face was that of a serene corpse. The sons of Gustav Klimt looked at their aunt lying there, curled up like a fetus, her face as expressionless as an embryo's. The youngest Gustav went up to her feet and touched her heels. I placed the palms of my hands beside his, on Klara's heels. Her heels were as cold as a corpse's. Klara remained with her eyes fixed on the white wall and was breathing steadily.

"What if this is self-anesthesia," I said. "What if she is killing herself to save herself from these shouts?"

"You are speaking about things you do not understand," said Dr. Goethe. Then he turned to the Gustavs. "Go along now, children. You have seen your aunt. It is time for you to go home."

We headed toward the door. I let the twelve Gustavs out into the corridor, and then, before I could leave, the youngest Gustav turned back. He went to Klara's bed, bent down close to her head, and set his lips as if to kiss her, but she was turned toward the wall and the bed was too high, so he could not reach her face. Then he went to the lower end of the bed and kissed her heels, which lay at the edge of the bed. He turned and ran out of the room.

The following day, I went to see Sigmund and begged him to insist that Dr. Goethe return Klara to her room, and shortly thereafter my brother told me his colleague had accepted the request. Upon waking I would always try to convince myself that I should visit Klara again, but soon I found an excuse not to. There was an epidemic of pneumonia and the Spanish influenza in Vienna. Hundreds of people were dying every day; schools, theaters, the opera, and movie houses were closed, and people were instructed to leave their homes only when necessary. In that year, 1919, immediately following the end of the illnesses that set in after the war, the Austro-Hungarian Empire, exhausted from the fighting, collapsed, and we remained in the part that henceforth was called Austria.

It was a Sunday afternoon when we learned from Sigmund that Sophie had informed him she was pregnant with her third child. Since her marriage six years earlier, she had not been to Vienna, and during that time Sigmund and Martha had visited Hamburg only twice. The Great War had intervened, and travel was impossible, and then, at the end of the war, rail lines between Austria and Germany were broken. During those months, my brother communicated with Sophie daily by telephone; one month before the birth, Sophie told him she was feeling quite ill. The following day his son-in-law, Max Halberstadt, told him there were complications in Sophie's condition and that she had been rushed to the hospital. A day later, Max called again to tell him that Sophie had died.

When I saw him for the first time after Sophie's death, my brother sat motionless, his gaze fixed somewhere in the middle of the table. As soon as he heard that we were beginning a conversation about Sophie, he said, "There is no greater tragedy than to experience the death of one's child."

"Death" and "child." At some time long before, when those two words were uttered close to each other, I felt something stab my womb.

"There is no greater tragedy than to experience the death of one's child," my sister Rosa repeated.

Martha's quiet sobbing could be heard in the room, mixed with the clinking of the knife and fork that shook in her clenched hands and struck her plate.

In the fall of that year, my sister Marie arrived from Berlin, several days after her daughter Martha had thrown herself from a bridge into the Spree River, where several years earlier her son Theodor had also drowned. Her husband had been dead for many years. She stayed with us until the beginning of winter, and whenever the conversation among the three of us—her, my mother, and me—died out, Marie noiselessly left the room and came back much later, her eyes red. She returned to Berlin at the end of that winter, when the snow was already melting.

IN THE SUMMER OF 1922, Mother, Rosa, and everyone in Sigmund's household went on vacation to the Vienna Woods. It was a muggy summer. Everything was steamy, and the city shimmered before one's eyes, as if it were about to melt in the heat. Some mornings, while it was still bearable to go outside, I walked to the building where both Sigmund and Rosa lived, and rang the door at my sister's to awaken my niece Cecilia. She was twenty-three years old, and beautiful in the way Rosa, the most beautiful of us five sisters, had been. One morning, I saw that Cecilia had opened the windows wide; it was one of those rare mornings that summer when there was wind, and the curtains were flapping like white

wings stretching toward the street. I entered the building, climbed
to their floor, and rang the bell. I waited, then rang again. Then I
put my hand on the door handle. It was not locked, so I entered the
apartment. All the doors and windows were open. The only sound
in the apartment was the sound of the breeze. I went to Cecilia's
bedroom. She was lying on the bed with a letter beside her, and
an empty pillbox on her nightstand. She was lying peacefully, as
though asleep. Her body was still warm. I looked at her, and I
thought of my sister Rosa. I sat on the bed beside the dead body in
a white nightgown. I picked up the letter, in which Cecilia explained why she had done what she had done. She had fallen in
love with a married officer and had become pregnant. He told her
he would not marry her. "I know that one cannot compare the
horror of shame with the horror of loss," she wrote to her mother.
"But the shame would have killed me anyway, and I would not
have been able to give a good life to the child I would bear. I would
not be able to look after it the way you looked after Hermann and
me. I would not be able to love it the way you loved us, nor sacrifice myself for it as you sacrificed yourself for us. And since I cannot give it the sort of life it deserves, the life I am obligated to give
it because that was what was given to me, it is best to give it no life,
and to take my own. I know that one cannot compare the horror of
shame with the horror of loss, and I cannot forgive myself that in
order to save myself from the horror of my shame I am giving you
two horrors, both shame and loss. But I know that you can forgive
me, and I beg of you that forgiveness." The handwriting was calm,
as if she had been writing some simple message, a note to say that
she was going out and would return soon. And then a white space,
and below, in an entirely different handwriting, were wobbly letters, surely written when she sensed she was sinking into what
resembled sleep: "Be strong, as always."

I set the letter on the pillow. I ran my hand through Cecilia's
hair, her long black hair. I spread it out on the pillow, across the

sheets of paper on which she had written her letter. I thought of Rosa, remembering the words she had spoken after her husband's death, when her children were young: "Now I am living only for them; if it were not for my children, I would breathe my last at once." I remembered the words she had spoken after her son's death: "Now I am living only for Cecilia. If it weren't for her, I would not live a moment longer." I placed my hands on Cecilia's belly, there where yet another life had ended, and I felt pain in my womb. I had placed my hands on Cecilia's belly the way one holds something alive, something that needs to be kept from decay, and my womb still ached. I then bent down and kissed her forehead.

My sister returned to Vienna that same evening. She spent the night on the bed, in embrace with the dead body. Sigmund and I sat in a corner of the room. Every so often, one of us got up and tried to persuade Rosa to go rest. She did not listen but remained lying there, stroking and embracing the body, whispering something inaudible, and only by the tone of her voice could we understand when she questioned and when she reproached her daughter, when she pleaded with her and when she cursed her.

"Now I have no one to live for" were the only words my sister Rosa would repeat after her daughter's burial. All other thoughts came and went; even those everyday things, those we repeat by habit, seemed as if they would never return to her mouth after she spoke them. The one thought alone returned again and again, as if with it she were trying to convince her body that it needed to expire. Her body became weaker and weaker by the day, and the doctors advised her to go somewhere to regain her strength. She went with Mother to Bad Gastein, and they returned half a year later.

The first evening after her return, my sister did not want to sleep alone in the apartment, so I spent the night at her place. Before we lay down to sleep, Rosa said to me, "I constantly ask myself whether I was a good mother. Did I give my children everything they needed? Did I tell them everything I needed to tell them? Did I say one word too few, or one word too many? I feel I said some things that should have been kept quiet, and I did not say some things that they needed to hear. But it is useless to think like this, because their lives are now a closed conversation, and mine as well."

She pulled out two photographs, one of her daughter, the other of her son, and she touched them with fingers dampened by sweat or tears.

Around this time, my brother became alarmed about a growth of some kind in his mouth that bothered him when he ate. The doctors told him it was his body's reaction to excessive smoking. He thought there was no need to tell his household about the minor surgical treatment; everything would be done in an afternoon, and he would be home again that evening. During the operation he lost a great deal of blood, and the hospital called Martha and Anna to have them bring him the items he would most need. The following day, however, he insisted on going home. I went to visit him that evening. Because the wound in his mouth was still raw, he could not speak, so he wrote his questions and answers on a sheet of paper.

A day later, his son-in-law, Max Halberstadt, telephoned him. He spoke with Anna and asked whether his son Heinerle, who had just had his tonsils out, could come to Vienna for a while. He was very sickly. The doctors had examined him, but aside from the problems with his tonsils they could discover nothing, and they said that it was likely the Hamburg climate did not agree with him.

From the moment we saw him, it was clear to us that he was not going to live long. Each of us kept that thought from the others; the thought was evident only in our eyes when we looked at him, but he just smiled when he noticed our contorted expressions riveted on his face. There was something old in that smile.

He smiled at us not in the way a four-year-old does but the way an old-timer, freed from fear, sneers at death. His grandfather Sigmund, excusing himself on account of his recent operation, his many patients, and his writing, left Heinerle to be cared for by his daughter Matilda in her home. Matilda was happy with this: She had had an operation in her early youth that left her unable to have children. It was her life's misfortune, and now she was happy to take the place of her deceased sister and provide motherly care to this youngster. She said that in the evenings she would hear sounds coming from the room where Heinerle slept, something like whispering or singing or sobbing. When she went in, she saw his lips slowly moving, emitting a barely audible sound, as if he were singing something. He sang or whispered or sobbed in his sleep. And it was like that every night.

Heinerle did not remember his mother. Sophie Freud Halberstadt died when he was thirteen months old; he knew her face from his father's photographs, and he had heard about her from his brother, Ernst, who was a few years older. When he saw her framed photograph during his first visit to his grandfather's home, he recognized her and said his brother had told him she was now lying in the ground. They rarely brought him to Sigmund's.

"Maybe Grandpa wants me to visit him," he said when Matilda brought him to our place.

"Of course he wants that, but it is difficult for him to have visitors," Matilda answered. "He was operated on two weeks ago."

In fact, he was busy. He was always receiving patients, and in the evenings he wrote.

"I had an operation two weeks ago, too," said Heinerle.

We knew that, but no one asked him how he was doing, whether his throat hurt when he swallowed; every day we forgot to take his temperature, although his father told us the doctors said it had to be done regularly. We were all thinking about Sigmund: Anna was concerned the wound from the operation would not heal properly; my mother was afraid it was perhaps a more serious illness and not an ordinary growth; Minna made sure he had peace and quiet so he could dedicate himself to his writing; Martha did not allow him to wear himself out working with patients; Matilda constantly procured new medicines; and I did everything not to be too conspicuous in my insistence on going to visit him as often as possible with my mother. So we failed to notice that Heinerle was getting thinner and thinner, that all that was left on his little head were a few straight blond hairs, below which his bulging eyes flashed and his greenish skin darkened. No one thought he needed conversation when we heard him whispering to himself while we talked about Sigmund, nor did we ask him what he was afraid of when we saw he was frightened by a glass turned upside down on the table.

One afternoon at the beginning of June, when Matilda had left him in my care while she went about Vienna in search of medicines for Sigmund, Heinerle said to me that it must be very beautiful now in the parks, and I just nodded my head. "And the flowers must smell wonderful," he continued. I murmured something in affirmation, and he added that the birds must be singing more beautifully than ever, and twice he whistled through his lips, imitating the chirping of birds. I did not see him often, but even from those few meetings I knew he never asked for anything. His desires were always hidden among his words of observation, his delight, or his disagreement. He looked at me in the expectation that I might recognize his wish. I did recognize it, and I kept silent. Heinerle sensed that silence, and fled from it by turning his gaze toward the flies that flew about the room.

"Is it true there are flies that live only one day?"

"Yes, it is. They are called mayflies."

"If you were to live only one day, then would you go to the park, would you smell the flowers, would you see the birds, or would you stay home?"

"I don't know," I said.

"Are mayflies afraid of death?"

"They cannot be afraid of it, because mayflies don't know what death is."

"Is it better not to know and not be afraid or to know and be afraid?"

"The best is to know and not be afraid."

"That is not possible," he said.

"It is possible," I lied.

He thought a bit, then asked, "But what do you do if you are afraid of death?"

In his voice I recognized my own fear when I was a child.

"We don't disappear when we die," I told him. "A person is like the hand inside a puppet that makes it move. When someone is born, that person slips into his body like a hand into a puppet. When the body dies, the person pulls out from it like a hand from a puppet."

"I've never had a doll that slips onto your hand."

I remembered he never asked for anything.

"One day I will make you a doll like that."

"I'll wait. I'm not a mayfly, so I have time."

When Matilda got to our place, and as she prepared to go home with Heinerle, something struck the window outside and frightened us. Heinerle said, "That was a bird. It probably thought the window was another sky." The two of us pretended we did not hear him when he added, "I would so like to go to the park and watch the birds." We all knew he never asked for anything. His desires were always hidden among his words of observation, his delight or disagreement. He looked at us, expecting us to recognize his wishes. We did recognize them, but we kept silent. Heinerle sensed these silences, and he fled from them by turning his gaze toward a spot on the wall, toward the flies that flew about the room, toward the window. Matilda left him alone at home more and more often when she went to buy medicines for Sigmund, and to bring them to him, and she told us that whenever she returned to her apartment she would find Heinerle seated on the floor with an open chessboard, his hands holding the figures, and he would be talking to them.

During the course of an examination, the doctors noticed a new growth in Sigmund's mouth. We worried increasingly about his health, and we did not notice that Heinerle was weakening by the day. We thought the temperature of his forehead was part of his excitement from the change of setting, his coughing due to a cold—up until the morning he could no longer get out of bed, and several days later when the doctors diagnosed miliary tuberculosis. He was placed in the children's wing of the Vienna General Hospital, and Matilda and I spent several days in his room taking care of him. When the doctors said his condition was taking an irrevocable turn for the worse, his father caught the train from Hamburg, hoping to find him still alive.

While I sat by Heinerle's hospital bed, I tried to turn his attention away from his body's torments. He was breathing heavily, and his breath was cut short by coughing that tore at his chest. From time to time he wiped his sweaty palms on his pajamas.

"Where's Grandpa?" he asked.

"He is sick," I said. Sigmund was preparing for his next operation. The whole family was also preparing for it. "He can't come."

He wanted to say something, but his words ended in coughing. I wiped his mouth, and he wiped his sweaty palm on his pajamas, then rubbed his forehead with his palm, and again wiped the sweat on his pajamas.

"You once promised to make me a doll," he said, and of everything he had said, that recollection was the closest he had ever come to making a request.

"I will make you one."

"When?"

"Whenever you want."

"Can you make it now?" He tried to prop himself up on the pillow, but he couldn't and so remained lying down. I adjusted his pillow, half resting it up against the wall, so that he could lie with his head elevated a bit.

"I don't know if I will find everything I need here," I said, and I looked around for fabric with which to make a puppet. Everything was white, all part of the hospital inventory. "I will make you a puppet at home, and I will bring it to you tomorrow."

"Please," he said. He had never pleaded before, as if he felt that even his pleas were too much like demands. "Now," and he wet his dry lips with his tongue.

I took one of the two white cloths that had been left on the nightstand by his bed. I pulled a thread from it and tied it around where the neck should be. From my purse I took out a fountain pen, and with the ink I dripped two dark blue eyes on the puppet's head.

"Here you are," I said, and handed him the cloth. "When we find everything else we need, we will make it hair, a mouth, and a nose."

He thanked me, and with my help put his hand inside the fabric.

"What will you name it?"

"Heinerle," he said. "The doll is me." He smiled. "You told me that when a person dies he comes out of his body like a hand out of a puppet."

"That is how it is," I said.

Heinerle coughed, then brought his fabric-covered hand to his mouth. When he took it away, the puppet's face was bloody. Heinerle's eyes rolled back, and he lost consciousness. I took the damp cloth that was lying on the nightstand and wiped his forehead. Heinerle regained consciousness. He looked at the puppet on his little hand. Then he looked at me. He tried to say something, but his tiny voice had completely dried up, and his gaze, turning toward the puppet with the bloody trace across its face, slowly died away. His hand fell to the bed. I closed his eyes and slipped his hand from the puppet. A strike at the outer windowpane startled me. I turned, but there was nothing there. Surely a bird had struck the glass, "thinking it was another sky," as Heinerle had said.

His father arrived that evening. The following day, he boarded the train to Hamburg, carrying his son with him in a small coffin.

That afternoon, Sigmund had his second operation. Several days later, against the doctors' advice, he left on a trip to Rome with Anna. On the second day of their trip, a scab tore from his unhealed wound, and it had been almost impossible to stanch the flow of blood that filled his mouth. When he returned to Vienna, he was diagnosed with cancer. In October of that year he had two more operations, and in November another. Glands beneath the upper part of his lower jaw were removed. His upper jawbone and palate were removed. A large prosthesis separating his oral and nasal cavities was inserted, enabling him to speak and eat.

The first time the family had lunch together after Sigmund's prosthesis had been inserted, we recalled Heinerle and the way he talked to himself. Then we talked about other things. While listening to the others talk, I rummaged several times through the pocket of my dress. There I kept a small piece of cloth, the hastily made puppet with the bloody trace across its face. I kept that scrap of cloth for years in the drawer with the photo albums in the cupboard where I kept my clothes, and sometimes I carried it with me. Once, when I was moving it from one place to another, I left it somewhere in the apartment. Later, I found my mother holding it, looking at the trace of blood.

"This must be blood," she said when she saw me come into the room.

"No, it isn't," I said. "Blood is red, and this has a brown tint."

"Then this blood must have dripped a long time ago to have turned brown, and for the brown to have faded like this." She opened the window. "I will let it fly away," she said, and she threw the scrap of cloth out the window.

IN THE LAST YEARS of her life, my mother became frail. Before that, she had possessed the gait of a young woman. She walked every day to see her friends (she was a half century older than some of them) and to play cards; once a week she went to the movie theater, and she never missed a theatrical premiere. When the first automobiles roared through Vienna and my brother was trying to learn to drive, she said to him, half in jest, half seriously, "My golden Siggie, buy me an automobile. I will learn to drive." She was like that up to her ninetieth year, and then it seemed that all those years when time had stopped had caught up with her, and suddenly she looked old; only the features of her face remained the same—sharp, as if chiseled in stone. She no longer wanted to see anyone who was not family. She walked unsteadily and did not leave the house unaccompanied, and even those walks ended quickly; she would stop, say that she no longer recognized the city, and then she would turn back toward home. She did not recognize some of her women friends she would meet by chance on her walks, and when they came up to her she would hide her confusion by asking general questions. And then she began not to recognize things, to get them confused. She once took out a knife to cut bread, but then, thinking it was a needle, asked me to bring a shirt so she could mend it. She arranged potatoes in the shoe cupboard. And that rag puppet with the faded bloody trace on it? It had likely turned into a bird the moment she held it, and she let it fly away.

It was August when my mother could no longer leave home. Every afternoon she leaned against me, and the two of us went out on the balcony. We sat for a long time and looked out at the street through the bars of the balcony railing. My mother used to comment on each passerby; now she looked with an absent gaze and said nothing. In the course of that summer, the features of her face, sharp her whole life, softened all at once. She had a look that now, in place of its former sharpness, had something that resembled tenderness but was actually disorientation; and her lips, rather than being pursed, now relaxed at the edges and drooped. She no longer looked like herself. One afternoon, while we were sitting on the balcony, my mother asked, "Will he come?"

"Who?"

"Sigmund."

"He will come. He always returns to Vienna at the end of September."

"He needs to come earlier this time."

Sigmund spent the first half of his summers in Italy, Greece, or at a spa, the second half in the Vienna Woods, where he had a cottage. My mother and Rosa went to the Vienna Woods with Sigmund's family, and sometimes they also went with him to the spa. That summer—1930, the last summer of her life—my mother stayed with me in Vienna. She sensed she would never again see the spas, or the Vienna Woods, and so in our conversations she recalled her former travels, what had happened when and where—events with her grandchildren, conversations with Sigmund, Rosa, Martha, and Minna—and then her voice would suddenly change, and she would say, "But those summers you stayed here alone." One of those afternoons, after I had carried chairs out to the balcony and helped my mother sit down in one of them, I noticed on the balcony railing a dead swallow. When she saw me putting it into a box, my mother asked, "What is that?"

"A swallow," I said, shutting the box.

"Will you keep it closed up inside?"

"It is dead. I picked it up to throw it away."

"Dead . . . to throw it away . . ." she said, then placed her hands on the arms of the chair, as if she wanted to get up. She turned toward me. "Will Sigmund come?"

"He will come," I said. "He always comes back after his holiday at the end of September."

"This time he will be late," she said.

"No. He will come at that time again."

"He will come at that time, but he will be late."

Whenever Sigmund called, I told him that our mother wanted to see him. Our mother had been going deaf for years, and she could not hear anything over the telephone. While I spoke with Sigmund, she understood from my words that I was speaking with him, and she looked at me with the gaze of the aged who— without fear, only hesitation—are preparing to die. As soon as I finished our conversation, she said to me, "Take me outside."

I grasped her under her arms, and slowly we went out to the balcony. Stooped, diminished, she sat in the chair with her arms on the arms of the chair, not to lean on them but as if clenching them to keep herself from falling to the floor. She was silent a long time, and then she said the words she had held in her mouth while I was speaking with Sigmund: "That means he is not coming." And she slumped even farther down in the chair. Everything around us was steaming from the heat. The street was empty; flies flew about in the air. My mother started to tremble, and she said, "It has never been so cold."

At one time, a time when I was helpless, when she crushed me with her words and actions, I longed for the moment when my mother would be physically weak, wished for the time when I would be able to pay her back, to avenge myself. Now she was helpless, and had she been only physically weak I could, perhaps, have returned the pain she had caused, but the Amalie Freud who cut with her words no longer existed. In her helplessness I recognized the helplessness of my childhood and my youth, and understood that each of my unfriendly words or actions toward that being who was slowly dying would be not revenge but cruelty against myself, against my memory of that child, that girl, against that young woman I once was.

At the beginning of September, my mother developed gangrene in her right leg. While I bandaged it, she seemed to look with resignation at the open wound. Whenever she rapped her cane on the floor, I knew she wanted to go out on the balcony. Supporting her, I led her out; she moved by hopping on one leg and leaning on me and on her cane. We sat and looked toward the street.

"I'm hungry," she said.

"We just ate lunch," I said.

"I am hungry for the food I ate as a child. I want bread. Just bread."

I brought some bread. She lifted it to her mouth, moistened it with her saliva, and crumbled more than swallowed it. Then she set the rest of the piece in her lap alongside the crumbs and looked a long time at the scraps. When she raised her head she said, "Look at that child flying."

"That is not a child," I said. "It is a balloon."

"A balloon," she repeated, as if she did not recognize the word. "Now even looking makes me tired," she added, and closed her eyes.

At one point her hands, which had been firmly holding the arms of the chair, relaxed, and her head rolled slowly forward, as if she were bowing deeply to someone. She fell asleep. It was a warm September day, but I knew she was cold, and I knew the cold made her dream of winter and frost. She dreamed that she had been left somewhere alone, and that snow was falling on her. I got up and went into the apartment for a blanket. When I returned, I saw that sparrows had gathered in my mother's lap and were pecking at the breadcrumbs. She was still sleeping peacefully—perhaps in her dream the sparrows were singing her a lullaby with their chirping. When I drew near her, the sparrows flew off; I brushed away the droppings some of them had left in her lap. Then I covered my mother with the blanket.

When she awoke, it was already growing dark. I gently helped her up from the chair, led her into the apartment, and brought her to her bed.

"Stay with me tonight," she said.

Although during the thirty years since my return home we had somehow grown close, some lingering trace of our former enmity remained, and something kept me from lying down beside her on the side of the bed my father had slept on until his death.

"I will sit," I said, placing an armchair by the bed.

We spent the night beside each other, barely saying a word. I sensed she wanted to tell me many things, but she said none of them. Thoughts and feelings shimmered around her like a blue light around the moon, but not a single one was turned into words. I looked at her; I had a premonition that this was her last night. And I remembered those nights of despair in my youth, a time when my mother, with ruthless delight, poured salt into the open wound of my soul. I remembered that during those nights I longed for this night, for her last night; ten thousand nights before this night I wanted revenge, and revenge could come at only the moment of her greatest powerlessness, to remind her, in her powerlessness as she was facing death, of my powerlessness and of her cruelty in my suffering. Yet now I looked at this Amalie who had nothing in common with that Amalie, and although the powerlessness of this dying woman reminded me of my former powerlessness, I either did not want or was unable to awaken in myself the cruelty she used to have within her and with which she pressed me so that I sank ever deeper, the cruelty with which, had I awakened it in myself, I would truly have been her daughter not only by blood but also by the cruelty that would make her suffer because of her own

cruelty, my cruelty that would take delight in her despairing
remorse.

I looked at her, and she looked at me; we said not a word. Before the night was over, she fell asleep; her dream, her last dream,
was calm, short. Before she awoke, she stretched out her hand, as
if seeking someone in her dream. She opened her eyes; I did not
recognize her look; it was as though she were looking not at me
but at some other woman. She stretched out her hand toward me.
I offered her my hand.

"Mama," she said to me.

When I heard someone call me Mama, for the first and last
time in my life, time collapsed. At one time, my mother's mother
had thought my mother was her mother and I was her daughter
Amalie. Now my mother thought I was her mother. She held me
by the hand awhile, and then her eyes rolled back, she began to
breathe heavily, foam formed on her mouth. I called the doctor.
When he arrived, he examined her and said she would die that
day. I sat by her bed, I held her hand; I listened to her raspy breathing. Somewhere around noon her hand let go of mine. I closed
her eyes, stood up, and went out on the balcony. A light September rain was falling, and I brought inside the two chairs my mother
and I had sat on during the summer afternoons.

After my mother's death, months passed and no one came
to the apartment, where I remained alone. Sometimes I went to
Rosa's. She spent the better part of the year at the baths. On Sundays we always gathered for lunch at Sigmund's, but after our
mother died he no longer came to my place on Sunday mornings.
Once a month, I made a beggar's gesture: I stretched out my hand
to my brother for money to live on. The nights were different now,
the quiet thickened in them, and I thought it would begin speaking to me. I became indifferent to maintaining the order of daily
routines: the dust piled on the floor and on the windowsills; spiderwebs hung on the walls and on the chandeliers; the dishes

remained unwashed for days and grew moldy. I ate as stray dogs eat, with no order to my meals, no set place to eat. I did not know where or at what hour I bit into my food, chewed, swallowed. In days that flowed one into another, I walked along the streets, my eyes cast down, the way lonely people walk, as though they believe their rejection by the world is written in their eyes.

Both fall and winter passed, and then, as I did every spring, I took two chairs out to the balcony. That spring and summer, I sat alone on the balcony, and I no longer looked toward the street but at the empty chair. That fall, when the weather turned cold, I gathered up my chair but left my mother's outside. I watched as the wind sometimes blew through it, carrying a dried leaf, or while some bird—a little sparrow, a crow, a pigeon—stood on it to rest, to sharpen its beak on the metal arms, or to leave its droppings. And then one winter morning I went out to the balcony, and I saw that snow had fallen on my mother's chair and covered her empty place.

On one of those lonely winter days, I was startled by the sound of the doorbell; no one had rung it for so long that I had forgotten it existed. I went to the door, unlocked it, and pulled it open. There on the threshold stood Klara Klimt. More than ten years had passed since I had visited her at the Nest with the twelve Gustavs.

"Do you remember me?" she asked.

I remembered, although the Klara I had known and the Klara who was standing before me were two different women; between them yawned the abyss that divides the shore of madness from the shore of normality. The mute and motionless Klara I had seen ten years before was the same Klara I had met earlier, when she went about Vienna with the little Gustavs, the Klara I had lived with at the Nest, the Klara I had met years before when life opened before us with its promise. This Klara stood on the other shore; aside from the ten years between our two encounters and the small shifts in her jawline and her demeanor, there was something else in her appearance and demeanor, something that shifts with the crossing from one shore to the other.

"I remember," I said. She hugged me.

We went into the sitting room. She looked through the door that led to the balcony and said, "Do you remember the time we stood here on the balcony? You looked toward the sidewalk and said, 'I want the day to come as soon as possible when I, too, will help my child learn to walk.'"

"I remember," I said. I felt my throat go dry. I began to cough.

"Are you sick?" she asked.

"Yes, I am," I lied.

"I will take care of you," and she hugged me. "I will sit here with you, and I will take care of you. I cared for my brother when he got sick. I took care of him, but he died anyway. You will not die. Now I know how to take better care. You will not die."

I asked whether she was hungry. We went into the kitchen, and while we were having some of the vegetable soup and bread left over from the previous day, she told me about the residents of the Nest who continued to live there. As she slurped up her soup, Klara said, "I owe you an apology."

"Why?"

"Because I didn't talk to you when you visited me. I wanted to talk to you, but I couldn't." She touched my fingers. "Forgive me."

"You didn't offend me. There is no reason to seek my forgiveness."

"Sometimes, when I am afraid to fall asleep alone in my room, I become silent again and turn to stone. Then they take me from our room." And she smiled as a person does when recalling good times past. "And they take me to one of those rooms where the patients scream, scream, scream. The screaming is a punishment for my silence. I lie there, and I feel I will suffocate, and I do not know what is suffocating me—is it the others' screams, or my silence? And when that feeling of suffocation becomes intolerable I start to speak. Not much, a word or two, just enough for one of the doctors or orderlies to hear me and return me to our room."

She got up, gathered the crumbs from the table, went to the window, opened it, and threw the crumbs outside.

"For the birds," she said, and closed the window. "Gustav always fed them." She smiled. It seemed as though all the layers of time had been wiped from her face and her brother were there in front of her. "Do you remember Gustav?"

"Yes," I said.

"I remember, too," she said, and she looked through the window where sparrows had gathered and were pecking at the crumbs. Klara began to speak quickly, in a monotonous voice. "Gustav runs around the rooms. Gustav pees behind the house. Gustav draws with charcoal on the fence post. Gustav masturbates. Gustav shouts at our mother when she bangs my head on the table. Gustav shows me a drawing of a naked woman fondling herself between her legs. Gustav has a stroke while we are eating. Gustav dies. We bury Gustav." She turned toward me. "Dr. Goethe told me that thirteen years have passed since then," and she shook her head in disbelief. "Is it true that so many years have gone by?"

"It is true," I said.

"And now even Dr. Goethe has died."

"He died?"

"Yes. Last month. Do you remember when . . . ?" And she began to tell the story of how we taught Dr. Goethe to knit.

It was getting dark outside. We went into my room and spoke for a long time; Klara continually began her sentences with "Do you remember . . . ?" She returned to the past, she raced toward it, or she raced after it, thinking it would escape her, as she at one time had fled from the present to some future of hers, to those things she longed to have happen, those things she wished to accomplish. We talked until we felt our eyes closing from exhaustion.

I left her there to sleep in my bed. I went to the bed where at one time my father and mother had slept. The thought that I had not gone to visit Klara all those years kept me from sleeping. The cowardly thought that she likely forgave me was not enough to assuage my conscience, because I knew she thought the fact that she had not spoken at that visit frightened me, cut me off. I knew she did not think that my obligation to visit her again—to ask how she was, to listen whether perhaps there was something she wanted to say or whether she wished to continue to suffocate in her silence—was stronger than my fear of her silence and of her stony stillness.

It was past midnight when the door creaked open and Klara came into my parents' bedroom. In her hands she carried the pillow from my bed.

"I'm afraid to sleep alone," she said, drawing near me. She lay down beside me and placed her head on the pillow she had brought from my bed.

I lay awake all night, imagining her nights, trying to hear those nights, because the darkness swallowed what could be seen, and I heard the cries that broke the silence of the darkness, I heard those who were condemned to be locked in their madness and to mix their madness with the madness of others: a voice calling to its children, a voice saying it was burning and the flames were engulfing its body, the raspy voice of a woman repeating how she killed her husband. Among all those voices, there was no sound of Klara's voice—in my attempts to hear her nights, among the cries during those nights, nights that stream into one another and flow into years, Klara remained mute, Klara yearned for quiet; Klara wanted only a small piece of this earth in which she could safely tuck her head and sleep through the night. During those nights I heard Klara breathe quickly, I heard her weep, I heard her pray, even though she did not know whom to direct her prayers to, since she had renounced God long ago, after he had renounced her; I heard Klara interrupt her prayer, and stop her crying, I heard her sniffling, and I heard her exhale; and then I heard her breathe slowly, and she seemed to push away some pain lodged in her chest. A clump has wrapped around the question "Why exist at all if one exists like this?" and she was happy as long as that clump enfolded the thought, because stripped bare, without that surrounding clump, the thought would be unbearable. And then she was overwhelmed with exhaustion from trying to cope with the noises—the whistles and shouts of the Nest increasingly seem to come from a distance, and they are no longer human voices but a sound created by the pangs of human pain, turned to rage, banging the gong of fate.

I heard those sounds in my imagination that night as I lay awake, and I expected Klara to scream as she slept, to answer in her sleep the voices that tormented her in her reality, the voices that did not let her fall asleep, and those she had become so accustomed to that, without them, the darkness frightened her. She slept peacefully. In the morning, when she awoke, she said, "It is wonderful to sleep on your pillow."

We lay in the large bed in which my parents had once slept, and we looked at each other. Klara spoke about her brother's sons. She talked about how the little Gustavs, whom she continued to call "little" even though they were now grown men, visited her at the Nest. She talked about their wives and children.

"When they come with their children, it seems to me that the whole world is coming. One has just started to talk; another has cut a tooth; a third has fallen and scraped his knee; a fourth has learned to fly a kite, and we spend the whole afternoon out on the grounds, looking at the sky," she said, and looked through the window at the sky. Then she turned toward me. "I would like very much for you to come to the Nest again sometime. So we can sleep just one more night together in our room." She took my hands between hers. "I will go now," she said. "I am going back to the

Nest. That is my place. That is what the doctors say when I beg them to release me. I ran away from them this time. But that is my place. That is why I will return there." She petted me, and while her left hand was still on my head she raised her right hand, ran it along the thinning hair on her own head, and petted herself. I hugged her. "I will run away again to visit you," she whispered into my neck. Then she went to the door, unlocked it, and cracked it open. She turned. "But I am going now. That is my place," she said. But before taking the step that would carry her across the threshold she remembered something and stopped. "May I take your pillow?" she asked. "It is wonderful to sleep on your pillow."

A LONG TIME PASSED before I went to visit Klara. When I entered her room, our room, she was sitting on the bed, with the pillow in her hands.

"Let's go to the dying room," she said.

The dying room, I remembered, was what we called the room where they brought those residents who were facing the end of their lives. Klara took me by the hand, clutching the pillow under her other arm, and we left the room.

"The Good Soul is dying," Klara said as we walked along the corridor.

In the dying room it smelled of death, a smell of raw, disintegrating flesh, of excrement, of sweat, and, in the middle of that stench, of bodies tossing on the eve of death, and bodies stiffly awaiting it. Several of the dying, laid out on mattresses on the floor, agonized with yet one more breath. It was cold, but it seemed that something was vaporizing in that dark room.

"This is Daniel," said Klara, pointing to a young man I did not recognize. He was chewing his blanket, and he held his hand out to us. "And there is Helmut," and she pointed to an old man who was lying motionless. I remembered that once, a long time ago, Klara had said that all normal people are normal in the same way, but each mad person is mad in his own way. And I thought, just as I had many years earlier when I entered the dying room for the first time, that in death everyone is different and everyone is the same. Everyone lets go of his spirit by exhaling, but each exhales in his own way.

Klara stopped and pointed at a curled-up body.

"There is the Good Soul," she said.

I continued toward the body lying on the mattress in the middle of the room. I bent down and pulled the blanket from the covered face. The Good Soul was looking somewhere off to the side. Her body was completely sunken, as if her skin had been pulled through her bones. Her lips were so stiff that she formed her words with difficulty; she continued to whisper something to Max. Only her eyes were still alive, although not with that full vitality she had had when we knew each other. Now they were alive as in a person who has seen everything, has endured everything, yet still possesses the desire to live at least one more day, the desire to continue to gaze into the emptiness and see there the one who has not existed for so many years. I looked at that vitality in her eyes, at the apples of her eyes that had shriveled and contracted, and had wasted to their hollows.

Drawing the blanket from her face had not stirred her, so I touched her hand. She remained motionless, in the same position, but turned her eyes toward me.

"Do you need anything?" she asked me.

I shook my head. I did not know what to talk to her about, so I asked what it was unnecessary to ask, because I could see: "How are you feeling?"

"Do not worry," she said. "Everything will be fine."

Something trembled inside me at her words; something scraped inside me, the same way her voice trembled and scraped.

"Do you remember me?"

"I remember," she said, "I just can't remember your name." She took my hand and placed it on her breast, above her heart. "Do you need anything?"

"No. And you?"

"Don't worry. Everything will be fine."

"I know," I said. "I know everything will be fine."

"Kiss me," she said, and she pressed my hand still tighter above her heart. It was as if in that moment her hand touched my heart, because at the Nest we all carried those words inside us, and we hid them from ourselves, just as we hid our reason from ourselves, or those words hid from us, and we searched for them, but instead of finding them we found madness. And now here they were, after so many years, spoken as simply as a thirsty person's request for water. "Kiss me," the Good Soul said again, and she closed her eyes.

I bent down and kissed her sweaty forehead. Then I said to her, "I must go now."

"If you need anything, come again," said the Good Soul, watching me as I went to the door.

"I will come," I said.

"And do not worry. Everything will be fine."

The Good Soul spoke to the emptiness for several more days, and she asked those who came to her bed in the dying room whether they needed anything, and assured them that everything would be fine.

But that day, after the visit, I repeated to myself the words the Good Soul had spoken—"Everything will be fine"—and they paled before the question, Why did she suffer, she who had done no wrong to anyone? I repeated her words to myself—"Everything will be fine"—but they did not bring comfort. Her words came back to me in a kind of insidious mocking echo. She lay there, and something within her believed that time was not just endless self-destruction, that the universe—the entire space that stretches around us to a point unfathomable to us—is not just an immense slaughterhouse. Something inside her believed it was so. I knew this by some thread interwoven amid the weariness of her voice, by the invisible ray beyond the pain in her eyes, but to me her words, which I pronounced with her voice in my head, still came back to me with a kind of insidious mocking echo.

SEVERAL DAYS LATER, the pale February sun began to melt the snow. I went out onto the balcony, and I noticed that the snow on the chair where my mother once sat had turned to liquid. It was not yet the season for sitting on the balcony; nevertheless, I set a chair for myself out there beside my mother's.

The snow still had not melted completely when Anna came to visit. She was then thirty-eight years old. Two decades earlier, she had begged her father to allow her to study medicine, but Sigmund did not believe that studies were for girls, and so she, as well as Matilda and Sophie, did not enroll at the university. Being forbidden an education did not distance her from him; she became yet more devoted to him, and she hated all the women who were close to him. She hated his sisters. She hated her Aunt Minna, because she often traveled with my brother. She hated the women who studied psychoanalysis alongside my brother, except for one of them, Lou Salomé, to whom she was connected by a close friendship, something that perhaps could have turned into a great and passionate love had she not promised her heart to an- other: her father. To his daughters, Sigmund often said, "The most intelligent young men know very well what their wives must have: sweetness, cheerfulness, and the capacity to make their lives easier and more beautiful." And several times when I saw my niece with that mature woman, Lou Salomé, I had a feeling that Anna had discovered in her that sweetness, that cheerfulness, that capacity to make her life more beautiful and more cheerful (al-

though Lou did not appear to anyone else as sweet, cheerful, or
capable of making someone's life more beautiful and more cheerful), and perhaps Anna wanted to make Lou's life more beautiful
and more cheerful, but she was hindered by the fact that she lived
for her father, and I imagined that, after his death, concern for his
works would give meaning to her life.

His immortal works. From her earliest youth, she was determined to devote her life to him; her daily routine consisted of the
arrangement of what Dr. Freud had written, in consultation about
his patients, the organization of his professional travel, assisting in
the management of his illnesses. Sometimes she related to him as
a daughter, sometimes as a spouse, sometimes as a child, most often as a scholar. But behind her cheerfulness and chattiness, behind her grand idea to serve her great father, one sensed a kind of
mute emptiness. Long ago, back in her childhood, her father, consciously or not, had laid the groundwork for that emptiness, turning Anna into his companion, his interlocutor, his confidante, and
his confessor. With her, he had also broken the ironclad rule he
had given to all psychoanalysts: patients cannot be people who
are close to them, whether parents, spouses, brothers or sisters, or
children, because that would allow for the manipulation of their
everyday life, and the analysis itself would fail. His daughter, however, was his patient; she told him her secrets, hopes, dreams, and
longings, extinguishing them before they became true longings,
which she would have set out after, and which would have separated her from him.

That winter morning when Anna visited me, she told me that
she and Sigmund were going to a spa, and that prior to that they
would stay several days in Venice. Minna was to have traveled
with them, but she had taken ill, and I could now go in her place.
I smiled, and nodded hesitantly. I recalled how, many years earlier,
when Rainer and I spoke for the last time, I reminded him that we
had once dreamed of living in Venice.

It was afternoon when we arrived in Venice. I did not see what I had once longed so intensely to see; a curtain fell between my eyes and Venice, a veil that through the years had become less translucent, ever darker, a curtain that divides us from everything around us, and makes it seem that even what is within arm's reach is of another world, a world that does not belong to us, and to which we do not belong.

My brother suggested we board a gondola.

"No," I said.

"But when you were a girl you said that when we got to Venice the first thing we would do was ride in a gondola."

"When I was a girl," I said.

Anna said she would ride the canals alone. Sigmund told her we would wait for her at a set time in front of the clock tower in Piazza San Marco. I saw how the gondolier helped Anna climb in, and then she waved to us as she moved down the canal; she called out to her father that she would tell him how her trip along the canals had gone. The meaning of her life was to exist for her father; even riding in the gondola had meaning for her only if she could tell him about it.

Sigmund suggested we go to the Palazzo Ducale, or to the Church of San Lazzaro or the Querini Stampalia Museum. I said it would be best if we took the shortest route to Piazza San Marco and waited for Anna there.

"Do you really not want to see anything?"

"I am no longer capable of seeing anything," I said.

"You speak as if you were dead."

"No," I said. "I speak as if I were between life and death. Neither here nor there. I believe that those things in what is called death are much more alive than what is in me now; when I die, I will be more alive in spirit than I am now. I am now at the transition between two existences, between life and death, neither alive nor dead."

My brother raised his hand and moved it in front of his face as if waving away flies. He did this whenever he thought what he had been told did not deserve a reply.

We set off along the narrow alleys and small bridges across the canals; surrounding me was one of my life's dreams, Venice, but I stared at the road in front of me, my head bowed. Although he had waved away my words, my brother could not contain his disagreement, and several minutes later, as we were walking along, he said, "You know, long ago I wrote that religions were born of the need for consolation, consolation for all the torments life gives us, comfort for all the pleasures life does not give us, comfort for the fact that death separates us from those closest to us, and from ourselves, comfort because after our short stay on this earth nonexistence follows. And this explanation of mine, that religious belief originates in the search for comfort, will last longer than any religious belief."

"Is that your comfort? The thought that you will live eternally through your works? The belief that the interpretations of dreams, the human unconscious, the death instinct and the life instinct will be remembered forever? Is that the comfort with which you promise yourself victory over death?"

At that moment, we heard singing from below the bridge we were crossing; for the first time during that walk, I pulled my gaze from my steps and looked toward the canal, where several young people glided past in a gondola, singing. I tripped and fell. My brother bent down and helped me up.

"Are you all right?" he asked.

"Yes," I answered. I felt a pain in my knee. I shook the dust from my clothes. Then we continued walking. I was hobbling.

"Does your leg hurt?" my brother asked.

"A little," I said. "My knee."

"Here," my brother said. "We will cut behind this corner and come out on the square."

When we reached the square, the first thing I saw was the clock tower. We still had an hour before we were to meet Anna.

"Let's go into Saint Mark's Basilica," my brother suggested.

"The Correr Museum is here somewhere," I said. "Do you remember when two of Bellini's paintings from that museum were exhibited in Vienna? You and I stood in front of them for hours."

My brother led me toward one of the palaces on the square. We walked through the halls without stopping, until we reached the one that held the works of Bellini. My brother immediately pointed to the painting of the Virgin Mary holding the young Jesus. Once again, after so many years, I encountered that sadness on the face of the child, the half-closed eyes that look out with the gaze not of a child but of someone who has seen much more than childhood. It is a look directed not in front of him but toward some great pain, some terrible loss, as if the child senses his destiny, and his separation from the one who stands behind him so peacefully and protectively at that moment, and who, many years later, beside the Cross, will be in despair herself, because she will be unable to do anything to prevent her separation from him, her loss. That pain has descended even onto the child's lips, and in the gesture of his hands—he has placed one high on his chest, above his heart, and with the little fingers of his other hand he holds his mother's finger, and with his index finger seems to point downward. His mother cannot see her child's sad disquiet; she is looking toward some other place, somewhere far away. The point where her gaze is directed is somewhere beyond the painting. Although the mother cannot see the disquiet in her child, perhaps she senses it. Perhaps she, too, knows what will be, but she knows it must be that way. She knows this is how it should be, and in this reconciliation she is calm. Her look directed toward the horizon outside the painting is perhaps a look into some other reality, where everything is preserved, and where everything that was, everything that is, and everything that will be acquires its true meaning.

"Here, this is what people expect from religion, this kind of parental protection," Sigmund said, pointing at the painting.

"Protection." I only whispered, but my brother took it as disagreement.

"That's it exactly—protection! They expect religion to protect them just as their parents protected them when they were children. Religion is a store of ideas born of the need to make man's helplessness bearable, created out of the memories of our childhoods and the childhood of the human race. It sees death not as an extinction, a return to inorganic lifelessness, but as the beginning of a new kind of existence. In the end all good is rewarded and all evil punished—all the terrors, the sufferings, and the hardships of this life are destined to be wiped away. Life after death, which continues our life on earth, brings to us all the perfection we may have missed here." He coughed. "Do we need to believe in such infantile ideas? Do we need to deceive ourselves in this way so that we can endure life more easily? Or is there a better way to endure one's own existence? If we knew we were left to our own resources, that would already be something. In that case, we would learn to use them properly. Man is not completely helpless. Beginning in the days before the Flood, science has taught man many things, and his power will increase still more. As for the great necessities of fate, against which nothing can be done, he will learn to endure them with resignation. Withdrawing his expectations from whatever follows in the life beyond the grave, and concentrating all his liberated forces into his earthly life, man will possibly succeed in making life for everyone endurable. And that is the most humane, the highest goal: for each person to have a life without burden."

"You know that is a utopia."

"And is that sufficient reason for me to seek consolation in a belief that death is not the end of existence? We need to reconcile ourselves to the fact that death is not a transfer from one type of existence to another but a cutting off of existence. It is simply nonexistence. Death is cold comfort—a person expects it to give what life has denied him."

"You are even more afraid of death than those who seek consolation in the idea of immortality," I said to him.

"But that does not compel me to give myself false hope, to flee from my fear."

"You do not have fear. You express your ideas about the nonexistence of immortality with such indifference, as if you were convinced of your immortality."

"I do not understand what exactly it is you are trying to say."

"I am trying to say that you speak about the cessation of one's existence as if you were condemning all of us to it but excluding yourself. There is something in your voice that says, Yes, immortality does not exist, everyone is mortal, expect for me. The coldness with which you condemn everyone to the cessation of their existence shows how much you believe that you, however, will continue to live."

"I have always had an unshakably negative view toward the idea of the soul's immortality."

"You are not promising yourself immortality through the eternity of your soul. You are promising yourself a different kind of immortality. Someone who does not believe that the soul is eternal can hope, nonetheless, that something of his will live on; that he will, by some means, outlive death, through what he has created. One can create works or children. Children, although they are blood of their parents' blood, are something other than the parents—often their negation, a repudiation as terrible as death. You have chosen the best path, my dear brother: you believe you will continue to live through your works. You know that humanity will read and reread your works, that it will discuss what you have said about being human, about man's dreams and his reality, about his conscious and his unconscious, about the totem and the taboo, about patricide and incest, about Eros and Thanatos. This is what you expect after death: to be a prophet of prophets, not one of those who said what man would be on this earth and above the earth but what he has within him, and what he can become, and what can be explained by what he has within him, not knowing it is within him. And even now, while you are still alive, you feed on that immortality. Conceited and arrogant, you condemn us from some other place to death, us mortals. As if we did not deserve even a tiny ray of our light to endure. Yes, only one who believes absolutely that he will exist after death can speak with such arrogance about death to those he consigns to nonexistence. Only allow me to consign something to you. All those who believe they will be immortal through what they have created—regardless of whether it is the children they conceived, and whose blood carries on their own, or their artistic or scientific works—all those people are horribly deluding themselves that this ensures their immortality. Know that all this is created in matter, and that one day this matter will be extinguished and will disappear. Know that even your works, which will be read and interpreted as long as mankind exists, will one day die, and your immortality will die with them, because one day even the last person will die. You must know that you, too, are mortal, that the immortality you believe in is not immortality but an endless dragging out of your death."

"Let us say that it is," my brother said. "Even so, your entire accusation that I am chasing away my fear of death with a belief in the immortality of my works does not prove the immortality of the soul."

"The question is not whether something of the person—let us call that a soul—continues after death. The question is this: If it does not have a higher meaning, is our existence here completely meaningless?"

While we were talking, we walked along the perimeter of the room, without looking at the paintings hanging on the walls, and, walking in circles, I thought of the circle of life and of the unending cycle of births, deaths, births, deaths, births, deaths, births. . . .

"The idea of a meaning to one's life is simply a concealed need for constant happiness," my brother said. "Or, perhaps more precisely, the need to search for meaning arises due to the impossibility of realizing constant happiness. What is called *happiness* in the strictest sense of the word is an unexpected fulfillment of pent-up needs, and by its very nature can be only an episodic phenomenon."

"Your definition of happiness has nothing essential in common with happiness. But your definition does imply that everything is filled with meaning, not only happiness. Is all the sadness in the universe error or chance? And where does this sadness go, together with all of the past, with everything that has occurred in time? Where do the thoughts, the feelings, go? Where are all the gestures and words that have been made and spoken since the beginning of time until this moment? If they have disappeared as if they never existed, why did they occur at all? Why were there all those joyful stirrings of the heart and the heart's despairing turns? Why were all those words of truth and of deception spoken? Why all those hopes and those disappointments? Why those wise thoughts and foolish thoughts? Why that joy and that grief? Why those evil deeds and why those good works? If time is not preserved, if every moment is not saved in some form, then time itself is meaningless, everything that occurs in time (and everything that occurs is in time) is meaningless, and everything that once was, that is now, and that will be is completely meaningless. Completely meaningless if time is a self-destructive category that inclines toward nothingness, a nothingness that devours everything that was, that is, and that will be.

"But there is that other possibility," I continued, "that all time exists *somewhere* in an eternal present, in some other dimension; there is the possibility for all times, for everything that has ever been, to exist, pulsing in parallel and synchrony, and for everything that is now, and everything that will be, to *be transferred* to that other dimension; and only there, and only in that way, through the encounter of all temporal layers and all existences, will everything comprehend its own meaning, which is unfathomable to us in our ephemeral existence. There what has already once decayed—and everything has decayed once already—will not decay, in the dimension where everything is preserved and saved for eternity. There, where through countless intersections each gesture and each word, each smile and each tear, each enchantment and each moment of despair, has its justification and its purpose, a purpose unfathomable to us now. This existence is, perhaps, only a riddle that will be unraveled when our existence, as it is known to us, will end, and then it will acquire its full meaning."

"Rather than your infantile conjectures, a person needs to ask himself a more modest question: What can people discover about the goal of their lives on the basis of their conduct, what they seek from life, what they want to attain? There can be no mistake about the answer: they strive for happiness; they want to become happy and to remain so. And those who torment themselves most with these questions concerning the meaning of life are those who, in their yearning for happiness, have succeeded least in attaining it."

"That is probably true," I said. "Those whose *earthly* purpose, the meaning of their daily lives, was taken from them, seek this greater, *celestial* meaning. Well, then, let that be a comfort; let those who struggle with meaninglessness in their daily lives be allowed this comfort. Although I know it is not just comfort. In cosmic time, everything is meaningless, because in it, everything will end and lose its meaning. But in eternity everything that ended in cosmic time will once again achieve its meaning, a meaning not given to us to understand and experience while we are in our time."

At that moment, Sigmund stopped and raised his hand as if waving away flies. He raised his hand again but did not wave it— he held it in front of his face, not in consideration of some thought about meaning and meaninglessness but because he was looking at his wristwatch. "Anna is waiting for us," he said.

I turned to the wall. We were standing immediately beside *Crucifixion*. It held no promise. On the face of Jesus there is only resignation at the horror; on the face of his mother, horrid despair. Resignation and despair, just as in that other painting *Madonna and Child*, only now resignation is filled with horror, Jesus' resignation at the moment of his expiring, and his mother, standing by the Cross, is in despair, her hands folded, her head bowed, her gaze blind to everything around her except the pain in her soul. Her eyes seemed wasted to their hollows, and in their place despair alone remained.

"Let's go," my brother said, and I set off with him, leaning on his arm, limping, turning back toward the mother and the son, toward their separation.

I SPENT THOSE SEVERAL DAYS in the hotel room. Anna and Sigmund begged me to explore the city with them, but I complained of the pain in my knee. I was, in fact, limping. I sat in my room and thought of my conversation with my brother. I thought of the humane sentiment he had expressed as we stood between the older Madonna with the crucified Jesus and the Madonna with the child Jesus: that the greatest aim the human race must strive for is to allow each person to live his life with the least possible suffering, and for each person to contribute to the realization of that ideal. On that February day in 1933, Sigmund truly believed this, but a different sequence of events was already in motion. Germany had a new leader, and our sisters had returned to Vienna. When the new German leader occupied Austria as well, my brother left for London with those whose lives he had chosen to spare; we, his sisters, were deported first to one camp, then to another. In those moments of suffering that my sisters and I lived through, his words that each person should strive for there to be the least possible suffering in this world sounded to me like ridicule.

On our last morning in Venice, after Anna and Sigmund had gone off to explore the city, my desire to see once more those two paintings of the Madonna and Jesus was more intense than the pain in my knee, and I left the hotel. I set off toward the square, and on one of the side streets I ran into a crowd. In the years that followed, I often peered at such crowds through the window of our apartment in Vienna, but this crowd was made up not of uniformed people but of masked ones. The Carnival of Venice was taking place, and every sort of creature ran past me: princesses and beggars, rulers and slaves, fish-people and bird-people. We were going in the same direction, but they were moving quickly, and as I fell behind I pressed myself against the wall of a house. I looked at their faces and bodies, at the feathers, scales, beaks, fins, and wings with which they had disguised themselves. Among them I saw a man dressed as a fool, with tight trousers, a bright shirt, and a hat with pompons. I pulled myself away from the wall and went toward him. The people were going by very quickly; they knocked into me, and I fell. I lay on the street with my hands protecting my head, and I saw dozens of feet running past me and heard happy shouts, songs, and laughter.

After the crowd had scattered, I stood up slowly and shook the dust from my clothes. I looked in the direction the crowd had taken, toward Piazza San Marco. At the entry to the piazza, a woman was sitting on the ground, with one arm outstretched for alms and the other holding a child. I stared at her and saw her raise her hand to wave at me. I raised my hand and waved back. She lowered her hand, and I realized that she had likely mistaken me for someone else, or that she was waving not at me but at someone else, or that she was not waving at anyone, that her gesture was, perhaps, meant to brush away her thoughts, to stop herself from contradicting herself. Then she pulled out one of her breasts and began to nurse her child.

Ten years passed from that moment to the end of my life, and I forgot the woman at the entry to the piazza nursing her child. In those ten years my sisters Paulina and Marie had to leave Berlin, and we lived once again in the apartment they had left when they married; after the occupation of Austria, Rosa joined us, too. My brother compiled a list of people who could leave Vienna with him, and we believed that, even from London, he would manage to pull us from Vienna. We believed this up until his death. We lived in poverty and fear, and then one day they loaded us onto a train and brought us to one camp and then another. And at the moment they led us into the room where we heard the hiss of gas and understood that we were standing face to face with our death, I remembered the woman nursing her child.

I was entering into death and I promised myself that death is nothing other than forgetting • I was entering into death and I told myself that a human being is nothing except remembrance • I was entering into death and I repeated that death is forgetting and nothing else

I was entering into death and I repeated everything I will forget • I was entering into death and I repeated to myself

I will forget how they brought us into this room • I will forget this bitter smell • I will forget how the old people around me are screaming fearful of their death • They scream or they pray • I will forget how I press my sister's hand and how she presses my hand • That will be my death • That forgetting

I will also forget Eva and her little daughter to whom I gave my mother's name • I will forget how Ottla went to her death together with hundreds of children

I will forget the years of fear • Years in which we were afraid that uniformed men would knock on our door at any moment and drag us off to the death camps • Or simply shoot a bullet into our old foreheads • I will forget how we hoped our brother would manage to pull us from Vienna • I will forget the day I learned that my brother had died

I will also forget the woman nursing her child at the entry to Piazza San Marco

That will be my death • That forgetting • I will forget

I will forget how the Good Soul was dying and how she said to me • Kiss me

I will forget that before she died my mother called me Mama • I will forget that this was the first and last time someone called me Mama

I will forget Heinerle and our conversation about the mayflies • I will forget how Heinerle slipped the puppet I had made for him onto his hand and how he then wiped his bloody mouth with it

I will forget how I found Cecilia with her hair spread on the pillow

That will be my death • That forgetting • I will forget

I will forget how I left my home • I will forget the years spent at the Nest

I will forget my mother's words • I will forget all my mother's words

I will forget how I cursed my father's seed and my mother's womb

I will forget that bloody trace on the wall of my room • The bloody trace • The only remains of my unborn child • I will forget

I will forget you as well my unborn child • I will forget how strongly and how briefly I was able to rejoice in you • That is my life • That is my death • I will forget

I will forget that I told my brother • Beauty is the only comfort in this world

I will forget that sweet pain and that bitter longing to give a new life • I will forget how I felt that my heart my womb and between my legs were beating together • Beating as one

That will be my death • That forgetting • I will forget

And I will forget you Rainer • I will forget how the water carried you away • I will forget your look filled with emptiness • I
will forget my hope that life would return to that emptiness • I will
forget that before your look was empty it was a look that cried inside and the tears fell inside you • I will forget that in the time
between when you had those two looks you had a different look •
I will forget that look of cruelty • I will forget everything Rainer •
Both the tenderness and the cruelty • I will also forget your question • Who am I • I will also forget your answer • I am nothing • I
will forget that because of you I felt I was nothing • I will forget my
joy when I learned I was carrying your child • I will forget how we
played with our shadows when we were children • I will forget how
I tore the little red pocket from my dress and gave it to you for
remembrance

That will be my death • That forgetting • I will forget

I will forget the quiet life and the quiet death of my father

I will forget Sarah and her fingers that held the dandelion • I
will forget Sarah and the clouds of butterflies around her • I will
forget Sarah and I will forget with what bashful longing she looked
at Sigmund • I will forget Sarah and her request • Do not forget
Klara and help her if you can • I will also forget Klara • I will forget
her care of the fourteen little Gustavs • I will forget her care of the
dead • I will forget how her firmness turned to frailty • I will forget
how she resembled a terrified bird

I will forget my vulnerability

That will be my death • That forgetting • I will forget

I will forget you Sigmund • I will forget everything about you
• I will forget everything down to my earliest memories from the
time when many things still had no name for me and you gave me
a sharp object and said Knife

I will forget that at the beginning of my life there was love and
pain • I will forget the first pain • I will forget the quiet dripping of

blood from a hidden wound • I will forget the first pain and the first words I remember • My mother's words • It would have been better if I had not given birth to you

I will forget that I was born

I repeated this while I waited for my death • I repeated that death is only forgetting and I repeated what I will forget

I will forget

Acknowledgments

I WROTE *FREUD'S SISTER* OVER A PERIOD OF seven and a half years, and I am immensely grateful for the support I received during that time from the following foundations and institutions: the Bellagio Center, the Rockefeller Foundation (Italy/USA); CEC ArtsLink (USA); the Central European Initiative (Italy); Château de Lavigny Writers' Residence/Fondation Ledig-Rowohlt (Switzerland); Društvo Slovenskih Pisateljev (Slovenia); the European Cultural Foundation (Netherlands); KulturKontakt (Austria); Ledig House International Writers Residency (USA); Nederlands Letterenfonds (Netherlands).

The novel has been edited for its English-language publication, and for this edition I would like to express my sincerest gratitude to Christina E. Kramer, for being so devoted to creating this beautiful translation; to Pierre Astier and Laure Pecher of Pierre Astier and Associates, for their care in helping the book find its way to the best publishers; to Peter Blackstock and Elena Mitreska, for valuing the novel; and, at Penguin Books, to John Siciliano, whose knowledge and love of literature find genuine expression in his work as an editor.

GOCE SMILEVSKI

IT HAS BEEN A tremendous pleasure and privilege to work with Goce Smilevski. I thank him for his careful reading of this translation and for his comments and suggestions. Thanks also to John Siciliano for his thoughtful editing and promptness in response to my queries. I thank Eleni Buzharovska, Rumena Buzharovska, Liljana Mitkovska, and Martin Sokoloski for help with queries on the Macedonian. David Kramer provided valuable editorial advice and the translation of excerpts from Mann's essay "Brother Hitler" and Kafka's story "The Bachelor's Misfortune." I thank Carol Anderson for her careful reading and numerous valuable suggestions, and Christina Santolin for research assistance.

The novel contains numerous quotations from and references to the works of Sigmund Freud. Quotations from *Moses and Monotheism* are based on the English translation by Katherine Jones. Smilevski has adapted excerpts from other Freud works, including his letters, *The Future of an Illusion*, *Civilization and Its Discontents*, and other essays. My translations of these and other quotations are based on the author's adaptations. In translating from the Macedonian, I have consulted the Penguin editions of *The Future of an Illusion*, translated by J. A. Underwood and Shaun Whiteside, and *Civilization and Its Discontents*, translated by David McLintock; Ernest Jones's *Sigmund Freud: Life and Work*, volume 1; *New Introductory Lectures on Psychoanalysis*, translated by W. J. H. Sprott; and *The Standard Edition of the Complete Psychological Works of Sigmund Freud*, edited by James Strachey. I consulted A. D. Godley's translation of Hippocrates and Francis Adams's translations of Aretaeus, as well as Robin McKown's *Pioneers in Mental Health*. The Goethe quotation is from Thomas Mann's lecture "The Art of the Novel," translated by Herman Salinger in *The Creative Vision*, edited by Haskell Block and Salinger. Quotes from Kierkegaard are from *Either/Or* translated by L. M. Hollander.

CHRISTINA E. KRAMER